THE FURY OUT OF TIME

BOOKS BY LLOYD BIGGLE, JR.

THE FURY OUT OF TIME

Lloyd Biggle, Jr.

WILDSIDE PRESS
SCIENCE FICTION

THE FURY OUT OF TIME

Published by:

Wildside Press
P.O. Box 301
Holicong, PA 18928-0301
www.wildsidepress.com

ISBN: 1-58715-053-0

Wildside Press Edition
September 2001

To Dean McLaughlin . . .

Part One

1

The day began strangely.

Bowden Karvel wrenched himself from a drunken slumber and took his first step without falling flat on his face. He wondered if it were an omen.

The trailer park reposed in an uncanny state of quiet. Puzzled, Karvel limped to the door of his trailer and opened it. A chill, gusty wind tore at his pajamas and spat fine particles of sand into his face. The November sun was coldly bright, and almost overhead. An F-102 jet flashed into sight, headed for a landing at nearby Hatch Air Force Base. Karvel watched it until it sank below the tree-choked horizon.

He stood for a moment in the open doorway, gratefully embracing the cold wind. The park's children would not be released for their customary frolic in mob formation until the day had warmed up somewhat, which accounted for the unnatural silence.

He limped to the bathroom mirror and studied his face with the distasteful detachment of one attempting to identify a corpse. With one hand he fingered a three-day growth of beard; with the other he held up his razor. His hand was steadier than it had any right to be.

He shaved slowly, dressed himself slowly. It was afternoon when he finished, but he had no hunger.

Nor any thirst. He had never experienced a craving for drink. He drank only when he had nothing better to do, which was, unfortunately, almost always.

He limped out into the cold, insistent wind and locked

the trailer door. "Another damned day," he said, and got into his car.

Whistler's Country Tavern was a long log building set far back from the road behind a screen of young pines. There was no sign. Whistler's customers knew where he was, and anyone traveling that narrow, winding, unimproved road who was not Whistler's customer was lost.

The military invasion was already under way when Karvel drove into the deeply rutted parking lot. On weekday evenings the tavern was merely crowded; on Saturday afternoons it was mobbed. Airmen from Hatch Air Force Base achieved spectacular feats of engineering in packing themselves into anything that possessed wheels and a hint of self-propulsion, and descended en masse on Whistler's Country Tavern, and Whistler hated them for it.

Karvel hesitated at the front entrance, told himself without conviction that he should eat something, and entered.

Bert Whistler, obscenely bald, formidably jowled, splenetically bad-tempered, was presiding at the bar like an irascible God on Judgment Day. He dealt out the momentary solace of beer to some, withheld it from others at a whim, and dismissed all complaints with a snarl. The airmen liked Whistler. There was no class consciousness to his incivility. He insulted colonels and the lowliest of enlisted men with superb impartiality.

His eyes fell on Karvel. His scowl deepened, and he raised both hands despairingly. Karvel grinned, pushed his way past the crowd by the door, and limped toward the kitchen.

Ma Whistler was bending bleary-eyed over greasy mounds of hamburger. She greeted Karvel with a toothless grin and unconsciously smoothed back her thinning strands of gray hair. "Have you had breakfast?"

Karvel shook his head.

"Kick somebody out of a chair, and I'll bring it."

Karvel nodded, and circled around to a small back room

that bore a crudely lettered sign, OFFICERS CLUB NO GENTLE-
MEN ALLOWED.

"Major Karvel!" a voice exclaimed. "Come and join us!"

A good-looking young captain jumped up from the large
circular table that filled the room, and whacked a lieutenant who was seated next to him. "Give Major Karvel your
chair," he ordered.

The lieutenant good-naturedly picked up his bottle and
glass, and moved aside. "Sit down, Major."

"It's *Mister* Karvel," Karvel said. "Thanks." He looked
about him and blinked his surprise. The day was continuing
as oddly as it had begun. "What do you mean, defying natural law by bringing females to Whistler's?" he demanded.

There were three young women seated at the table, all
of them in attractive civilian clothing, all of them young,
and pretty, and curvaceous. The sight was rare enough to
be unsettling. Whistler had lost his easygoing, friendly local
trade when the Air Force took over. A male civilian at Whistler's during the off-duty hours was made to feel as unwel-
come as a Communist at a Birch Society meeting, and
although a WAF occasionally appeared with appropriate
bodyguard, no female civilian dared approach the place.
Even Whistler's elderly, rheumatic wife frequently closed
her kitchen in disgust and locked herself in their living quarters, and such was the tavern's local reputation that Whistler couldn't hire a waitress.

The captain performed introductions. "Miss Sylvester,
Miss Carson, Miss Drews. Major Bowden Karvel. Major
Karvel is retired, which is why he's trying to call himself
mister. The ladies are television actresses, Major. You've
probably seen them on TV."

"You know better than that," Karvel said.

"They're on the program 'Wayward Girls.' Miss Sylvester
is the star."

Karvel studied her gravely. She was blonde, she had a
lovely face, and her curves were as sensationally proportioned as her eyelashes. "I'm sorry to hear it," he murmured
politely.

She fluttered the eyelashes. "Sorry?"

"Sorry you're a wayward girl."

The soaring, musical lilt of her laughter was unsettling to even such a confirmed misogynist as Bowden Karvel. "Oh, I'm not one of the wayward girls," she said. "I play the part of a probation officer."

"You can understand why I was confused," Karvel told her. "None of my probation officers ever looked like you."

"Never mind Major Karvel," the captain said. "He just doesn't approve of there being two sexes."

Miss Sylvester arched the delicate lines of her eyebrows. "Goodness! He must be awfully behind the times!"

"He thinks women are one part flesh and blood and three parts optical illusion," the captain went on, "and you have to admit—"

"They don't have to admit a thing," Karvel said. "Optical illusion is the one art the twentieth century excels in, and should be respected. Enjoy it as much as you like, but keep your mind off the structural implications, which are none of your business."

"I don't know which of us he insulted," Miss Sylvester said, "but *somebody* ought to slap him."

The captain laughed, and playfully clipped Karvel on the chin. "By the way, Major—have you seen Sergeant Walling lately?"

Karvel shook his head.

"He's complaining about those collections of yours that are on display in the library. He says they take up too much space, and he wants them out of there."

"They give the establishment a very important intellectual tone. I thought the men found them interesting."

"Maybe they did two years ago, but the novelty's worn off. Walling says it interferes with the powers of concentration to be surrounded by carcasses of insects, not to mention the rocks-in-the-head feeling one gets from looking at rocks day after day, and as for the seashells—"

"The rocks in Walling's head are no responsibility of mine. But I'll have a talk with him."

"You'd better. He's threatening to feed the insects to the birds. I forget what it is he's going to do with the rocks and shells."

"I haven't any place to put them. I'll appeal to his generous nature. Anyway, he's got nothing to complain about. My collection of stuffed alligators is still down at Homestead."

Ma Whistler pushed her way into the room with Karvel's breakfast. He looked at it helplessly.

"Eat it!" she snapped. "You die twice as fast drinking on an empty stomach."

Karvel ate, chewing each tasteless mouthful interminably while mustering courage to swallow, and listened to the cheerful banter that was tossed about the table. He said nothing more—he had already said too much, for he did not belong there. Crippled, tossed onto the retirement heap at the age of thirty-six, he felt decades too old to associate with these young officers and young women whose aspirations were unsullied and whose futures were still bright. He continued to nod or shake his head when spoken to, but he did not hear the questions; and afterward he remembered very little of what happened during the next hour.

For no particular reason, the disconnected impressions he retained stood out vividly:

The odd question Miss Sylvester asked, with an equally odd flutter of her eyelashes. "Exactly how far is this place from the base?"

Whistler's new and inexperienced bartender serving a Manhattan with an olive in it, and getting it dashed into his face.

Lieutenant Phineas Ostrander charging in, waving his moose call and shouting "Geronimo!"

And there was the strange civilian who appeared suddenly in the tavern doorway, and called out, "Hey! Can you tell me how to get to Highway 41?"

Whistler, at his disrespectful worst, filled the ensuing silence with a snort. "What way you going, 41 east or 41 west?"

The stranger stared. "What difference does that make? It's just one highway, isn't it?"

"Mister," Whistler said scornfully, "you better know the difference between east and west before you start asking for directions."

Karvel became aware that hands were reaching for his, that the girls and their escorts were leaving. He started to get to his feet, found his artificial leg hooked around a chair leg, and was still struggling to free it when they walked away.

He returned his half-eaten breakfast to the kitchen and told Ma Whistler that he'd done his best. Leaving the tavern by the kitchen door, he circled around to the plot of ground in the rear that Whistler chose to call the tavern gardens.

Whistler's gardening consisted of cutting weeds at irregular intervals, but during the summer months he had kept three gaudy umbrella tables behind the tavern for the use of favored customers, none of whom cared what he called the place. The chairs were comfortable, the service and insults no worse than those suffered inside the tavern, and the view, because Whistler's Country Tavern was perched precariously on the rim of a deep valley, was magnificent.

On that Saturday the tables were missing. Of all of the day's singularities, this was the most irksome. Karvel limped back through the tavern, invaded the sacrosanct region behind the bar, and demanded an explanation. Whistler straightened up to his full five feet five inches, wiped his hands on the soiled white apron that magnified his paunch, and eyed Karvel in flabbergasted silence.

"The tables," Karvel said again. "Where are the tables?"

Whistler's arms flapped protestingly. "Stored. Stored for the winter."

"It isn't winter yet."

"It's gonna be winter."

"It's always going to be winter. It was going to be winter last month, but the tables were there. It was going to be winter last spring, when you bought the damned things. I want my table."

"Nobody wants to sit outside. It's too cold."

"I want to sit outside," Karvel said. "Cold is one of the few genuine discomforts that modern civilization hasn't corrupted. You ought to try it sometime."

Airmen, crowded four ranks deep along the bar, cheered on the argument. "How about that?" a hefty chief master sergeant said. "Taking the major's table when it ain't even winter yet. Whistler's a cheapskate!"

Others took up the chant. "Whistler's a cheapskate!"

Whistler ignored them. The unexpectedness of Karvel's attack had rocked him off balance, but only momentarily. He loved an argument, and his uncouth features concealed a mind of surprising resourcefulness. Karvel grinned in anticipation of a devastating rejoinder, but before Whistler could speak the sergeant waved for silence.

"Nobody buys until the major gets his table. Right?"

"Right!" the airmen chorused.

Whistler wavered, shaken by the thought that winning an argument might cost him money. He glared at Karvel. Then he descended to the basement, and came crashing up the stairs with a table.

Karvel was genuinely fond of Whistler, and he would have preferred to win his point without the low blow to the cash register. The damage was done, however; he placed a bill on the bar, told the men to have one on him while it lasted, and left the room to a rousing chorus of "He's a Jolly Good Fellow."

He followed Whistler outside and resumed the argument, this time over the number of chairs required for the comfort of Bowden Karvel. They compromised on two. While Whistler waited impatiently for his order, Karvel draped his jacket over one chair, sat down in the other, and composed himself to have the last word.

"The usual?" Whistler said finally.

"No. This isn't one of my good days. When I spend money for whiskey, or even for the diluted paint remover you peddle as whiskey, I want to be happy enough to enjoy it. Just bring me a bottle of pop."

Speechless, Whistler glared at him. Speechless he departed. The bartender brought the pop. Karvel sipped it slowly, and admired the view.

The patchwork of brown fields and riotously colored trees dropped away precipitously in a breathtaking expanse of landscape. Swift-moving clouds were crisply white against immaculate blue. The wind that knifed its way up out of the valley and tore at the gaily colored umbrella was cruelly cold, but Karvel did not reach for his discarded jacket.

Sounds of arriving and departing cars drifted to him fitfully from the parking lot. In the main room of the tavern two choruses of exuberant airmen began to shout songs. Thumping gusts of wind capriciously blended the strains of "Roll Out the Barrel" and "Yellow Rose of Texas," to the enhancement of neither. Lieutenant Ostrander kept time with blasts on his moose call. A whistle sounded shrilly, and another answered.

Karvel resignedly raised his glass. At such moments he felt himself insecurely balanced between the glories of nature and the vulgarities of man, and in grave danger of toppling the wrong way.

He spent the next half hour feeling very sorry for Bert Whistler.

The tavern owner was torn between shipping the whole Air Force off to the nearest mental hospital or following the path of least resistance to the bank. Karvel considered it a tragic study in human degradation. Whistler hadn't wanted to be rich, or he wouldn't have built his tavern miles away from anywhere. Then the Air Force located a new base in his neighborhood, and his income skyrocketed. Money, Karvel thought, could be as habit-forming as dope.

Though Whistler's insults were often hilarious, Karvel had never known a man so devoid of a sense of humor. He tolerated the airmen's gags not because he appreciated them but because he never quite seemed to see the point. He said nothing at all when some wag hung up the OFFICERS

CLUB sign, or even when the words WAF'S WELCOME appeared mysteriously over the door of the men's room. He'd watched without protest when Lieutenant Ostrander nailed up an enormous streamer that read, IF YOU WANT ANYTHING JUST WHISTLE.

But this last sign produced results that Whistler found not just unamusing but also unnecessary. It appealed to the competitive spirit of his customers. The base was sifted for whistles, men wrote home for whistles, sirens, horns, and assorted noisemakers, and vied with each other to see who could order beer with the loudest, shrillest blast. All of this Whistler endured stoically enough, but when Lieutenant Ostrander broke out his moose call the sign came down.

Now it was rumored that Whistler was at work on a sign of his own, to be hung over the front door. It would read OFF LIMITS TO AIR FORCE PERSONNEL.

But Karvel knew that the tavern owner would never have the nerve. The money-making habit had him hooked.

Eventually Karvel dismissed Bert Whistler and his problems to lose himself in contemplation of the scenic beauty spread out before him. Man's normally corrosive touch had been unusually benign in that lovely valley. The farms were well-kept and prosperous. The groves of trees that were splashed about the landscape with such generous abandon concealed most of the farm buildings. On the distant, curving valley rim the trim structures of the Mueller farm perched in doll-sized daintiness, but there were few other signs of human habitation—a narrow, graveled road that ran up the valley and several times crossed the stream that meandered there; a few silos that rose behind the trees like lonely, stubby fingers; an abandoned barn far off across the valley; a patch of white or red where a house or barn could be glimpsed through the trees; here and there the steep slope of a mansard barn roof. Cattle grazed where the fields rose too abruptly for farming.

It was altogether lovely, and it was *unhurried*. It offered the illusion of permanence. One could look away or close

one's eyes with the certitude that the beauty would be un-
changed when one looked again.

The afternoon wore on slowly. There were seven empty
pop bottles on the table and the sun hung low over the distant valley rim when Karvel closed his eyes and opened
them just in time to see, far off in the valley, a solitary tree
falling.

Even on that wind-blown autumn afternoon the event
was incongruous, but it made no immediate impression on
his consciousness. Then a dozen trees of a row that lined
the stream were toppled, and *that* brought Karvel to his
feet. Afterward he had no recollection of shouting, but a
moment later Bert Whistler was beside him, and Karvel
could only point silently.

Trees continued to fall, in a widening circle. Half of a
small wood lot went down, and a flick of an eye later the
abandoned barn across the valley disintegrated into splin-
ters.

"What is it?" Whistler demanded.

Karvel shook his head. The path of destruction was spiraling outward with incredible speed, cutting an ever-widen-
ing swath and at the same time leaving a widening spiral
untouched. Beyond an undamaged grove of trees a silo top
vanished abruptly. Karvel strained to see what had happened to the farm buildings, but the grove screened them.

Trees continued to fall. A herd of cattle was bowled over,
and an instant later the destruction reached the distant rim
of the valley and sliced through the Mueller farm. The barn
collapsed, the house dissolved in a cloud of erupting brick.
Outbuildings and a concrete silo were untouched.

"It's coming closer each time around," Karvel said to
Whistler. "It'll be here in a moment. Better get everyone
into the basement."

Whistler gawked at him wildly and turned away muttering to himself. "Crazy! A tornado in this weather!"

The screen of young pines at the left of the garden suddenly bent to the ground, and an invisible force smashed

into Karvel. He lay twenty feet from where he had been standing, dazed and bleeding. The table, minus its umbrella and bottles, was spinning away down into the valley. The tavern was untouched.

Whistler waddled over to help him to his feet. "Crazy tornado," Whistler said. "Didn't even *hear* anything. You all right?"

Karvel did not answer. The pain in his chest sharpened to agony when he inhaled. He had the impression that his good left leg had been torn from its socket at the knee, and his various aches were too numerous and well-distributed for inventory. He dabbed at the moisture on his face with his handkerchief and identified it as blood.

"Your head's bleeding," Whistler said unnecessarily. "Can you walk?"

"Let's try," Karvel said.

With Whistler's support he made his way around the building to the parking lot. Every step and every breath was genuinely exquisite torment, but he noted wryly that the law of compensation was still operating. The intense pain in his left knee had absolutely cured the limp in his artificial right leg.

Far up the road a pickup truck had veered into the ditch. A carload of airmen had pulled into the parking lot a moment before, and Karvel pointed and snapped an order. "See if anyone's hurt." With Whistler's sturdy figure still supporting him, Karvel turned toward the tavern. Just inside the door was a pay telephone. He fed a coin into it and found to his surprise that it was working.

He got through to Hatch Air Force Base and asked for the Combat Operations duty officer. "This is Major Bowden Karvel," he said. "I'm calling from Whistler's Country Tavern. I suggest an immediate base tornado alert."

"*Tornado* alert?" the officer repeated blankly.

"I'd guess that you have five to ten minutes. Allow fifteen as a safe margin. If nothing has happened by then, it's missed the base. Civilian and off-duty casualties will need all the medical personnel and equipment you can lay your hands on. Send whatever men are available to help clear away the wreckage. Most of the farms in the area are badly hit. We'll need an officer to take charge—Hello!"

The line had gone dead. Karvel hung up, and with Whistler's help moved across the crowded room to the Officers' Club. The sole occupants were Lieutenant Ostrander and his moose call. Ostrander was dreamily arranging empty beer bottles into a monogrammatic *PO*. Karvel cleared the table with a crashing gesture of disgust.

"Take six men and get over to the Mueller farm. Look for survivors."

"*Survivors,* sir?" Ostrander's youthful face assumed contortions of astonishment. "What the devil's happened?"

"Move!"

Ostrander moved. Karvel pointed Whistler toward the main room and plucked the chief master sergeant from behind a bottle of beer.

"I want every road in and around the valley checked carefully," he said. "You may find cars wrecked, and you'll find a lot of buildings flattened. Leave a rescue party wherever you think it'll do any good. Use your own judgment. Send back reports on what you find, and let us know where medical supplies and ambulances are needed."

"What happened, Major?" the sergeant asked blankly.

"Get moving, and you'll find out." Karvel turned to Whistler. "You may have to convert this place into a temporary hospital. Tell Ma what happened, and leave her in charge here. You get over to the base and try to convince someone that we've had a major disaster. That idiot in Combat Operations didn't believe me. He'll ask the weather officer, and the weather officer will say there couldn't be a tornado today, and he'll forget about it."

The parking lot was emptying rapidly when they got outside. Karvel saw Lieutenant Ostrander's party off, and helped the sergeant get the main rescue force under way. Bert Whistler watched silently.

"I been thinking, Major," he said, as the last car pulled out. "It wasn't no tornado. What was it?"

"I don't know." Karvel moved toward his own car.

"Your head's still bleeding, and you really look awful. You better wait for one of them ambulances."

"I'm going to drive around by Mueller's and come back up the valley road. You get over to the base and raise hell. Insist on seeing Colonel Frazier personally, and tell him I sent you. I have a hunch that a lot of lives are going to depend on how quickly we can get people out of smashed houses. You saw what happened to Mueller's?"

Whistler nodded, and helped him to get settled behind his steering wheel.

"Can't you bend your leg at all?" Whistler asked.

Karvel shook his head impatiently.

"Good thing you got hand controls," Whistler said. He closed the door and stepped back, and Karvel drove away without a backward glance.

At the Mueller farm he found Lieutenant Ostrander and his men working quickly and efficiently on the mound of brick that had been the house. A small body lay on the ground, partially covered by an Air Force blouse. "One of the younger kids," Ostrander said. "The rest of the family's either dead or unconscious. We haven't heard a whisper."

The lieutenant was no longer the congenial buffoon with the moose call. He was pale and tense, but superbly competent. He snapped an order at two men who were trying to pry a rafter loose, and ran to help them.

Karvel watched him approvingly. He would have to write a letter of appreciation for Lieutenant Phineas Ostrander —though he doubted that the base commander would believe it.

He suppressed an impulse to go to their assistance. His knee was already badly swollen. He was certain that he had at least one fractured rib, and he found himself wincing in anticipation of the occasional deep breath his body demanded. The gash in his head continued to ooze blood. He'd left his jacket at Whistler's, and at this end of the valley, no longer warmed by the setting sun, he soon felt shudderingly cold. He started his motor and turned on the heater.

"There's something I want to see while I can still hobble around," he said, when Ostrander returned. "Carry on, you're doing fine."

At the neighboring farm only a corncrib had been damaged. Karvel sent the farmer and his three sons to help Ostrander, and drove on. Fallen trees partially blocked the road, but he managed to steer his car around them. He stopped once and painfully got out to examine a smashed car, but he paused only long enough to assure himself that the man, woman, and two children were all dead. He could not have gotten them out in any case—that would take torches or cutting tools.

He turned onto the valley road, edged his car around more fallen trees, and kept a firm grip on the brake handle during the steep descent. Twice he stopped briefly to look about. The pall of death hung heavily over the mangled fields. Cattle lay in clusters, their entrails smashed from their flattened bodies. A car was parked where the road leveled off, and pale-faced airmen were at work about a shattered farmhouse. They had recovered two bodies. The fury had commenced near this farm, and the awesome record of its force challenged the imagination. Buildings were pulverized, and enormous old trees had been flung to the ground.

A staff sergeant recognized Karvel and hurried over to report. Karvel waved him back to work. He pulled a piece of dead branch from a brush pile to use as a cane and limped haltingly across the road and into a pasture, pausing once to ponder the nature of a force that could snap fence posts and barbed wire. He reached the stream and splashed across it. Turning aside to avoid dead cattle and fallen trees, he moved painfully toward the first tree he had seen toppled.

He sat down on it and gazed unbelievingly at the shredded trunk and the splintered edge of the stump from which it had been wrenched. He was still sitting there an hour later when Colonel Frazier, the Hatch Air Force Base commander, strode up accompanied by his wing intelligence officer, Major Wardle. The colonel asked him what the hell he thought he was doing, and Karvel shook his head and did not answer.

He had seen the dullish-black sphere that rested in a hollow fifty feet away. It was some ten feet in diameter, and it had no more place in that quiet pasture than did the Empire State Building. Karvel had marveled at it, but he had been unable to investigate. By the time he'd reached the tree even a shallow breath was impaling him with pain, and he had the queasy feeling that he might pass out if he ventured one more step on his injured leg.

But he had found something close by that piqued his curiosity at least as much as the sphere. It was a butterfly, a tiny thing no larger than his thumbnail, that had alighted on the tree beside him. Karvel captured it before it could fly away, and he was still staring at it when the colonel arrived.

If the sphere was an improbable ornament to a rural landscape, this butterfly was a flat impossibility.

2

Gerald Haskins sat quietly in a corner of Colonel Frazier's office, chair tilted back against the wall, and puffed on a cigar. The colonels were arguing again, but Haskins was paying very little attention to them. He was really interested in only two kinds of people—those who could tell him what he wanted to know, and those who could do something he wanted done. These officers could not qualify on either count, but this neither surprised nor disappointed him. High-ranking officers were rarely of any value to Gerald Haskins, except in helping him to find the kinds of people who interested him.

He had flown out from Washington with two of them, Colonel Harlow Stubbins of Air Force Intelligence, and an Army Intelligence officer, Colonel James Rogers. Colonel Frazier had immediately taken them on a prolonged tramp about the countryside, and Haskins's feet hurt. He did not resent this, but he doubted that it had been necessary. He was marking time until some of the people who interested him were ready to tell him something. Then—perhaps—he could decide what he wanted done.

Colonel Stubbins said peevishly, "I'm not going to be stampeded into any conclusions until I've had a talk with your Major Karvel."

Colonel Frazier nodded agreement. "As you say, he *is* the most important eyewitness. I'll warn you, though, that an interview with him isn't going to clear up anything. Quite the contrary."

The army colonel, who was displaying the reticence military etiquette seemed to demand of a guest in an alien domain, entered a mild protest. "You said he was a good man."

"A very good man," Colonel Frazier said. "I don't think he's ever had a commander who called him anything but brilliant. He'll describe what he saw, and describe it very well, but even a good description is not an explanation."

Haskins leaned forward. The front legs of his chair struck the floor with a thump that produced a trio of irritated scowls. "I'd like to see Major Karvel's 201 file."

"I don't have it," Colonel Frazier told him.

"The man is stationed at this base, and you don't have—"

"He isn't stationed here. He's a retired officer—disability retired. It's a tragic story. He was one of the new group of astronauts, and doing a tremendous job, as everyone who knew him expected. Then he got involved in a freak auto accident. Rather, he took to the ditch to avoid piling into an accident that had already taken place. He saved several lives, which I hope is some consolation to him because he lost a leg. Naturally NASA isn't going to put a one-legged man on the moon, and our medical boards even take a dim view of one-legged men flying jets. Karvel could have had a responsible desk job with either NASA or the Air Force, but he refused. He's just not the desk type. I suppose you'd say he couldn't stand it to stay in the Air Force, but once he got out he couldn't stay away from it. He's been living in a nearby trailer camp, and I'm very much afraid he's gotten himself onto a nonreversible treadmill to Hell. It's a damned shame."

Haskins broke off the twitch of suspicion he'd felt, and filed it. "Where *is* his 201 file?"

"At the Air Reserve Record Center, in Denver."

"I'd like to skin your medical officer," Colonel Stubbins said. "Why the devil did he have to operate this morning?"

Colonel Frazier smiled. "It didn't occur to me to ask. The last time I questioned the judgment of a doctor was when I was a second lieutenant. It was also the first time. I learned—"

"I didn't have to learn not to argue with a doctor," Colonel

Stubbins growled. "Nevertheless, what happened yesterday may be at least as important as what happened at Hiroshima back in 1945, and I don't like having to sit here waiting for someone to tell me when I can talk to the one man who knows anything about it."

"As far as Colonel Vukin is concerned, the only important consideration was that Karvel was badly injured and in considerable pain."

"What sort of operation?" Haskins asked.

"Medial collateral ligament damage," Frazier said. "In the knee. If you know what that means—I don't. Karvel also had three broken ribs and a bad cut on the head, with a concussion. And an assortment of bad bruises. I suppose they sewed up his head. I don't know what the ribs and the bruises required. According to Vukin, his principal means of transportation is going to be a wheel chair for some time to come. His left knee will be in a cast, and he won't be able to use crutches because of the broken ribs. The amazing thing is how he accomplished as much as he did, considering the condition he was in. Vukin says the ribs alone should have made him a stretcher case."

"All the more reason why we should see him as soon as possible," Stubbins said. "The knock on the head didn't impair his thinking?"

"No. He was his usual brilliant self right up to the moment Vukin put him under with an injection of something. The crew of surveyors was his idea. He thought the path of destruction was a perfect spiral, with that damned sphere—"

"Unidentified object," Colonel Rogers murmured.

"—with the U.O. at dead center, and up to the last report he was absolutely right."

"You should have questioned him when you had a chance," Stubbins said.

"I told you he gave me a detailed description of what he saw. Force X travels with incredible speed. It forms a widening spiral with a widening gap. It knocks down trees and smashes buildings—as we saw. It makes no noise, and it's invisible. Whistler told us almost as much, and none of it helps us to deduce what Force X is."

Stubbins lifted his hands helplessly. "Let's go down to Hangar Seven."

The other colonels nodded, and got to their feet. Haskins remained seated, thoughtfully contemplating the stub of his cigar. "I'd like to make a phone call," he said.

"Go ahead," Colonel Frazier said, donating the office with a sweep of his hand.

"I'll be along in a moment," Haskins said.

He waited until the door closed after them, and then he went to the desk and gave the switchboard operator a Washington, D.C., number. When he reached his party he did not waste words. "Major Bowden Karvel." He spelled it. "U. S. Air Force, disability retired. The works."

Gerald Haskins had his own practical outlook on the general fitness of things, and "unidentified object" seemed a ridiculous misnomer for the heavily guarded sphere in Hangar Seven. To have a piece of apparatus securely enough in hand to commence dissecting it, and still be unable to label it with anything more aptly descriptive than U.O., was the height of military futility. He was happy that the dissecting was being done by his own bright young men, who were carefully drawn from the two kinds of people who interested him.

Hangar Seven was a small maintenance hangar, but its drafty dimensions still dwarfed the unidentified object into illusory insignificance. The sphere rested approximately in the center of the hangar, surrounded by workbenches, laboratory equipment, and seventeen puzzled scientists.

Colonel Stubbins strode up to the nearest bench and demanded, "Got anything yet?"

The scientists looked up at him, not startled but quietly disdainful, and unanimously decided to ignore him. Haskins kept his amusement to himself, wondering if soldiers would never learn that *civilian* is not necessarily a military rank below private.

He stopped to talk with a young scientist who seemed fascinated by a thick cylindrical object. "The controls?" he asked.

"One of them. A control capsule, I suppose you'd call it—or an instrument capsule. They snap in and out. Easily."

The three officers gathered around them to listen.

"I don't know if they're machined, or cast, or stamped," the scientist went on. "I've never seen anything like them. I also can't find any way to disassemble them. We took one over to the hospital and had it X-rayed. Nothing. Maybe the case is lined with lead—or something. These capsules come in two sizes, of exactly the same shape except that they're keyed. It would be impossible to put one into the wrong hole."

"Any special significance to that?" Colonel Stubbins wanted to know.

The scientist shrugged. "Perhaps not. Of course it could mean that the instruments are in some way expendable and have to be replaced frequently. Or that the U.O. is being mass-produced and the keys are to prevent assembly line errors. Or both."

Stubbins blanched. "Mass-produced! All we'd need would be a fleet of these things, aimed at population centers!"

"So far we haven't found any way to aim this one—if that's any consolation," the scientist said. "We also don't understand what the controls are supposed to control—if they *are* controls. We have turned up one interesting point. That hole at the top of the instrument panel is definitely designed for one of these capsules. So one control, or one instrument, is missing."

Stubbins looked at Frazier. "Did one of your men swipe a souvenir?"

"All my men have done is guard the thing. None of us, not even myself or Major Wardle, looked inside. Until Haskins's men got here we didn't even know how to open the hatch."

"Karvel?"

"Never got within fifty feet of it, and it's been under observation ever since he first saw it."

"Could anyone have gotten into it before he saw it?"

"It's possible," Frazier admitted. "But I don't think it's very likely."

"What about the men who were doing the rescue work?"

"I'll have them asked," Frazier said. "Yes, Sergeant?"

"Colonel Vukin called, sir. You can see Major Karvel now."

"Tell him we're on our way," Frazier said. "Want to come, Haskins?"

Haskins nodded. "Mind if I bring a couple of people along?"

"I don't mind. Vukin said he'd admit the four of us, and a stenographer, and that's all. A hospital room is not, and I quote, 'the Roman Colosseum.' We also have a time limit—fifteen minutes."

"Starting now, or when we get there?" Haskins asked with a grin.

Frazier grinned back at him. "I suppose we'd better hurry."

They stopped at Wing Headquarters to pick up Sergeant Gore, a stern-looking, middle-aged WAF who carried her stenographer's notebook with authority. Lieutenant Colonel Vukin, a tall, somber man who might have been more appropriately cast as an undertaker, met them at the hospital's main entrance and did not bother to welcome them.

"How's the patient?" Colonel Frazier asked.

"Considering the concussion, and the loss of blood, and the nine stitches in his head, and the couple of miles he managed to walk on that knee, and the various iniquities he committed with three broken ribs, he's in fairly good shape. I want you to remember that he breathes—and therefore talks—with difficulty and considerable pain. Under no circumstances is he to be excited. I'll take your word for it that it's imperative that you talk to him, but you'll conduct your business quietly and allow him plenty of time between questions, or I'll throw you out—individually and severally."

"Surely, Colonel, sir," Sergeant Gore said, wickedly dead-pan, "you wouldn't throw out a lady."

"Any female who is party to a ruckus in a patient's room is *ipso facto* no lady, and gets bounced. Come along."

Vukin entered Karvel's room first, and exclaimed, "What the devil! I left strict orders—"

Major Karvel already had company. The officer seated beside the bed, a plump, jolly-looking captain with a chaplain's cross on his blouse, smiled at them innocently. The tavern owner Whistler, whom Haskins had met that morning, was sprawled across the foot of the bed. Karvel was sitting up supported by pillows, and if he was in pain he concealed the fact expertly.

"I should have thought of it," Colonel Frazier muttered. "A chaplain is the one person who can talk back to a doctor!"

Vukin recovered his power of speech, and pointed at Whistler. "Out!"

"Bah," Whistler said, not moving. "Wait'll the next time you try to buy beer."

"Have you finished?" Vukin asked the chaplain coldly.

"Now, Colonel—you know perfectly well that my obligations to your patients don't end until you bury them. And not even then, of course, but after that I can manage without the use of your facilities." He got to his feet, and clasped Karvel's hand. "I think the major represents more of a challenge to my profession than he does to yours. Some men have mountains in their souls—mountains they are compelled to climb. Major Karvel owns an unusually lofty range. The summits are not only out of reach, but they are quite lost in the mist of self-doubt. I've never been able to decide whether I should be helping him to the top, or showing him a way around."

"Did you ever try just giving him a kick in the pants?" Whistler asked.

The chaplain smiled. "It isn't the sort of task one can ever consider *finished*. One never knows what one will find on the other side. More mountains, perhaps." He nodded to the colonels, and winked at Karvel. "Coming, Bertram?"

Whistler got leisurely to his feet. He said to Karvel, "You oughta be grateful for the knock on the head. At least, now you got an excuse."

"Just a moment," Colonel Stubbins said. "As long as he's here, why don't we go over the whole thing with both of them?"

"You already talked to me," Whistler said. "Anyway, I don't like to stay in a small room with so much brass. Afraid I'll get lead poisoning, or something."

Sergeant Gore suffered a sudden attack of coughing, and by the time Colonel Stubbins had stopped glowering at her Whistler and the chaplain had left. Colonel Vukin motioned an orderly with extra chairs into the room. Introductions were performed, Colonel Frazier got everyone seated, and there was a brief pause while Colonel Stubbins eyed Vukin suspiciously.

"This meeting is confidential," he announced.

"In that case I'd better close the door," Vukin said, and did so, and went to stand at the head of Karvel's bed. The three colonels shrugged in turn, and Haskins concentrated his attention on Major Bowden Karvel.

His left knee bulged with a cast, and the pajama leg was tucked neatly around the stump of his right leg. His head was heavily bandaged. His pajama jacket, open at the throat, revealed the binder about his chest.

That he appeared to be less than medium height was probably due to his wiry build. There was a touch of gray in the hair that the bandage did not cover, and he looked older than his thirty-six years; but his face revealed none of the defeat, or self-pity, that Haskins had half expected to find there. His bearing was that of a man who intended to get up and fight again.

"Did you get the surveyors, sir?" he asked Colonel Frazier. There was a twang to his speech that Haskins could not place.

Frazier nodded. "They haven't finished yet, but so far they confirm everything you said. That sphere—unidentified object, we're calling it—represents dead center, and whatever it was—"

"Force X," Colonel Rogers murmured.

"—Force X spiraled out from there. The tree you picked out last night was the first obstacle it struck."

Colonel Stubbins cleared his throat ostentatiously. "If you don't mind an interruption—" He looked at the others. No one minded. "This is an important point, Major. Did you notice anything at all *before* that tree fell?"

"No, sir," Karvel said.

"Think carefully, Major. That U.O. didn't materialize on the spot. It had to come from somewhere. We'd like to know how it got there."

"I can't help you, sir. I'd been sitting there in Whistler's garden for maybe three hours when things started to happen, but obviously I didn't spend that time staring fixedly in any particular direction." He was speaking slowly, with frequent pauses. "I may have been looking toward that tree for a minute or two before it fell, but I couldn't swear to it, and I didn't see anything."

"He couldn't have seen anything anyway," Colonel Rogers said dryly. "I told you the U.O. wasn't visible from Whistler's, not even with binoculars. It was resting in a depression."

"He might have seen it arriving," Colonel Stubbins said. "It had to come from somewhere, and it didn't pop out of the ground. If it floated down by parachute, for example—"

"In that case, where's the parachute?" Colonel Rogers demanded.

"I only used that as an example. The U.O. wasn't hauled in by truck, or there'd be tracks. It didn't fall out of a plane, or get dropped from one, or it would have been smashed or at least embedded in the ground. Also, the base radar would have picked up the plane. It didn't arrive under its own power—"

"We can't be certain about that. Shall we get on with it?"

"Ten minutes, gentlemen," Colonel Vukin said crisply.

"The condition of the grass it was resting on should give

you some idea of how long it had been there," Karvel said.

"We have something better than that, Major," Colonel Rogers said. "A farmer drove a jeep across that pasture shortly after one o'clock yesterday. He passed within twenty feet of the spot—we measured from the tracks—and he thinks he would have noticed the U.O. if it'd been there. We think so, too. As for the condition of the grass—"

"Never mind," Colonel Stubbins said. "Major Karvel says he didn't notice anything before that tree fell. Let's leave it at that. What happened next, Major?"

"I doubt if anyone ever saw a tree fall the way that one fell," Karvel said thoughtfully. "The trunk was knocked right out from under it. As I found out later, it fell with its upper branches on the stump, and the lower part of the trunk was shredded, as if someone had wielded a gigantic sledge hammer."

"What did you think at the time it happened?"

"It just vaguely registered as an odd way for a tree to fall."

"And then?"

"The spiral pattern was obvious almost at once. It—your Force X—kept getting broader, as did the space between the spirals. It left the valley first in the vicinity of the Mueller farm, but it kept cutting back. I didn't see it again after it hit me. By the time Whistler picked me up it was no longer in sight."

"You didn't see it again," Colonel Stubbins mused. "Did you actually see Force X at any time?"

"Bad semantics," Karvel said with a grin. "No, sir. All I saw was what it did."

"There was no optical distortion, or anything like that?"

Karvel shook his head.

"Or—when it came close to you—any sound?"

Karvel shook his head again. "The destruction was highly audible, but I neither saw nor heard Force X. I *felt* it, if that's any help to you."

"What did it feel like?"

"Like a silent, invisible, speeding truck."

"Was there any odor?" the army colonel asked.

"No, sir, not that I can recall."

"Very well," Colonel Stubbins said. "Force X was invisible and silent and odorless, and it spiraled. The other survivors didn't see or hear or smell anything, and the crew of surveyors confirms the spiral. What else can you tell us?"

"In the way of facts, very little. I can offer a few conclusions. Or guesses."

"We'd like to hear them."

"For one thing, Force X gradually got weaker. In the beginning it was knocking the trunks out from under the trees. Later the trees fell normally. I'd say this was fortunate for me. If Force X had struck me with the impact that it had down in the valley, you would have found me looking like those dead cattle. For another thing, although Force X weakened, it didn't slow down. I've thought about this, and I discussed it with Whistler. We're both certain that Force X didn't lose any speed at all. In fact, it was constantly accelerating."

Colonel Stubbins took a moment to ponder that. "I suppose you know that you're postulating a physical impossibility."

"I'm not postulating anything, sir. I'm just trying to describe what I saw. The best analogy I can think of is the turntable of a phonograph. Every point on the diameter of a phonograph record is making the same number of revolutions per minute, but in terms of distance traveled the outer edge is going a whale of a lot faster than a point located close to the center. The outer edge of a ten-inch record travels roughly thirty-one and a half inches with each revolution. A point one inch from the center travels a little over three inches in the same time. To the best of my recollection your Force X made regular revolutions, which means that it had to be accelerating tremendously. Otherwise, I would have had a distinct impression of the spiral slowing down as the force moved away from the center. Each successive revolution would have taken longer, because the force had farther to go."

"Interesting," Colonel Stubbins said. "But still impossible.

Think of the resistance it was encountering! Everything it struck *must* have slowed it down, even if infinitesimally."

"Not to mention air and ground friction," the army colonel put in.

"Was it traveling on the ground, sir?" Karvel asked.

The colonels stared at him.

"It left no marks on the ground, and it didn't strike anything at ground level. That first tree was struck roughly a foot above the ground. Your Force X followed the contours of the ground, but in addition to accelerating it was also slowly rising. By the time it got to Whistler's, it, or the bottom of it, was waist high, and I have the broken ribs to prove it."

"I suppose your injured knee also proves it was waist high," Colonel Stubbins said.

"It didn't strike my knee. That was injured when Force X knocked me over, or maybe when I landed."

A brief silence followed, which Colonel Vukin broke with the words, "Five minutes, gentlemen."

Colonel Stubbins glared at him and turned back to Karvel. "At least there's no argument about Force X becoming weaker. The damage decreased steadily until it stopped altogether. And since Force X did become weaker, of course it slowed down. The strength would be proportional to the velocity."

Karvel shook his head. "No, sir. A phonograph record. The revolutions were as regular as a clock ticking. I'll swear to that. If it sounds impossible, just tell me one thing about this Force X that *is* possible."

"Does Whistler agree with you? About the regular revolutions, I mean."

"He does. We're also in agreement about how long we watched together, and of course you won't believe this, either. Within ten seconds after the first tree fell, I let out a yell. Whistler was passing the rear door, and he heard me. He came out to see what was going on. He says he ran, but that's a little hard to believe. By walking fast, he made it in less than ten seconds. Within another twenty seconds the spiral pattern was obvious, the Mueller farm had been struck, and I could see that the tavern was in danger. I told Whistler to get everyone into the basement, and he started away. Then it hit me. Allow another fifteen seconds. I make it less than a minute from that first tree to the tavern, and all of those times are estimated conservatively."

"Indeed." Colonel Stubbins cocked his head meditatively. "Considering the spiral, Force X traveled a good many miles between that first tree and the tavern. Less than a minute, you say?"

"I wouldn't believe it myself, sir, if I hadn't seen it. But I did see it."

"Even on a straight line it's several miles from Whistler's to the tree. Following a spiral path, Force X probably traveled—oh, say ten miles for each mile of diameter. The surveyors can give us the exact figures. What you're saying is that Force X covered perhaps fifty miles in less than a minute, which would require an average velocity of . . . uh . . . something in excess of three thousand miles per hour."

"Something like that, sir," Karvel said with a grin.

"And since Force X was accelerating—you say—it must have been traveling considerably faster than that when it struck you."

"That's the way I have it figured."

Colonel Stubbins leaned back disgustedly. "If you'd been struck by anything going that fast, your present physical dimensions would be a fraction of a millimeter thick by a good many yards square."

"I can't disagree with you, sir. That I survived at all is an impossibility, but what's one more impossibility among so many?"

"Frankly, Major, I was hoping for something better than that from you—something rational, let's say. What would be your evaluation of Force X as a military weapon?"

"I don't know. Against a specific target, it would depend on how accurately it could be delivered. Against a general target, such as a population center, it would frighten me."

"At least there's one point we can agree on. If Force X had started its spirals in New York City's Times Square, we'd have a catastrophe on our hands that almost defies description. We have to decide immediately whether this U.O. was delivered here by a foreign power, and if so, why this particular area was chosen—if it was chosen. The U.O. could have been aimed at this base, but Hatch Air Force Base isn't as important as all that. Are we being given a few days to survey the damage before we receive an ultimatum, or was the U.O. intended for a major Midwest city and sent with unbelievably bad aim? The military implications— What's that, Rogers?"

"We're wasting our time," the army colonel said. "Obviously the major can't help us on the critical point, but ask him anyway, and let's get out of here."

"Ah—yes. Major Karvel, we're assuming that the U.O. and Force X represent cause and effect, because the U.O.'s position is the precise center of the spiral. Among other things we'd like to know whether Force X commenced the instant the U.O. arrived, and since you didn't see the U.O. arrive I don't suppose you can help us."

"No, sir. I don't suppose so."

"Time, gentlemen," Colonel Vukin said.

Colonel Stubbins ignored him. "Have you anything else to tell us about this, Major?"

Karvel hesitated for a moment, shook his head. "No, sir."

"Thank you, Major. Except for that fat tavern owner, you're our only witness of any consequence. If you think of anything else, I want to know about it immediately."

"Yes, sir."

Stubbins got to his feet, pushed his chair back, and started for the door. Sergeant Gore closed her notebook with a snap and followed him. Colonel Frazier walked over to the bed.

He said softly, "I have a message of commendation for you from the governor. Your prompt action in getting the rescue work started saved some lives, not to mention bringing speedy aid and comfort to the injured. I also want to apologize for what I said last night. On reflection, I decided that there was no way for you to know that Force X wouldn't reach the base, and considering the destruction you'd seen, your action in suggesting a tornado alert was entirely proper."

"Thank you, sir."

"I also want to compliment you for resisting what must have been a powerful urge to wave that damned butterfly under Colonel Stubbins's nose."

"Thank you, sir, but you deserve the credit. You convinced me last night that I shouldn't wave it."

Frazier turned away, his facial expression enigmatic. Colonel Rogers stood waiting in the doorway. "Coming?" Frazier asked Haskins.

Haskins shook his head. "I'll walk back."

Frazier nodded, and went out. Haskins moved a chair close to the bed, and calmly seated himself. When Colonel Vukin advanced on him, he said good-naturedly, "Cut the act, Colonel. I'm not part of the chain of command. I have one question for the major."

"How do you feel, Karvel?" Vukin asked.

"No worse than I did an hour ago."

"Ring when you want him thrown out."

"Let me know as soon as you hear from the professor," Karvel said. He turned to Haskins. "What's the question?"

Haskins felt his hand reaching for a cigar. He moved it away reluctantly. "What are you holding back, Major?"

Karvel met his eyes steadily. Vukin left, muttering something that Haskins did not understand. A nurse opened the door, said, "Oh, excuse me," and closed it. Still Karvel's gaze did not waver. Haskins, who spent his waking hours meticulously evaluating those human animals who attracted his attention, knew that he was being measured himself, and he resented it.

"Who are you?" Karvel asked finally.

"Gerald Haskins, just as I was when Colonel Frazier introduced us. Shall I have him come back and vouch for me?"

"No. Your credentials must carry some impact, or you wouldn't have gotten in here."

"And so I say again, Major—what are you holding back?"

Karvel closed his eyes. "I don't really know if I'm holding

anything back," he said slowly. For the first time Haskins became aware of his rapid, shallow breathing, and realized that Colonel Vukin had not been pulling hospital rank on his superiors for the fun of it. Karvel was a sick man, and—after his interview with the colonels—a very tired one. "Until I find out," he went on, "I'm going to keep my mouth shut. How about letting me ask a few questions."

"Go ahead."

"What are the chances that the U.O. came from outer space?"

"None at all," Haskins said, "unless it was enclosed in something else. The external surface is a relatively soft alloy. It would have burned in the upper atmosphere."

"I suppose you won't know if the thing is self-propelled until you break into it."

"We've already broken into it," Haskins said. "That was no problem. All we had to do was open a hatch. It was a bit more complicated than it sounds, but only because no one ever saw a hatch like this one. It operates on the principle of an iris diaphragm—something like the adjustment on the lens aperture of a camera. We opened it, but we still don't know if the U.O. is self-propelled."

"Hatch? You mean a *passenger* hatch? Was the thing designed to carry passengers?"

"It was designed to carry one passenger."

"Then you *really* have a problem. Was there a passenger, and if so, what happened to him?"

"No problem at all," Haskins said peacefully. "There was a passenger, and when we opened the hatch he was still there. Unfortunately, he was dead. Extremely dead. Smashed the way those cattle were smashed, only more so. The U.O. required extensive cleaning before we could begin to study it comfortably. Now may I ask you a question?"

Karvel nodded.

"What are you holding back?"

"I won't know until I've talked with an expert. I've invited one, a college professor, and he's promised to come as soon as he can get away. When and if he arrives, you can ask him about it."

"Give me his name and address, and I'll hurry him up."

"He's detained by the circumstance of his wife's having a baby," Karvel said. "I don't question the potency of your influence, sir, but I doubt that even you can hurry that."

"What kind of an expert is he?"

"A lepidopterologist."

"It sounds like an extremely rare species of expert," Haskins said dryly. "I was thinking of drafting a substitute, but I doubt that a . . . lepidopterologist, was it? . . . is that easy to locate on a Sunday morning. I'll wait for your professor. And because he is a . . . lepidopterologist . . . that means you are holding back—"

"One butterfly," Karvel said. He raised a hand tiredly as Haskins started to speak. "No amplification, and no more questions. Please."

Haskins obediently moved toward the door. "Thank you, Major. I'll be seeing you."

3

Professor Kent Alexander arrived shortly after two, and was detained in the lobby until Haskins reached the hospital. Colonel Vukin introduced them, and Alexander gave Haskins a cigar, told him it was a boy, seven pounds four ounces, and asked what had happened to Karvel.

"He was in an accident," Haskins said.

"He sounded incoherent on the telephone. Or maybe it was a bad connection. I thought he said he'd found—"

"Let's see it before we talk about it," Haskins said. "I'll take him up, Colonel. Thank you."

He hurried the professor away before Vukin could object.

"Are you interested in butterflies?" Alexander asked.

"Only in this one," Haskins said.

The professor was something of a disappointment to him. Gangly, youthful-looking, shy, he had the appearance of a flustered undergraduate—or, Haskins reminded himself, of a new father. He decided to postpone judgment.

The professor bounded into Karvel's room ahead of him and burst into laughter. "Aren't you getting a little old for this sort of thing? What does the other guy look like? Here—have a cigar."

"I didn't touch him," Karvel said. "And no, thanks. It may be weeks before I can inhale properly. What took you so long?"

Haskins closed the door, and unobtrusively took possession of a chair in the corner.

"I was driving carefully," Alexander said. "I want my son

to be at least a day old before he's an orphan. And man, am I tired. Didn't get a wink of sleep last night. Hospital waiting room. Gruesome experience. It's enough to give one a wholesome respect for nature. Who'd want to go through that more than once a year?"

"Your wife probably agrees with you," Karvel said.

"At least she had an anesthetic. Where *is* it, man? If you've made me drive a hundred miles just to investigate one of your hallucinations, I'll choke you."

Karvel opened the nightstand drawer, took out a small cardboard box, and opened it. The professor stared, whipped out a pocket lens, and stared again. His breath hissed audibly. "Bowden," he whispered. "I'll name the boy Bowden, though Doris swears he'll go through life answering to his middle name if I do."

"What do you think of it?" Karvel asked.

"I don't know what I think. I can't think. The thing is absolutely impossible. It's a monster. Where'd you get it?"

"I was sitting on a fallen tree, and it circled me a couple of times and lit right beside me."

"You're sure you saw it fly?"

"Positive. What I'd like to know is whether such a drastic mutation can occur at one crack, or whether it would require gradual evolutionary changes over a large number of generations."

"You've got me. I'm no geneticist."

"What's your answer as a lepidopterologist?"

"Yes to both questions. Because the changes *are* so drastic, it's hard to believe that they all occurred in a single mutation. On the other hand, if a long series of evolutionary changes had taken place, some of the intermediate stages should have come to light. A lot of people collect butterflies, and someone, somewhere, would have found a monarch with a thorax like this one, or eyes—did you notice the eyes?—or wings, or . . ." He paused. "I'm not sure even now that you're not pulling my leg. It's hard to believe this even when I'm looking at it. My God—a bialate, bipedal butterfly!"

"It's real. I told you—it flew around me a couple of times and landed right beside me, which was a colossal piece of luck. If I'd had to take even one step to catch it, it would have gotten away."

"Why?"

"I couldn't walk."

"You lack the true scientific spirit. I'd run a mile to catch this, whether I could walk or not."

"Sure you would," Karvel said disgustedly.

Haskins chose that moment to leave his chair. "May I see it?" he asked.

Alexander held the box under his nose. Haskins scrutinized the impaled butterfly, shrugged, and returned to his place in the corner. He was wondering if Karvel, with the professor's assistance, was trying to pull *his* leg.

"If it did require a series of evolutionary changes," Karvel asked, "how long would they take?"

"I haven't the faintest idea," Alexander said. "As I said before, I'm no geneticist."

"I'm not asking for a scientific paper. Just an educated guess."

"I haven't got that kind of an education."

"An uneducated guess, then."

"I can't even give you that. I'll make some inquiries, though. Can I take it with me?"

"You might as well," Karvel said. "If a certain colonel sees it again, he'll try to make me eat it. Push those inquiries, will you?"

"Sure. There's a man at the college who might be able to help. Ferguson, his name is. He'll know whom to ask, anyway. What do you think of it, Mr. Haskins?"

"It looks like a butterfly," Haskins said.

"I suppose so," Alexander said, with a puzzled frown. "It looks like a butterfly, it *is* a butterfly, and yet it can't be a butterfly. Put another way, it doesn't look like a butterfly, it isn't a butterfly, and yet it's got to be a butterfly."

"Are you sure he's an expert?" Haskins asked Karvel.

Karvel nodded. "Stop talking nonsense, and tell Mr. Haskins what's different about this particular butterfly."

Alexander seated himself on the edge of the bed, bent over the box with his pocket lens, and announced in hushed tones, "It has two wings!"

"Don't most butterflies?" Haskins asked. "They'd have a little trouble getting around on one, wouldn't they?"

"Good God! *All* of the Lepidoptera—moths and butterflies —have *four* wings!"

"Is that so? Sounds like a good point. I've never paid much attention to moths and butterflies."

"And it has only two legs," Alexander went on. "It should have six. The thorax has only a single segment. It should have three, each of them with a pair of legs and two of them with pairs of wings. The abdomen is shortened—not just smaller, but structurally simplified, with fewer segments. The eyes—the damned eyes aren't even compound! This is obviously a monarch butterfly, but it's only about a fourth as large as it should be."

"In other words," Haskins said, "it's a freak."

"*Freak* isn't strong enough. It's a dratted monster!"

"Abnormalities occur in all living things. Man has two legs, but babies have been born without legs. A butterfly with only two wings—"

"It isn't that kind of abnormality," Alexander protested. "It isn't a butterfly with two wings missing. It's a butterfly with a single pair of wings shaped and adapted to do the work of two pair."

"All right. You're the expert, and I'm not equipped to ask intelligent questions, much less argue with you. It's a mutation, a sport, or maybe it's the result of a long process of evolution. Could such a mutation be induced by radiation, Professor?"

"I don't know. I'd have to consult a geneticist."

Haskins smiled, shaking his head. "Consulting experts is exactly like running into debt. Once you get started, there's no end to it. I gather that you favor the mutation theory over the evolution theory."

"I don't remember saying so, but I suppose I do, mainly because no butterfly has ever been found with *any* of these changes."

"The professor knows nothing about related events," Karvel said to Haskins.

Haskins met his eyes squarely. "Are you assuming that the events *are* related, Major?"

"I am. No butterfly has ever been found with any of these changes. Suddenly one is found, with all of them, in close association with an object and an occurrence that are equally strange. Aren't we entitled to make such an assumption?"

"I'd be the last to deny it."

"What the devil are you two talking about?" Alexander demanded.

Haskins ignored him. "You're entitled to make any assumption you like. Assumptions, or suppositions, or hypotheses are highly useful work animals, but for display purposes they aren't worth a damn. Can you put your assumption to work?"

"Look at it this way. Say an airplane of unknown design crashes in the valley below Whistler's. We don't know where it came from, but nearby we find a butterfly that has previously been identified only in Tibet. Wouldn't it be rational to form a working assumption that the plane came from Tibet?"

"I doubt it," Haskins said. "I'd want a guarantee signed by the butterfly itself that it actually did come from Tibet, and hadn't been an unnoticed local resident for years. I'd also want to know what world travelers had passed through the neighborhood recently. In actual fact, I'd probably ignore the butterfly and concentrate on the airplane. I have a bias against assumptions involving animate objects."

"He had a whack on the head," Alexander said. "Are you humoring him, or what?"

"I'm humoring myself. Go ahead, Major. For the moment we'll assume that the Tibetan butterfly proves the airplane came from Tibet. What then?" He watched Karvel closely.

Either the man was better-tempered than he had any right to expect, or his self-control was impressive.

"How about it, Alex?" Karvel said. "Do you deny that this butterfly *could* be the result of a long period of evolutionary change?"

"Not really. Evolution seems to move toward simplification and specialization, and most of these changes are actually anticipated in many current species. Butterflies once had six wings, perhaps even eight. Today they have four, and the hind wings are frequently smaller and of little use in flying. Some species already have their front legs reduced to small brushes. Maybe the evolutionary trend toward a bialate, bipedal butterfly with a simplified body is already under way, but one just doesn't expect to come face to face with the end product. Even that couldn't account for what's happened to this butterfly's eyes, unless you want to say that evolution had to make them better because they couldn't get much worse. As for your related events—"

Karvel cut him off with a wave of his hand. "The reason none of the intermediary stages of this butterfly have come to light *could* be because they haven't occurred yet, and this butterfly hasn't occurred yet, either. It will occur only in the future."

"Are you sure this isn't a mental hospital?" Alexander asked, in an uneasy aside to Haskins.

"Not today," Haskins said, "though I'm not making any guarantee about tomorrow. How far into the future, Major?"

"Consult your friendly geneticist. A few years, a few centuries—perhaps thousands of years."

Haskins glanced at his watch, thinking that it was time he got back to Hangar Seven. He said absently, "Continue, please."

"I've finished. If a Tibetan butterfly in connection with an airplane would suggest that the plane came from Tibet, then a future butterfly, in connection with the inexplicable arrival of an inexplicable U.O., would suggest that the U.O. came from the future. As a working assumption, of course. If any inconsistencies turn up—"

"You back down easily, Major."

"So far I haven't been able to find a single inconsistency."

"What about Force X? Did that come from the future?"

"In a sense. If an object smashes through a brick wall, you'll expect to see a few bricks fly. If an object smashes through a temporal barrier, you might reasonably expect some comparable reaction."

"A few bricks—of time?"

"Or an eddy of time. Or a whirlpool."

"A whirlpool," Haskins mused. "A spiral of time. I'm sorry Colonel Stubbins isn't here. His reaction would be interesting to watch."

"I only told you because you asked for it."

"So I did. And having gotten it, I couldn't complain even if I wanted to, which I don't. Tell me this, Professor. While this future butterfly is evolving, what changes might take place in the human race?"

"What a question to ask a lepidopterologist! Oh, I vaguely recall some speculation on the subject. The man of the future may be totally bald. Vestiges such as the appendix and perhaps the tailbone might disappear altogether. There may be changes in the teeth, as one devastating result of the civilized diet. The feet will be modified by the corrosive restrictions of shoes. Experts have produced long lists of such things, but I don't remember much about them except that they always give me the impression that I'd rather not be around to meet their subject."

"The passenger," Haskins said softly, keeping his eyes fixed on Karvel, "has no body hair. His feet have four toes, but his hands have five fingers. He has no teeth, and something about his jawbone has given this base's chief dental officer nightmares. He is nearly eight feet tall. The body's internal structure is equally interesting, though they're having a bit of a problem in getting it reassembled for study. A smashed corpse makes a messy kind of jigsaw puzzle. The most intriguing thing thus far is that they haven't been able to find any stomach. The clothing, incidentally, which one of my jocular experts describes as a two-piece toga with cod piece, is of a fabric not yet identified. As for the U.O., its instrumentation is so advanced that it has my experts behaving like kindergartners. It is nuclear-powered, but we haven't been able to decide just how the power works, or what it's supposed to do. The numerical system employed on the controls and instruments—if they are controls and instruments—is unlike any numerical system known to us. If it is a numerical system, that is. The U.O. is constructed in part of wholly unknown alloys or unknown metals or both. Your assumption—"

"Is still working," Karvel said.

Haskins got to his feet. "You can take the butterfly with you, Professor, under these conditions. You will guard it well, you will show it to no one, and you will say nothing, either publicly or privately, about it or anything you have heard here. You will photograph it, and study it carefully, and you will write a report of which there will be only one copy that you will deliver to me personally. Have I made myself clear?"

Alexander looked crushed. "You mean I can't publish—"

"Not now. Next month, next year, five years from now—perhaps. Have I made myself clear?"

Alexander nodded.

"As for your assumption, Major—it seems to be consistent with the facts that we have, but so would an assumption that the U.O. belongs to a previously undiscovered civilization located in the depths of the Amazonian jungle. We already have a long list of such assumptions, and if you don't mind, I'll keep yours on file as a last resort. It raises questions that are far more complicated than those it answers, one of them being how your flimsy butterfly managed to arrive intact when a sturdy, vertebrate, human-type passenger was smashed."

"Now I feel better," Alexander said. "For a moment I thought you were taking him seriously."

"I'm in a very serious business, Professor. I take everything seriously—whether I believe it or not. I'll be waiting for that report."

He shook hands with both of them, and walked over to Wing Headquarters to borrow Colonel Frazier's office. He called his favorite Washington, D.C., number.

"Read me the file on Bowden Karvel," he said.

He listened, puffing thoughtfully on the professor's cigar, and for a long time after he had hung up he sat wreathed in cigar smoke, feet planted untidily on the polished top of Frazier's desk, thinking. When the colonel attempted to reclaim his office, Haskins waved him away irritably.

He was wondering if Major Bowden Karvel was one of the kinds of people who interested him.

He telephoned Washington again. "About Karvel," he said. "I want him recalled to active duty and assigned to me. Never mind the medical problem. I know the man is missing a leg, and I also know that he's hospitalized at this moment, but I want him. Immediately. Just have the order issued, and if there are any repercussions I'll probably be finished with him before they catch up with us." He hung up.

He doubted that Bowden Karvel would ever be able to tell him anything he wanted to know. The man's appetite for general knowledge was too rapacious, and his interests too volatile. Haskins did not disparage those qualities, but neither did he patronize them. He knew from experience that when he wanted information a brilliant amateur was a poor substitute for a well-schooled professional.

Neither could he think of any job that Karvel might be qualified to do for him. His immediate concern was to put the major under military control, so he could order him to keep his mouth shut. If a man with his qualifications and background ever started spouting to the press about future butterflies and bricks of time, there'd be the devil to pay. To keep his mouth shut, and to keep a firm check on his awesome flights of imagination—those would be the problems.

"Though it is odd," Haskins mused, "that his theory is the only one without an obvious inconsistency."

4

Professor Charles Zimmer was a mathematician, and he was expounding some obscure theory of numbers to Gerald Haskins. Bowden Karvel, seated nearby in a wheel chair, listened absently and wondered if Haskins understood what the professor was talking about. Karvel did not.

In Karvel's lap lay a stack of photographs of the U.O.'s interior. Uppermost was a close-up of the central feature of a strange, bafflingly simple instrument panel.

"How about 'positive' and 'negative'?" Karvel asked suddenly.

The professor's smile spread over his plump face in concentric wrinkles. He took the photograph. "If that were so," he said, "the symbols on either side of the norm could be reasonably expected to exhibit similarities. In fact, they should be identical. I consider these symbols as representing a scale of regularly changing values, but whether it should be read from left to right, or vice versa, I would not even hazard a guess. Without some understanding of the function of this gadget, I am not even prepared to state positively that the symbols relate to numerical values."

He returned the photograph to Karvel.

"In that case," Karvel said, "how do you account for the fact that the central symbol is the largest, with the other symbols decreasing in size in either direction?"

"That's why I referred to the central symbol as the 'norm.' Such an interpretation is reasonably obvious. Consider the temperature gauge on an automobile. Between the two extremes of hot and cold there is some kind of mark to indicate the normal operating range. I would consider that this central symbol serves a comparable purpose."

Karvel looked at Gerald Haskins. He had come to think of him as a personification of the Anonymous Man. He was so average in every way that he was almost invisible in a crowd. Everything about him was medium: his height, his build, the color of his hair, the price of his suit—even his age, though the wrinkles around his eyes suggested that he might be older than he looked. Only the ever-present cigar struck a jarring note. It was expensive, and Haskins was a heavy smoker.

It had occurred to Karvel that such a consistent mediocrity had to be deliberate.

Now Haskins was delivering a warning shake of his head with moderate firmness, as he always did when Karvel seemed about to theorize in public. Karvel muttered, "Thank you," and wheeled himself away.

Lieutenant Ostrander hurried after him and took charge of the wheel chair. Haskins caught up with them a moment later, and they moved in silence toward the center of the hangar and the U.O.

"I suppose he's going to write a report," Karvel said.

Haskins nodded.

"What can he possibly have to report? He doesn't even know what the problem is."

"Does anyone?" Haskins asked. "What's your interpretation of those symbols?"

"I think they're a calendar."

Haskins whirled, and received a sharp rap on the shin from the wheel chair. He stooped and rubbed his leg vigorously, but there was more amazement than pain in the stare he directed at Karvel. "Calendar?"

"I think three of those instruments work in conjunction to select the U.O.'s destination. When I asked about 'positive' and 'negative' I was thinking of movement forward or backward in time."

Haskins gave his shin a final rub and straightened up with

a smile. "At least you're consistent. You'll have to admit, though, that the professor's objection is valid. If the controls measured time, the symbols on either side of the norm would exhibit similarities. Five centuries forward or five centuries backward. That sort of thing."

"Nonsense. If the central symbol represented the year 2500—and I'm not suggesting that it does—the forward count would be six, seven, and eight, and the backward count four, three, and two. Where's the similarity?"

"Eventually—"

"Eventually, nothing. Our numerical system builds from its simplest components, so we have a pattern of repetition neatly organized by tens. The U.O.'s numerical system uses an individual symbol for each number, without any repetition. Offhand I'd say it would be a difficult system to learn, but that wouldn't bother the people who built the U.O. because they're so much smarter than we are."

Haskins grinned at him. "You're in good form today, Major. Come along to my meeting, and shake up the security officer."

Karvel waved a hand, and Ostrander obediently turned the chair toward the partitioned office at the end of the hangar.

Except for Haskins it was to be a military meeting, and Colonel Stubbins was waiting impatiently for him in the doorway. Karvel said softly to Ostrander, "Go have a smoke, Phinney. If the higher ups' subconscious minds ever get you linked with me, your career will be blighted."

Haskins chuckled, and placed a hand on the wheel chair. "Go ahead, Lieutenant. I'll look after Major Karvel. They won't want to let you in anyway, and since you're in my party I'd have to insist, and a routine meeting isn't that important. I'd rather save my ammunition."

Haskins pushed the chair through the doorway, and Colonel Stubbins followed them and closed the door with a bang.

None of the six officers present paid any attention to Karvel, and he paid very little attention to the meeting. The security officer, a Captain Meyers, delivered a long report, replete with statistics on sentries and security checks and clearance cards and who owned them, and a new cover plan he was working on to replace one that had apparently been under severe criticism. Karvel's mind wandered back to the U.O. instrument panel, and he was startled, many minutes later, to hear his name spoken.

"We seem to have lost Major Karvel," Colonel Stubbins said dryly. "I am in the process of polling those present to see if they have any comments, Major. I apologize for the interruption."

"That's perfectly all right, sir," Karvel said, ignoring the undercurrent of laughter that circled the room. "I fully approve of these elaborate security precautions, even though I don't agree with the reason for them. If the Russians actually wished that U.O. onto us, as some of you seem to believe, I can't see them wasting time and risking agents to break in here. They already know more about it than we do. I'm convinced that they didn't send it, and that they'd eagerly offer a first mortgage on the Kremlin for a good description of it, with Lenin's Tomb and the Berlin Wall thrown in for a photograph. So I am in complete agreement with Captain Meyers. I've heard two of you remark privately that his arrangements are thorough to the point of being ridiculous, and that's the way it should be. We can't be too careful."

"Thank you, Major," Colonel Stubbins said. "We all feel easier about it knowing that you approve. Next—"

"I'm not finished, sir. I wouldn't say that this matter disturbs me, because I don't think it makes any difference, but there are some intriguing inconsistencies in the security arrangements." He paused, making certain that he had everyone's attention. Haskins was scowling and shaking his head, but Karvel ignored him. "If the Russians *did* send the U.O., they're going to be more interested in the valley below Whistler's than they are in this hangar. They're going to want to know the precise place the U.O. landed—"

"It's a little difficult to place the whole countryside under guard, Major," Captain Meyers said testily.

"—the precise place, and perhaps the precise time. Of

course it's too late to worry about that now, because their agents would have been on hand when the U.O. arrived, and left as soon as they got the information they wanted. It might be interesting to find out who the agents were, though. I point out that the personnel of a television program was visiting the base for allegedly honorable purposes, and three of the actresses were at Whistler's last Saturday afternoon. Odd that they should turn up on that particular day, don't you think? I remember one of them asking exactly how far the tavern was from the base, which in retrospect seems a peculiar question. Whistler's new bartender might be worth a casual investigation. There was a stranger who turned up at the tavern asking for directions to Highway 41, and looking for Highway 41 on Whistler's road is a little like looking for the moon in a coal mine. It makes one wonder what he really wanted—and, of course, where he went when he left Whistler's. And what other strangers conveniently managed to get lost about the valley on that particular afternoon. As I said, none of this disturbs me. If the Russians didn't send the U.O., what they find in the valley won't do a thing for them except whet their appetites to break in here. But if they did send it—"

Five minutes later Karvel managed to leave the room unnoticed in spite of his necessarily cumbersome departure and the fact that Haskins got up to help him through the door. The initial surge of argument had collapsed, and Colonel Stubbins was removing Captain Meyers's hide, one sentence worth at a time, while the others looked on uncomfortably.

"It was your idea," Karvel said, when they were safely away.

"I was about to thank you," Haskins said. "If they will now concentrate on who was where last Saturday, and leave us alone somewhat, perhaps we'll get some work done."

"I wouldn't say that your own guards are any improvement over the military."

"They make it difficult to get in or out, but they don't

bother you while you're here. Feel like having an early supper?"

"No. I'll have Ostrander bring me something later. Have they found any wires yet?"

"In the U.O.? No, no wires. Each instrument capsule is a self-contained unit. We're still trying to figure out a way to break into one without damaging it."

"What about the fuel?"

"We're working on it."

They reached the first guard post, at the hangar door, and two men in civilian clothes searched them routinely but thoroughly. They were not halted again until they came to a gate in the tall, barbed-wire-topped fence that had been erected around the hangar. Getting back in was much more time-consuming.

Ostrander caught up with them and helped Karvel into the car. "We'll drop Mr. Haskins at the Officers' Club," Karvel told him. "Then I'd like to go back to the B.O.Q."

Ostrander folded the wheel chair, stowed it away in the trunk, and cheerfully took his place at the steering wheel. The ready and efficient way he'd assumed the role of personal nursemaid was irksome to Karvel. In some previous incarnation Ostrander had been a millionaire's well-trained houseboy, and he had not lost the touch. When Haskins suggested that Karvel should have an assistant, he'd asked for Ostrander, thinking that the assistant was to help him on the U.O. project. It turned out that Haskins meant someone to assist him up and down stairs.

Twenty minutes later Karvel was settled in his wheel chair in the small room he was occupying temporarily in the Bachelor Officers' Quarters.

"When do you want to eat?" Ostrander asked.

"I don't. Let's skip it."

"Something to drink? Pinky Selton has some pretty good brandy."

"Nothing, thanks. I'll see you in the morning."

Ostrander left obediently, and Karvel lapsed into a sullen, brooding silence. In a lifetime of frustrations, he had never

felt as frustrated as he did now. He was weary of being
hauled about in a wheel chair, and furious with Colonel
Vukin for prohibiting crutches. He was mentally exhausted
from formulating ideas that Haskins's cavernous mind swallowed up unthinkingly, and more ideas to counter objec-
tions to ideas he'd already expressed. He was feeling
intensely resentful of Haskins, and bewildered as to why
the intelligence agent—which Haskins certainly was—had
wanted his help in the first place. He had an overwhelming
urge, active service or no, to hook his trailer onto his car and
depart.

Any destination would do, as long as it was satisfactorily
remote from the damnably inert U.O. in Hangar Seven.

Eventually he fell asleep.

He awakened suddenly, surprised to find himself in the
wheel chair. He moved it a few feet, pushed himself erect
on his artificial leg, and pivoted to drop onto the bed. As
he fumbled with his shirt buttons, his mind gyrated uneasily.

Where was Haskins? The Anonymous Man had made a
practice of dropping in each night for a quiet chat. Had he
found Karvel asleep, and left without waking him?

It was ten after midnight. The B.O.Q. reposed in a state
of unnatural silence. Karvel maneuvered himself back into
the wheel chair and rolled it toward the door, again cursing
Colonel Vukin's ban on crutches.

As soon as he opened the door he heard reassuring noises
—the faint vibration of snoring from a room across the corridor, hushed laughter floating down the stairway from the
floor above. He rolled the chair along the corridor to the
next room, Ostrander's, and knocked softly. He waited,
knocked again, opened the door.

Ostrander was not there. The bed had not been touched.

He swung the chair toward Haskins's room. Haskins was
not in, and the ash trays were empty of cigar stubs—incon-
trovertible proof that the Anonymous Man had not been in
his room since morning.

Karvel closed the door silently and rolled back to his own room. He took his blouse from the bed, wriggled into it, and propelled the chair around the corner to the building's main entrance. He had halted at the door and was sourly contemplating the outside steps when a late-returning lieutenant hove into view and sprang to his assistance.

"Going somewhere, Major? Want some help?"

"Thanks," Karvel said. "If you'd take the chair down, and then help me—it isn't easy—" He winced as the lieutenant put an arm around him. Ostrander managed it much more adroitly, and without hurting him. "Thanks. I'll be all right now."

"I doubt it, sir. Not if you're going very far."

"I'm going to Hangar Seven."

"You can't, sir. It's been put off limits."

"It isn't off limits to me."

"Then I'd better take you."

He ignored Karvel's protests and got the wheel chair rolling at a brisk pace. As they rattled along the deserted, heavily shadowed walk Karvel reflected that he was doing an idiotic thing. He did not want to go to Hangar Seven. He wanted to go back to his house trailer, and have a sound, drunken sleep, and wake up with a blissfully shattering hangover in a world where no U.O. existed. Would Haskins's men be working at this hour? He didn't know. Probably the U.O. would be locked up for the night.

"Lieutenant—" he said.

"Too fast? It is a bit bumpy along here."

The chair rattled on, reached the well-lighted complex of walks that converged on Wing Headquarters, and turned off toward the hangar area. The night was moonless, but clear and dazzlingly star-splashed. There were no planes up. Red obstruction lights gleamed brightly atop the control tower and dotted the invisible horizon, but the runway lights and the blue taxiway lights were on low intensity.

They were approaching a well-lighted gate, where two sentries stood lonely vigils in sentry boxes, when abruptly the siren cut loose. Karvel glanced at the lieutenant, saw his lips form the words "Practice alert," and nodded. He pushed up his sleeve to see the second hand on his wristwatch.

The rumble of the alert aircraft blended with the dying wail of the siren. The field lights brightened, and the roar of the jets crescendoed as the first plane moved onto the runway. A scattering of spectators hurried to the fence to watch. The first plane took off, and Karvel nodded his satisfaction and shouted to the lieutenant, "A minute and fifty-two seconds."

They watched until the fourth plane was airborne and a heavy silence had settled onto the field. "Ready to go?" the lieutenant asked.

Karvel nodded; and then, as familiar laughter rang out—brilliant bells of merriment tinkling in the darkness—he snapped, "Wait!"

He peered at a row of shadowy figures standing by the fence. One of them noticed him at the same time, and bounded forward.

"Major Karvel!" Ostrander exclaimed. "What's up?"

"I don't know," Karvel said. "Is something supposed to be up?"

"I'll take over, Steve," Ostrander said. "Many thanks."

Karvel added his own thanks, and told the volunteer he was free to go to bed. The others had gathered around, and Miss Sylvester said wonderingly, "It *is* Major Karvel. I was so sorry to hear you had an accident, Major. It was that tornado, wasn't it? We must have gotten away from there just in time."

"You did," Karvel agreed gravely. "But it was no accident."

"It wasn't?"

"The tornado did it on purpose."

Her laughter rang out again. "You have such an interesting accent, Major. I've never heard one just like it. Where are you from?"

"That's another of the troubles with the human race," Karvel said wearily. "No one knows where he's going, so we make a science of figuring out where we've been. I'm not from anywhere, and I have a birth certificate to prove it."

"Never mind Major Karvel," a voice said.

"I know," Miss Sylvester said. "He doesn't approve of there being two sexes. I'd like to know what he intends to do about it."

"Nothing, tonight," Karvel said. He nudged Ostrander. "Let's go over to Seven."

"Right," Ostrander said, not eagerly. "Night, folks. See you later—maybe."

They moved off, and Karvel growled, "What's *she* doing here?"

"The same thing the rest of us were doing. Watching the scramble."

"What I meant was, why is she still on base?"

"They're filming a TV program here. One of the 'Wayward Girls' is joining the Air Force."

"Several of them already have. Has Security checked her out?"

"Oh," Ostrander said. "Is that why Haskins was talking with her tonight?"

"I wouldn't be a bit surprised."

They passed the gate sentries and rolled smoothly along the paved road that led to the hangars. At Hangar Seven they ran the long gamut of identification and search, and finally they were allowed to enter the darkened building. One of the civilian guards obligingly followed, and turned on the lights.

"Were you looking for someone?" he asked. "They all went outside to watch the planes."

"They?"

"Some of those scientists. I don't think they were doing much anyway. Just sitting around talking about football."

"I have a hunch," Karvel said, as they moved toward the center of the hangar, "that our esteemed scientists are stumped."

"You mean you aren't?" Ostrander asked.

"Not stumped. Frustrated."

"Haskins would say it amounts to the same thing."

"The U.O. is enough of a problem. I'm not going to try to figure out Haskins."

"Who do you suppose he is?"

"CIA, at a guess. He knows all the right people, and when he wants something, nobody asks him why."

Karvel signaled a halt by a filing cabinet and took out the folder with the instrument panel photos. He laid aside the enlargements of individual instruments and sat back to study a shot of the full panel.

It seemed so simple, and yet it was so utterly incomprehensible. The raised symbols—tiny, angular maze, jagged serpentine, tangled, unsymmetrical web—did they mark off centuries, or miles, or light-years? Or some strange concept of velocity, such as centuries per minute?

The small, buglike lever was poised to crawl curvingly from symbol to symbol, over the hump of the outsized integer—if number it was—that occupied the central position. No symbol was repeated anywhere, and the symbols on the lesser instruments were, if anything, more intricate in design.

"Is it possible to have a numerical system where the smaller numbers are the most complicated?" Karvel asked.

"Sir?"

"Never mind. I was wondering— What's the matter?"

"Frankly, sir, I'd rather be up there."

"I told you yesterday you could chuck this assignment whenever you like. I don't require a pilot, or even an officer, to push my wheel chair. How about it? Shall I tell Haskins to draft an enlisted man for me?"

"I'd feel as though I were running out on you, sir."

"You wouldn't be. It won't take me five minutes to train a new man for the job. I'll take care of it in the morning. Now let's see if we can eliminate a little of my frustration before we call it a day. Has anyone explained this small hole at the top of the instrument panel?"

"They think there's an instrument missing. It's the same size as the holes that take the smaller capsules, but none of them will fit into it."

"Of course not, since each one is keyed for its own hole. Interesting, but maybe not critical. We both know that there are a number of instruments on the panel of an F-102 that the plane would fly without, even if not so conveniently."

"The U.O. flew all right—if that's the word for it."

"I don't think we can be certain that it flew all right," Karvel said. "It killed its pilot. But never mind. We aren't likely to figure out the function of what's missing until we've made some headway with what we have. Where are the capsules?"

"Maybe they put them back."

Ostrander took a flashlight from a workbench and went to the U.O. The dilating hatch opened smoothly and silently when a hand placed on a recessed handle was moved in a circular motion; it closed automatically when released. Ostrander opened the hatch and aimed the flashlight. "Yes. They put them back."

"Did they try to manipulate the things at all?"

"Sure. They manipulated them for hours. It wouldn't surprise me if they'd worn them out."

Karvel propelled his chair toward the U.O. and pulled himself erect, balancing awkwardly on his artificial leg. "I wish I could get inside," he said.

"Tell me what you want done, and I'll do it."

"Pull three of the capsules—the large one in the center and the ones on either side. The way I see it, they *have* to be the destination selectors. I want to know if they can be given settings that are opposite to the settings they arrived with."

Ostrander climbed through the hatch. He seated himself on the circular metallic hump in front of the instrument panel, and bent forward against the curving wall. The position was cramped, and his knees partially obscured the instruments. "This thing was designed for midgets," he complained.

Karvel leaned through the hatch, aiming the flashlight. "Interesting. No one mentioned that to me."

"They must have noticed it. If they tried to sit here, they *had* to notice it. Let me have that photo."

"You'd better pull them," Karvel said.

"Nuts. What would that prove? What difference does it make what can be done with them when they aren't in place?"

Karvel handed in the photograph. "Don't force them."

"There's hardly any resistance. There. Precisely opposite. All three of them."

"That is strange—about the seat, I mean. The dead passenger wasn't a midget. Nearly eight feet tall, Haskins said."

"He must have been awfully uncomfortable."

"Maybe that thing isn't supposed to be a seat."

"Sure it is. You can tell that just by looking at it. It's *shaped*. It certainly isn't the shape of my bottom, though. Let me have the flashlight."

Karvel traded the flashlight for the photograph and eased himself back into the wheel chair. The hatch opened again a moment later, and Ostrander babbled excitedly, "I found the light switch!"

"Which one is it?"

"The lowest gadget on the right. It lights up the whole interior. That metal projection at the top glows with a white light. Want to see it?"

"I can see it from here. Turn it off, and get out of there."

"Right," Ostrander said.

"Better not touch anything else. I've found out what I wanted to know, which wasn't much, but at least I feel a little less frustrated. We can go to bed now."

"Right."

Ostrander's head jerked back, and the hatch closed. Suddenly, with a tremendous *swish*, the U.O. vanished. Papers sucked from a nearby bench swirled about the hangar floor in a fluttering spiral, and then lay still. The excited scientists came at a run, shouting questions, arguing. Later Haskins arrived, with a raging Colonel Stubbins.

Through it all Karvel sat silently in his wheel chair with the crumpled photograph in his lap, and said nothing.

5

It was another November Saturday. Karvel had been lying awake for hours, staring at his trailer ceiling, when the knock came at the door. The handsome, boyish, light-encircled face of Phineas Ostrander hovered just below the dark paneling, one of its variegated moods following another, the frowns, the laughter, the whimsies, the buffoonery, all so real, so terrifyingly *alive*.

The knock came again. Wearily Karvel took his crutches, which were contraband from the base hospital, and started for the door. His ribs hurt when he used the crutches, but not as much as his muscles ached with the strain of trying to get around without them.

He opened the door. Gerald Haskins said matter-of-factly, "You look terrible," and pushed past him into the trailer. Bert Whistler followed, remarking that there was nothing wrong with Karvel's appearance that a little embalming fluid wouldn't cure.

"Did you come to invite me to the court-martial?" Karvel asked Haskins.

"Nonsense. Stubbins wouldn't dare. Five men heard you tell Ostrander not to touch anything. Anyway, Stubbins has no authority over you. You're on special assignment to me."

"I sent Ostrander in there."

"So? Both of you had clearance to work on the U.O. Sit down. When did you eat last?"

"I don't remember."

"Fix the man some breakfast, Whistler."

Whistler rummaged through the cupboards and glanced into the refrigerator. "There's nothing to fix. Just a jar of coffee. I'll go get some stuff."

"Do that," Haskins said. "Bring enough for three." Whistler drove off, tires screaming in the loose gravel.

"A real nice guy," Haskins remarked. "He'd give you both of his legs, if it were possible."

"I know."

"But he drives like a lunatic. Have a cigar? What have you been doing?"

"Climbing mountains."

"Climbing— Oh. That chaplain."

"Captain Morris. He spent yesterday evening with me. My mountains fascinate him."

Haskins nodded absently. "I'm sorry I didn't get to talk with you before. There's one thing I wanted to ask you. What were you and Ostrander *really* trying to do?"

"I don't know what Ostrander was trying to do. He'd found the light switch—"

"So had we. We tried each of the instruments, but with all of the others removed. The light switch was the only one that produced any result. We were gradually building up to the same thing Ostrander achieved, but it would have taken us a while."

"So killing Ostrander didn't even accomplish that much."

"Nonsense. I feel certain that if it hadn't been Ostrander it would have been one of the scientists. The U.O. was just too much for us. We don't know much more about it now than we did when we started."

"Do you think there's any chance at all that Ostrander survived?"

Haskins shook his head. "You didn't see the other passenger. I'd say no chance whatsoever."

"What makes it worse is that I was thinking of making the trip myself. I'm sure something could have been designed to protect the passenger."

"What were you going to protect the passenger against?

Time? Well, you can have a shot at designing a protective device that would keep out time!"

"Not time. Pressure. The pressure built up in passing through time. Never mind. There's no use arguing about it now."

"What sort of a device did you have in mind?"

"Something along the line of deep-sea diving equipment."

"Yes," Haskins mused. "That might have worked. The passenger was crushed, which certainly suggests that he was subjected to a purely physical pressure. Mention the possibility in your report. The scientists have been taking your assumption seriously since they saw the U.O. vanish. Smoke bothering you? Here, I'll open a window. We did chalk up one significant gain. We now have a practical nuclear fuel. It's a simple liquid allotrope of uranium, and we can produce it in quantity as soon as we find a use for it. But you only answered part of my question. What were *you* trying to do?"

"I'm not sure. I thought that three of the instrument capsules selected the U.O.'s destination—in time—and if they were precisely reversed the U.O. could be sent back to where it came from. It's just possible that those responsible for it aren't aware of the destruction it causes. Returning it to them would be one way of bringing that to their attention."

"Where were those three capsules set when Ostrander pulled the switch?"

"He had them set where I wanted them, and if he left them there— Was there enough fuel in the U.O. to get it back where it came from?"

Haskins nodded. "The fuel container was nearly three-fourths full when it arrived, and we took only a small sample for analysis. Here's Whistler. You two are leaving today on a long vacation. We'll go over the whole business when you get back."

"Don't be silly. I'm in the Air Force, thanks to you. I go where I'm told. And Whistler is in bondage to his cash register."

"You belong to me, and I'm telling you to take a vacation. Go collect butterflies or something. Take a month. Take two months, if you want them. You'll be incapacitated at least that long. Whistler will drive the car and run errands for you."

"Who'll run the tavern?" Karvel asked Whistler.

"It don't need no running," Whistler said cheerfully. "What d'ya think I got that new bartender for? Ma takes off whenever she feels like it to visit her sisters, but I ain't had a real vacation in years."

"That explains your nasty disposition," Karvel said. "All right, we'll go together. But not to collect butterflies. If even a one-wing butterfly was to light in my lap, I'd shoo it away."

They left that afternoon. Karvel took an imaginary compass reading on Lieutenant Ostrander's laughing face, and chose a route that seemed to lead in the opposite direction. Whistler's driving technique was a hair-raising blend of insolence and impetuosity, and they would have made excellent time had he not insisted on a professional visit to every bar that crossed his line of sight. They spent more time in bars than they did traveling, and before the end of the first afternoon Karvel made a startling discovery. Whistler never drank anything stronger than beer, and he drank very little of that.

"I got too much respect for my insides," he said.

"I wish you had some respect for mine. How much lousy whiskey have you sold me in the last six months?"

"Why should I sell you good whiskey? Guys that drink like you taste with their stomachs."

By the time they reached Kansas City, Karvel had convinced himself that Colonel Vukin was right. It was too soon for crutches, and Whistler handled the wheel chair as if it contained a load of nitroglycerin. He gave Karvel a luxuriously comfortable ride, maneuvering around bumps, easing the chair over curbs, coming to a dead stop at corners.

Karvel would have preferred more speed with the chair and less with the car, but he suffered in silence.

Another imaginary compass reading, and they turned south into Oklahoma and then Texas, with Ostrander's face behind them and Karvel's personal range of mountains filling the horizon.

"If you aren't going to drink, why are we spending all this time in bars?" Karvel asked impatiently.

"I like to watch bartenders work. I been studying them all my life, everywhere I go. The good ones, they got a philosophy, and no two of 'em work just alike."

"There can't be that many ways to pour a glass of beer."

"You're thinking about the mechanics. The philosophy is how you treat your customers. Look at this guy. He flatters everybody. Me, I give 'em insults. It don't matter as long as it's genuine. Even a drunk customer can see through a phoney philosophy."

"This comes as a shock. I've never thought of you as a philosopher."

"That's 'cause I'm so good at it," Whistler said.

They drove west across New Mexico and into Arizona, and finally rented space in a trailer camp in Tucson. For a week Whistler visited bars, and Karvel soaked up sunshine and asked himself what he could have done to keep Ostrander from trying one more switch, and both of them became so bored that they stopped insulting each other. Then, late one night, Gerald Haskins came knocking at their trailer door.

He handed Karvel his briefcase as casually as though they had parted two minutes before. "Hold the door," he said, and was back a moment later with a motion picture projector and a screen.

"Goody!" Whistler said. "Movies."

"We have another U.O.," Haskins said.

"Ostrander?" Karvel asked quickly.

Haskins shook his head. "Set up the screen, will you, Bert?"

"No trace at all of Ostrander?"

"*Another* U.O., I said. It wiped out a little village in northeast France, which means that it belongs to the French. It was only through a stroke of luck that we even found out about it."

"Was there a passenger?"

"Yes. Just as smashed as the last one. The French have agreed to exchange information with us. Colonel Stubbins is already in France, and some of my men went over with him. I had business to wind up on the West Coast, so I had the first reports flown to me there. I thought I might as well get your reaction on my way east."

"You're going to France?"

"Tomorrow. Ready, Bert? Where can I plug this thing in?"

Haskins threaded in the film and adjusted the focus, and they were looking down into a valley at the demolished village. Rubble clogged the streets except for a lane that a bulldozer had carved out. Three tents stood in the foreground, and the wooded hills across the valley were scarred with the widening loops of the spiral.

"How many people were killed?" Karvel asked.

"They think seventy-three. The entire village. As you can see, it was built on a curve. At that point Force X was just wide enough to take all of it. The only survivor was the priest, who happened not to be home."

The camera moved closer. They could watch workmen shifting stones and moving rafters and shoveling rubble. A young priest stepped carefully amidst the debris, head bowed, hands clasped behind his back—a pathetic, lonely figure who had no soul left to attend to but his own. The dust had scarcely settled about the village, but it was as lifeless as Nineveh because its people had died with it.

"What's the name of the place?" Whistler asked.

"St.-Pierre something or other. Just a moment. Here it is —St.-Pierre-du-Bois."

"Never heard of it."

"It's less well-known than Paris," Haskins said dryly.

"You said northeast France. I been all through there. I

was stationed there more than a year, during the war. I don't remember no St.-Pierre-du-Bois."

"You wouldn't," Karvel said. "It was too small to have a bar."

Haskins stopped the projector. "The rest is a close-up of the U.O.," he said. He reversed the film to a shot of the entire valley, and dipped into his briefcase. "A farmer named Cras was walking on the road north of the village when Force X struck him. Before he died he made a statement. I want you to read it."

It consisted of a single paragraph. Cras had been hurrying home to supper. There was still enough light to see the village clearly, but he hadn't been looking at it directly. Out of the corner of his eye he saw the church steeple fall. He stopped and stared, and the village wasn't there. A moment before it had been, but now there wasn't a single house standing. Just rubble piled up and flung about, and a cloud of dust rising over everything. He started to run, and then something struck him, and that was all he remembered.

"Any comment?" Haskins asked.

Karvel shook his head.

"Getting hit by Force X is the one thing you're expert in. Compare the Frenchman's experience with yours, and see how many new assumptions you can come up with."

Karvel pushed himself to his feet and hobbled to the screen. "Cras must have been closer to the center of the spiral than I was. Are we facing north? Then he was somewhere along this road. Where was the U.O. found?"

"Where the large tent is," Haskins said. "They haven't moved it yet."

"Here's the loop that took the village, and on the next time around it took this tree by the road—he couldn't have been *that* close—and then it got the trees south of the village. Cras must have been about here, which means that Force X approached him across open fields. He had no warning at all. Just a moment."

"What's the matter?"

"The spiral goes clockwise. The spiral that struck me was moving counterclockwise."

"Are you sure? Yes, I see it now. That's very interesting. I'll have something to say to my men for having missed that. Can you think of anything else?"

Karvel shook his head.

Haskins turned off the projector and got out a cigar. "There are several interesting things about this U.O.-2. For one, it arrived with its fuel tank, if that's the proper term for it, virtually empty. This naturally raises the question as to whether the stuff we analyzed really is a fuel. We've sent a batch to the French for experimental purposes, but we can't be positive yet that this is what makes a U.O. go."

"Their first experiment is likely to be their last one," Karvel said.

"They've been warned. For another thing, the passenger is absolutely unearthly. There is no possibility of it being related to any known Earth species. The French consider this proof positive that the U.O. comes from outer space."

"Are you certain that it's a different U.O.?"

Haskins nodded. "We took shavings for metallurgical analysis, which left marks. This U.O. doesn't have any."

"Did they look for butterflies?"

Haskins caught his breath. "I don't think so, but I'll see that they do. Can you fit this unearthly passenger into your time theory?"

"Easily. We'll soon have contact with other worlds. Eventually there'll be contact with inhabited worlds, and those inhabitants will probably visit Earth. I see nothing strange in the idea of an unearthly being visiting us from the future."

Haskins bit firmly on his cigar, and emitted a series of short puffs. "Pressure," he whispered, as though the word awed him. "Tremendous pressure. Do you have any idea how much pressure that U.O. is built to resist, inside and out? Neither do we, and we probably wouldn't believe it if we knew. It isn't spherical by accident, and it's made of a strange alloy that is soft, but becomes hard under pressure. The more pressure, the harder it gets. For all we know, from the tests we've been able to make, that condition maintains to infinity. That soft metal—under pressure—is the hardest substance known to man.

"The instruments are designed—we think—so that pressure won't damage them or change their settings. Under pressure they lock in place. The engineers who designed the U.O. knew that there'd be killing pressure, both inside and outside, but they made no attempt to protect the passenger. Why?"

"*We* knew that there'd be killing pressure, but we made no attempt to protect the passenger we sent back to them."

Haskins gaped at him. "You mean—stowaways? *Both* of them? No." He shook his head. "No. One I could accept, but not two. This can't go on, you know. Twenty-eight people were killed by U.O.-1, and another sixty were injured seriously. Seventy-three were killed by U.O.-2. We were lucky both times. We may not be so lucky with U.O.-3."

"What are the chances of my taking a ride in U.O.-2?" Karvel asked.

"None," Haskins said bluntly. "The French have been highly cooperative in exchanging information, but that's to their advantage as well as ours. They won't be receptive to suggestions as to what they should do with the U.O. I personally think that their investigation is a mess, with nothing being done right, but that's their privilege. We had our chance, and we blew it. Any passenger in this one would be French."

"That's what I was afraid of."

"It's too bad, really. If you weren't so banged up, I'd say it was an ideal job for you. No one has better qualifications, and you have no family at all, which is important. Even if you made the trip safely, you couldn't come back. Do you know that?"

"Unless I could hit the Sahara Desert dead center, there wouldn't be any welcoming committee for me."

"The same would apply at the other end. You wouldn't have diplomatic immunity, and if you killed a few thousand

people when you arrived you'd start your negotiations under a handicap."

"That's a risk we'd have to take."

"There's no doubt that the job is made to order for you,"
Haskins said slowly. "A freak accident cost you outer space,
and saved you for man's ultimate frontier—time." He smiled.
"If your theory is correct. But U.O.-2 belongs to the French.
It's a shame. I'll put it to you frankly. The U.O.'s are utterly
beyond us. We aren't ready for them, technologically or
morally. The man who could put a stop to them just might
be the savior of twentieth-century civilization."

"Will you put the proposition to the French?"

"No. I know they'd refuse, and it might make them suspicious. We're working together nicely, and I want to keep
it that way." He glanced at his watch. "You're staying here
for a while? I'll keep in touch with you. If there were anything for you to do in France I'd take you along, but there
isn't. Will you roll up the screen, Bert?"

He shook hands with both of them and was gone as suddenly as he had arrived. Whistler stood in the trailer door,
watching the diminishing taillights and muttering to himself.

"St.-Pierre-du-Bois. I still think I shoulda heard of it."

"What did you do in the army?" Karvel asked.

"I was mess sergeant in a lousy replacement depot. I
wanted to kill Germans, so they made me a cook."

"So you killed Americans instead. What would you rather
do—stay here by yourself and study philosophy, or—"

"You're going to France."

Karvel nodded.

"You think you're going to swipe that U.O. and take a ride
in it."

Karvel nodded again.

"I can see it now—you carting it away in your wheel chair,
with an army of Frenchmen chasing you!"

"I know it sounds ridiculous. It's a thousand to one against
my getting close to the U.O., and another thousand to one

against my finding it refueled and ready to go. After that, the odds start getting long. But I'm going."

"I'm coming with you."

"There isn't time. The longer I wait, the less chance I'll have. The present security arrangements look pretty feeble, but any minute the French may decide to put the U.O. behind fences and locked doors."

"What does that have to do with taking me?"

"Do you have a passport?"

"That won't take long," Whistler said confidently. "I know a bartender in Washington—"

Karvel laughed.

"—that knows everybody. You need me. You need somebody to drive your car, and push your chair, and run errands. Like I told you, I been all through that part of France. I parley enough French to be understood, and I know at least four hundred dames, and four thousand black market operators—every other Frenchman was a black market operator in those days—and all the taverns."

"The black market operators I can understand," Karvel said. "And the taverns. But I never would have suspected the four hundred dames. All right. I think I can manage a more direct connection with the State Department than through your bartender. I'll start packing, and you telephone for the plane schedules."

6

Seven days later Karvel took the Night Ferry at Dover, leaving behind in England the cast from his knee, a substantial portion of his bank balance, and a mystified firm of engineers. In Dunkerque he left an equally mystified customs official, who was overtly suspicious of the heavy, wheel-mounted trunk that Karvel's various papers and documents alleged to contain routine business equipment.

"I'm in the salvage business," Karvel explained, with as much aplomb as he could muster. "Marine salvage. Underwater work. This is diving equipment."

His papers were in order, and he had a beautifully forged letter from the Port Authority of Strasbourg concerning a construction project. In the end the customs official could discover no reason why Karvel and his trunk should not be admitted to France, though he spent some time in trying.

Whistler was waiting with a small panel truck. He hurriedly got the trunk loaded, and they drove away into an overcast French dawn.

"The wheels were a mistake," Whistler announced. "A trunk with wheels is unusual. The French don't like things to be unusual."

"Later on, you'll appreciate the wheels," Karvel told him. "I have all I can do to move myself around. You'll have to handle the trunk."

"We'll have plenty of help," Whistler said confidently.

"What about the U.O.?"

"It's still there. The bigwigs have gone—Haskins and his

bunch, and the French civilians. They were staying in Thionville and commuting every day, but they moved out last night. I think they finished studying it, and now they're trying to figure out what to do with it."

"Is it still in the tent?"

"Sure."

"I can't understand why they'd leave it there."

"They want to make it easy for us, why should we worry? I guess you made out all right in England."

"No one could understand why I'd be putting diving equipment through such a small opening, but it was my money. Did you have any trouble?"

"Naw. I arranged things without hardly showing my face. You got nothing to worry about. Just leave everything to me."

Karvel smiled. "You've arranged to have the U.O. fueled and ready to go?"

"Oh, that. I don't know what you'll find when you get there, but I guarantee to get you there. I got a plan."

They traveled southeast along the sparsely traveled roads of northern France, following a route that avoided the larger towns. Their leisurely pace soon became irksome to Karvel. "What's the matter?" he asked. "Lost your nerve?"

"Relax," Whistler said. "We got plenty of time. We don't want to get to Thionville much before dark."

"Why not? I'd like to see St.-Pierre-du-Bois by daylight."

"You couldn't get close enough for a look anyway. They got roadblocks up. Anyway, it wasn't nothing to see even when it *was* a town. I been through it dozens of times, and never noticed it. Like you said, it was too small to have a bar."

At noon they stopped to stretch their legs and make a roadside meal of long loaves of French bread, and cheese, and raw red wine. Karvel's left leg was badly in need of stretching. He sat on the grass and massaged his knee while Whistler paced back and forth, chomping on bread and cheese and casting wicked aspersions on the morals, habits, and institutions of the French peasantry.

"I wish I could speak French," Karvel said. "It'd be interesting to find out what they think of you."

Whistler halted his pacing and regarded Karvel quizzically. "I don't think I ever asked you. Why do you want to take a ride in that thing?"

"Good question. I wish I had a good answer." To find Ostrander? There wasn't a chance in a million that the lieutenant was still alive. To save twentieth-century civilization? It was doomed anyway. No civilization was immortal, and Karvel would not lament the passing of this one.

He said slowly, "Have you ever visited an orphanage?"

"No. What does that have to do with it?"

"I was brought up in an orphanage. There may be worse environments for a child than that particular institution, but I hope not. My earliest resolution in life was that I'd never make any child an orphan, or any wife a widow."

"So that's why you never got married," Whistler said. "I guess that's why you lost your leg, too—trying to keep from making some dame a widow."

Karvel did not answer.

"What's all that got to do with taking a ride in the U.O.? Just 'cause you had a rough time as a kid is no reason for not having fun now. So it was a lousy orphanage. So what? We got lousy legislatures, and lousy colleges, and lousy hospitals. Why should orphanages be different?"

"You don't understand."

"I understand that you're a damn fool. Here you are, still young, with a good pension for life and nothing to worry about, and you're bellyaching about being an orphan. I been an orphan myself for nearly ten years, and you never heard me complaining."

"I suppose an honest answer would be that I'm running away."

"That's even sillier."

"It is," Karvel agreed.

It was also true. His escape to the stars had been frustrated, but now he saw that it would have led him into a trap. Amidst the lonely splendor of the moon, or the arid wastes of Mars, or the steaming clouds of Venus, he could not have been free from this civilization that he hated, but helplessly dependent on it. Each delicious breath of transported air would have been a bitter reminder of the unseverable ties that forever bound him to this Earth and this century.

A psychiatrist had once told him that he was still attempting to run away from the orphanage, something he had tried —unsuccessfully—dozens of times. Karvel declined his offer of an easy cure. His own idea of destroying an urge was not to think it out of existence, but to satisfy it.

The U.O. offered the only genuine opportunity for escape, except through death, that he was ever likely to have, and he fully intended to annihilate any Frenchmen who got in his way.

"It's your neck," Whistler said. "If you're sure you want to go, I won't worry about why. I ain't had so much fun since the war."

They drove more slowly as the afternoon waned, and reached Thionville at dusk, precisely on schedule. There they turned north, and soon left the main Luxembourg highway to follow a narrow, winding road. From a hilltop Karvel had a disconcerting view of drab farmland, sparse forests, and a distant village of stone houses pinned to the landscape by its church spire. Abruptly it was dark.

"One good thing—it'll be a black night," Whistler said.

"How much further is it?"

"Just a few miles. I figure we'll start at eleven, so you got time for a nap, if you want it."

"No, thank you."

The long, tedious ride had done nothing to alleviate the tension that had been building in Karvel ever since they left Tucson, and he was more worried than he cared to admit. For all of Whistler's confident planning, the odds against success remained overwhelming.

"Here we are," Whistler said finally.

They turned into a rough lane, and at the end came upon

a cluster of stone buildings. There were lights in the house, and the door opened as they got out of the truck.

"Jacques?" Whistler called.

"*Oui.*"

A ruddy, corpulent, middle-aged Frenchman assisted Karvel over the threshold, shook his hand, and said with a grin, "Hi. Okay."

Jacques's wife put food on the table, and Karvel munched at it absently, only half aware of what he was eating, and listened to Jacques and Whistler spout French at each other. Whistler's fluency amazed him, but as they talked Karvel quickly sensed that something was wrong. Whistler's manner changed rapidly from incredulity to anger, and then to disgust, and when finally he turned away Karvel had never seen him so chagrined.

"They're going to chicken out," he announced.

"What's the matter?"

"He says the whole French army is guarding the place, and with submachine guns. He doesn't want any part of it."

"I don't blame him. I hadn't counted on submachine guns myself. Or on an army."

"Aw—that isn't what he saw. It's just what he thinks he saw. This really messes things up. Jacques runs a sawmill. He got permission to haul away the trees knocked down by Force X, and he's been all over the place. I ain't even been near it. There wasn't no point in an outsider snooping around and getting their backs up if it wasn't necessary."

"Does Jacques know what we're trying to do?"

"He thinks we're news photographers, trying to get pictures of the village. The official word is that an ammunition truck blew up there, but the French still haven't let reporters near the place."

"He thinks we're trying to get pictures—at night?"

"We got a whole trunkful of special equipment. I guess we'll have to figure out another plan. We can't use the road, and I wouldn't try to find my way through the woods at night. Anyway, we'd need Jacques's men to help with you and the diving stuff. It's all up- and downhill."

"I suppose there's only the one road."

"With two roadblocks on each side—one at the nearest crossroad, to turn traffic around the village, and another just before you get there."

"If we make the effort at all, it'll have to be at night," Karvel said thoughtfully. "Ask Jacques if he'd be willing to take us to some point at the edge of the forest south of the village. We probably wouldn't be able to see anything, but at least we'd get an idea of the route. Then we could decide what to do."

"They could take the trunk part way, and hide it in the woods."

"We might have a devil of a time finding it. No. Tell him there won't be any equipment and we won't go a step closer than the edge of the forest. We only want to know the best way to get there."

They talked again. Whistler, so blunt and caustic in English, seemed expansive and congenial in French, but Jacques was not easily persuaded. The submachine guns had impressed him.

"It's a long walk, and it'd be tough-going even in the daytime," Whistler said. "He doesn't think you can make it."

"I'll make it."

"He's willing to try if some of his men will come along. I guess he figures they may have to carry you."

"They won't, but he can bring all the men he wants. Did you offer to pay them?"

"Doggone well, for a walk in the woods."

"Then let's get started."

Whistler drove the truck into a barn, and the three of them got into Jacques's tiny car. It started up with a roar all out of proportion to its size.

"That motor isn't original equipment," Karvel observed.

Whistler nodded. "I think Jacques is a part-time smuggler."

Four hours later Karvel lay on the ground at the edge of the forest, looking down at a brilliant circle of light. The three dark tents stood out starkly. Somewhere beyond, hidden by the darkness, were the mortal remains of St.-Pierre-du-Bois. They had walked for nearly an hour across rough ground and up- and downhill and through the forest, and Karvel felt utterly exhausted.

He also felt completely disheartened. He had expected guards, but not a full company of infantry, and he had not reckoned at all with the light. Naïvely, he had envisioned a stealthy approach through the darkness, and the overwhelming of a bored sentry or two.

The thing was impossible. Even if they got the diving equipment down to the tents, he still had to pass it through the U.O.'s hatch, assemble it inside, get into it, set the instruments by memory, and throw the switch—and with no assurance that there was any fuel in the U.O., or even that the instruments would be in place. The sentries were alert, and had weapons they knew how to use, and they couldn't be expected to stand around picking their teeth while all that was happening.

He had no right to lead Whistler or anyone else into deadly danger with such a minute chance of success. He said firmly, "It's impossible. Let's forget it."

Jacques hissed for silence.

"By the time we get within a hundred yards of the U.O., we'll either be dead or captured," Karvel whispered. "One would be as bad as the other. I've heard that the inside of a French prison isn't nice."

"What do you want to do?"

"We've known from the beginning that this expedition was a silly idea. Now we know just how silly. Let's find ourselves a place to stay, and we'll talk it over in the morning. If it still looks as stupid as it does right now, we'll go home."

Whistler whispered to Jacques, who spoke softly to the three men crouched behind them. They helped Karvel to his feet, and started away. Karvel had not moved ten feet when he bumped into a tree, stumbled over a bush, and went sprawling.

Instantly a shout rang out. *"Halt-la!"*

One of Jacques's men darted away, scrambling noisily along the edge of the forest. A flashlight beam flickered after him, and another challenge was shouted a short distance to the east. They froze where they were, and waited. The valley was suddenly alive with lights and movement. Flashlight beams searched the hillside. A squad of soldiers clumped noisily past, and broke into a run when shots rang out where Jacques's man was hotly pursued.

"Let's get out of here!" Whistler hissed.

He took one of Karvel's arms, and Jacques took the other. Crouching, blindly feeling their way forward, they moved back through the trees. Machine guns rattled again, and a volley of stray shots whipped past them. Finally they staggered over the crest of the hill, and the sounds of pursuit faded.

They did not pause until they had topped the next hill, when Karvel shook off his support and sank panting to the ground. Jacques and Whistler conferred in whispers.

"Lucky for us that someone ran for it," Karvel muttered.

"At least *that* plan worked," Whistler said with satisfaction.

"Plan? You *planned* that?"

"Just in case. I promised Maurice a bonus if he brought it off. I hope nothing happened to him. We haven't come a mile yet. Maybe we better get moving."

"I don't think they'll follow us through the forest. They don't know we won't shoot back."

"Jacques thinks they'll set up more roadblocks as fast as they can. By the time we get back to the car they may have us boxed in."

"Like you said, we'd better get moving."

They struggled forward again. The slopes were endless and steep, the ground underfoot uneven and treacherously sown with obstacles, the night totally black. For some time the alarms and confusions of the valley continued to reach them faintly, but the shooting had stopped. Finally they reached the cars and found a grinning Maurice waiting for them. Karvel gave him a firm handshake, and Whistler called for a flashlight and solemnly counted out the bonus.

Jacques held a short strategy conference. They had to negotiate two miles of narrow, rutted forest track to reach the road. The question, Karvel gathered, was whether to tear out of there at top speed with lights blazing, or to try to sneak out without lights—which would take infinitely longer. They voted for speed, piled into the two cars, and were off.

They bounced recklessly along the zigzagging track without incident until they rounded the last turn and saw, where the arching trees met the highway, a waving flashlight. Jacques growled something that would have been profane in any language, and pumped a signal with his brake pedal.

"I hope you have a plan for this," Karvel remarked.

"From here on, it's their plan," Whistler said.

At the road they veered sharply to the right and came to a stop. The car behind them pulled alongside, veering to the left, and the two young soldiers stepped forward innocently. They had not even unslung their weapons. Suddenly spotlights struck them in the face, and the cars roared off in opposite directions. Karvel tensed himself and waited for shots, but none came.

"I guess we're in good hands," he said dryly.

"That's just the beginning," Whistler said.

At the next crossroad they took another roadblock by surprise. It was set up to stop southbound traffic, with a car parked across the highway; they passed it going west, and skidded around the car on screaming tires. Again there were no shots, but Karvel looked back a moment later and saw headlights following them.

For the next ten minutes Jacques drove the narrow, meandering road with furious confidence, negotiating curves with a recklessness that made even Whistler wince. They tore through a village, made a screaming turn, and thundered along a straightaway. The lights did not gain on them, but neither did they seem to lose ground.

Jacques spoke excitedly. Whistler answered, and turned to nudge Karvel. "He's worried that we'll hit another roadblock. He thinks he could talk his way out of it if we weren't with him. We'll get out at the next village."

"Sure. Ask him if he'd mind slowing down."

"He'll stop. You just be ready to jump."

A cluster of dark houses flashed past, and then a larger cluster with a crossroad. Jacques suddenly cut his lights and braked to a stop with his handbrake. Karvel and Whistler scrambled out, and he drove straight ahead without lights. They hurried toward the nearest house and took cover behind a parked car. Seconds later the other car approached, slowed at the crossroad, and impulsively turned left. Whistler gave a grunt of satisfaction and plucked at Karvel's sleeve.

They felt their way around to the rear of the house. Whistler knocked softly, knocked again, and then tried the door. It opened. He pushed Karvel ahead of him, stepped inside, and closed it.

They heard footsteps approaching. The light went on. They were in a kitchen, and facing them at the other side of the room was the fattest woman Karvel had ever seen. She was clothed tentlike in a faded nightgown, and she determinedly pointed the rifle one of her ancestors had carried in the war of 1870.

For a moment she stared at them. Then the rifle crashed to the floor.

"Bertie!" she squealed, and hurled herself at Whistler.

They spent the next day in a dusty garret. A dark cloud scudded overhead, wept whimsically onto the streaked window, and passed by. Another followed, and another. The unheated room was chill and damp. Karvel decided that he did not like France.

Late in the afternoon Jacques drove up, followed by Maurice in Whistler's truck. Jacques was abjectly apologetic. He hadn't expected to encounter sentries so close to the forest.

"Did your men get away all right?" Karvel asked.

Jacques shrugged. Their car had received four bullet holes

when they ran through a roadblock, but those were easily fixed. Did Karvel wish to try again that night? Or perhaps that afternoon?

"Try what?" Karvel demanded.

Jacques waved his hands triumphantly. The soldiers were gone, he said, and so were the roadblocks. He had driven straight through the valley and found it deserted. Now Karvel could take all the pictures he wanted.

"In that case, we can manage by ourselves," Karvel said. "Pay him off."

"I already paid him," Whistler protested.

"Give him a bonus for keeping his mouth shut."

Jacques accepted the money delightedly, shook hands with both of them, and drove off with Maurice. Karvel and Whistler left immediately, but not before Christine, their bulky hostess, gave Whistler a parting hug that made his eyes pop. She tearfully waved good-bye as they drove away.

"So that's your taste in women," Karvel said. "I've always wondered."

"She didn't used to look like that. When the light went on I didn't even recognize her. I thought it was her maw."

"How come she recognized you?"

Whistler gave Karvel a wounded look. "*I* haven't changed!"

They circled back to the St.-Pierre-du-Bois road and turned north. A thick drizzle was falling. Whistler drove slowly, and the distance seemed far greater than Karvel remembered it.

"They may not all be gone," Whistler said. "Are you sure it's wise to barge right into them?"

"We're just a couple of dumb foreigners trying to get to Strasbourg. We'll ask for directions, and see what's going on, and then we'll decide what to do."

They topped the last hill, and Whistler stepped on the clutch and let the truck coast. The shapeless mass of the stricken village lay in the valley below. There were no sentries—and no tents.

Whistler steered the truck off the road, and Karvel flung

his door open and reached for his crutches. He swung himself awkwardly over the soft ground toward the square imprints where the tents had crushed down the weeds. At the center of one was a churned hollow where the U.O. had rested.

Karvel stooped, picked up a piece of cardboard. Under it was moist, pungent earth and an earthworm slithering away from the light.

He did not know whether to weep or curse. Whistler said nothing.

Karvel wrenched a crutch free from the ground, and turned back. Whistler hurried ahead of him to open the door of the truck. "What do we do now?" he asked.

"As I said before, it was a silly idea to begin with. Let's finish our vacation."

7

The Mediterranean was a vast azure mirror tilted toward infinity. Karvel, stretched out peacefully under a beach umbrella, projected his thoughts at the horizon. He saw a shadow merge abruptly with the umbrella shadow, but he did not bother to look up.

Gerald Haskins said peevishly, "Just where the devil have you been?"

"Following orders," Karvel said. "Taking a vacation."

Haskins crouched beside him, and hissed, "If you had any idea of the trouble I've had finding you—"

"What I particularly enjoy," Karvel said, "are the cloud reflections. If only someone would keep the gulls away, the scenery would be perfect. I hate to see gulls messing up cloud reflections. It makes me think of a beautiful woman with fleas."

Haskins sat down heavily. "Why didn't you get in touch with me?"

"I did. I sent your office a picture postcard the day I got here. I said, 'Having a wonderful time, wish you were here,' but I didn't expect—"

"My men don't usually report by picture postcard, and some idiot probably filed it in the wastebasket. A luxury hotel in a little French resort town is the last place I expected to find you, and it's just about the last place I looked."

"To each his own taste, but why did you bother? Sooner or later we'd have run out of money, or gotten bored, and headed for home."

"Good God, man! Don't you read the papers? Don't you pay any attention to what people are talking about?"

"I can't read French, and neither can Whistler. He can talk the stuff like crazy, but he can't read it. He isn't much interested in literature anyway."

"Where is he?"

"He's found an illegal bistro with a female bartender. She fascinates him. He hangs out there twelve hours a day, studying philosophy."

"Did you know that a massed army of reporters has been searching three continents for you and causing all kinds of trouble at home? The Air Force has been accused of shang-haiing you into a mental hospital."

"Retribution," Karvel murmured. "I know at least three generals who have wanted to do that for years."

"That's nothing compared with what they'd like to do now. Let's go where we can talk. Where are your crutches?"

"Abandoned. I am now able to limp about with a cane. The doctor's only restriction is that I can't kick anyone be-fore Christmas—not even myself." He got up resignedly. "You can carry the umbrella."

Haskins said nothing more until they reached Karvel's hotel suite. He locked the door and gave each room and closet a quick but thorough inspection while Karvel watched in amusement.

"It's a habit I've picked up," he said. "Well, I suppose you want to know what's happened."

"The approach of old age has eroded my curiosity. There really isn't much that I can't stand not knowing."

"We have another U.O."

"Ostrander?"

Haskins shook his head.

"I suppose you're calling this one U.O.-3. Just incidentally, what happened to U.O.-2?"

Haskins stared at him. "Where *have* you been?"

"Here, and not reading the papers. Remember?"

"Well. The French called a high-level conference. All the major powers were represented, including the Russians."

"The *Russians?*"

"U.O.-2 positively established their innocence. Not even the Russians could have contributed the passenger in U.O.-2. It was the considered opinion of many scientists that they couldn't have contributed the passenger in U.O.-1, either. Anyway, the French got everyone's opinion, and then they went ahead and did what they wanted to do, it being their U.O. They sent it back to where it came from—they hope—with a pointed diplomatic message in forty languages requesting that the senders cease and desist."

"Did they send a diplomat to present the message?"

"It was just barely considered. The conference took note of what had happened to the two passengers who arrived with the U.O.'s, and decided that a dead diplomat would be negotiating under a severe handicap. I wasn't there to argue the point. It was an extremely high-level conference, and it was rushed. Just as it was getting started some French gangsters got the idea that the French army was guarding something valuable there in the valley by St.-Pierre-du-Bois, and tried to steal the U.O."

"The French should have let them have it. It would have served them right."

Haskins smiled. "I don't know what they thought it was, or what they thought they could do with it. The business sounded highly exaggerated, but it caused uneasiness in high places. The U.O. was hauled off to Paris, and the conference was pushed to an indecently hasty conclusion. Anyway, the French sent the U.O. back—they hope. We furnished the fuel, and the instrument settings were the same as those we think Ostrander used. A string was attached to the proper control, and they backed off and pulled it. Within a week the whole story had been leaked to the press, but by that time I suppose you were down here enjoying the sea breezes and boycotting newspapers."

"Nice of you to look me up just to tell me all this."

"I looked you up for two reasons. One, I had to find you before someone else did. The French were given a summary of your time theory, and *that* was leaked to the press, too.

To put it conservatively, there's been hell to pay. We suspect that your life is in danger."

"Over a theory?"

"You haven't been reading the papers. That was one reason. The other is the new U.O., which is actually U.O.-1 back again. No, no trace at all of Ostrander. There's another passenger, similar to the first one and just as smashed. We were really lucky with this one, because it hit the New Mexico desert down by the Mexican border where there isn't anything or anybody to damage. We don't even know how long it had been there before it was spotted. Would you like to take a ride in it? You'll have the best protection scientists can devise for you. We're building a cylinder inside the U.O., with a controlled leakage system."

"I don't know," Karvel said. "I'll think it over."

"You'll *what?*"

"Think it over. Has listening to so much French blurred my speech?"

Haskins got to his feet. "Start thinking," he said coldly. "You can have until dinnertime. It may take me that long to line up a plane for us."

For the next hour Karvel sat looking out at the Mediterranean. Finally he stirred himself, and packed their few belongings. Whistler came in just as he finished.

"I saw Haskins downstairs," he said. "Just to wave at, but I figured we'd be leaving."

"Check us out," Karvel said. "I want to see if I can get ahold of some newspapers in English."

"It was a nice vacation."

"It's still a nice vacation. I just decided to move it somewhere else."

Karvel left the hotel by a side entrance. Whistler was waiting with the truck, and he asked, "Where to? Marseille?"

"If I were Haskins, that's where I'd expect us to go. So we'll go to Italy."

Karvel concentrated on the newspapers, and after he'd read for a few minutes he said, "Did you ever have the im-

pression that you were the only sane man in a world full of
lunatics?"

"Ever since the Air Force moved in on me," Whistler said.

They crossed the Italian border and leisurely followed
the coast road south. "How far are we going?" Whistler
asked.

"I think we'll sell the truck and diving equipment in
Rome, and take a train to Switzerland."

"Isn't it cold in Switzerland?"

"Probably. When you get tired of Swiss bartenders, you
can learn to ski."

"Why are you running away from Haskins?"

For a long time, perhaps for most of an hour, Karvel did
not answer. Then he said, "It'd be silly to go back to France.
I can probably get in touch with Haskins through the em-
bassy in Rome."

Whistler shrugged. "There isn't such a thing as a Swiss
bartender. They're either French, or German, or Italian.
And I don't want to learn to ski."

"I wasn't running away from Haskins," Karvel said. "I
was trying to run away from myself."

"Either way," Whistler said, "I don't think you'd have
made it."

Rome, then to London to meet Haskins, and finally Washington, D.C. Somewhere en route Karvel crossed the threshold of unreality. When he saw the waiting throng at Dulles
International Airport he knew intuitively that the world
from which he'd sought to escape had been snatched from
under him, and that he would fervently hate the world
that replaced it. He had lost forever the right to contemplate his unscaled mountains in comfortable obscurity. Always they would be awash with the hot glare of television
lights, and his every climbing step would feed the greedy
curiosity of millions, and be recorded, and measured, and
debated.

"Is this necessary?" he asked Haskins.

"Think of the fuss they've made over the astronauts. And

the astronauts only went up to collect scientific data, or to test some gadgets, or maybe for the ride. You're going—"

"For the ride. Couldn't you have launched me quietly some dark night, and made the announcement afterward?"

"You've read the papers," Haskins said quietly.

"Yes. . . ."

The screaming headlines, the thousand variations on the thought "WHAT DOES THE FUTURE WANT FROM US?" And the absurdly speculative answers: natural resources, slaves, markets, havens from atomic holocausts . . . absurdly speculative, and at the same time terrifyingly plausible. What *did* the future want from us?

"This business was building toward global hysteria," Haskins said.

"From here, it looks as if it's already arrived."

The surging crowd was no more than an unrelenting clamor and a blur of faces until an elderly man, clerical collar visible above his black overcoat, sprang into the lane the guards had cleared for Karvel, leveled a revolver, and pulled the trigger. The gun clicked off a second misfire as the guards swarmed over him. Karvel was hustled away.

"He wasn't even a clergyman," Haskins said later, at the hotel.

"That makes me feel much better," Karvel said dryly. "Why did he pose as a clergyman?"

"I thought you'd read the papers."

Karvel stared at him. "I didn't read anything about the churches declaring open season on me!"

"Not on you. On time travel. What do you think of its religious implications?"

"Does it matter?"

"It certainly does! You're going to be asked—repeatedly. Is time travel a religious sacrilege as well as a violation of the laws of nature? Many serious-minded, intelligent people are troubled about this, but the dangerous ones are the nuts who've gotten the idea that you're about to go back in time and catch the best of Christ and Moses on a tape recorder, for commercial distribution. Or to make a Technicolor film of the Crucifixion. Supposing you interfered, and destroyed the foundations of Christianity? Or brought back alleged documentary evidence that the saints were lechers, the prophets rabble-rousers, and the cherished beliefs of all the religions mere fiction? Let enough people convince themselves that this is remotely possible, and you have—"

"Global hysteria."

"Right. Your time theory is fantastic, but so were the events that engendered it. Where *does* the U.O. go when it vanishes?"

"My answer will be that I hope to find out."

"You'll say you don't believe in your own theory?"

"I'll say it's only a theory. And if it's correct, I will be traveling in time for only one purpose: to put a stop to traveling in time."

"Good!" Haskins nodded approvingly. "Very good. Time travel or no, the important thing is to stop it, and that's what we're working to do. It's an explanation with moral force, because it happens to be true. We've *got* to stop it."

Karvel went his well-guarded way, and learned to ignore the crowds and the popping flashbulbs. There was an appearance before a congressional committee, at which he answered a few questions noncommittally and the congressmen made speeches. There was a much-publicized meeting with the President of the United States, and that same evening Karvel was the guest of honor at a formal reception for foreign dignitaries. His leg gave out in the receiving line.

There were long, serious discussions with State Department officials, who seemed reluctant to entrust a critical diplomatic mission to a man with military training, though none of them were volunteering to go in his place. There were press conferences, where Karvel stood blinking under the TV lights and fended off unanswerable questions.

There were letters, thousands of them, from all over the world. Some of the writers were sincere, some were obviously demented, and many defied classification. Karvel read through them until he reached the first proposal of marriage, and then he left them for Haskins to deal with.

All of it was unreal. Karvel began to ask a question of himself: "*What* U.O.?" The dullish black sphere seemed more imagined than remembered.

Then a time bomb was found in the hotel lobby. Haskins removed his entire entourage immediately, and early the next morning they were flown out to Hatch Air Force Base. A regiment of army troops was already on hand to assist in guarding the base, and the U.O. had been brought in from New Mexico and again reposed in Hangar Seven. The scientists' decision was to launch the U.O. from the general vicinity where it first arrived.

The protective device was already in place inside the U.O.—a reinforced cylinder that looked disquietingly like a huge coffin.

"Arm and leg joints are the principal problem in designing diving equipment," Haskins said. "Since you don't have to walk around, or use your hands, we're solving the problem by not having any joints."

"Fine. How do I throw the switch?"

"You don't. We'll do it with a string, the same way the French did. The cylinder is padded to give you the most comfortable ride you've ever had. Want to try it out?"

"Where's the latch on the lid?"

"There isn't any. The pressure will seal it shut, and should diminish almost at once when the U.O. stops. As soon as you can raise the lid without resistance, you'll know it's safe to climb out."

"I see another advantage to this arrangement," Karvel said.

"What's that?"

"If anything happens to me, the mess will be confined to that coffin. Our friends in the future will have a lot less cleaning up to do before they send the thing back."

"Oh, shut up! We've installed six radios, to work on various wave lengths. Three are for voice use, and three will send out automatic signals. We're wondering how long we'll be able to track you. Now inside with you, and see if it fits."

Karvel eased himself into the cylinder and tripped the oxygen valve and the radio switch as Haskins lowered the lid. He lay at an angle across the U.O.'s interior, with his feet lower than his head. He had more than ample room to move about, and the foam padding was superbly comfortable.

"Not bad," he said through the radio. "If it's a long trip I can snooze a little."

"There'll be smaller cylinders for any supplies or equipment you want to take along," Haskins said. "I'd suggest plenty of food and water and clothing. You might land in a desert or wilderness, where you'd have to use the U.O. as a supply base, and I won't guarantee any particular kind of climate. What else do you want?"

"A rifle, if there's room, and a pistol. A knife that can function either as a tool or a weapon. Canteen, flashlight, matches, blankets—the works. Say the equivalent of a B-52 survival kit. Within seconds after the U.O. stops I want to be outside and fully equipped."

"I agree. We'll split your supplies two ways—the survival stuff that you can grab and run with, and a large reserve of field rations, water, clothing, and the like in case you need a base of operations for an indefinite period. What will you wear on the trip?"

"It may be warm in here. A cotton flying suit, I think, and I'll pack winter flight clothing. When do I leave?"

"We'll need time to get your equipment together, and to arrange with the television and newspaper people to give you a proper send-off. Day after tomorrow? About 10 P.M., I think, so we can get live coverage without disrupting the regular TV schedule. You can have a heavy meal at noon and a light meal in the evening."

"And with any luck," Karvel said cheerfully, "I'll arrive wherever it is I'm going just in time for breakfast. It would spoil my whole day if I was to miss breakfast."

The U.O. stood somberly in a blaze of light. Cameras ringed it. Karvel shook hands with Haskins, with the scientists, with a phalanx of military brass and distinguished observers. He noticed Whistler, standing disconsolately at one side, and hurried over to give him a farewell hug.

"I wish you were going along," he said.

"If there ain't any Air Force where you're going, I wish I was too."

Karvel shook his hand and limped toward the U.O.

"How about a wave for Telstar, Major?" someone called.

Karvel turned, and resisted the impulse to thumb his nose. He waved one hand as he dilated the hatch. The interior of the U.O. was illuminated.

"Are we leaving that on?" he asked a hovering scientist.

"I think not. Just until you're ready."

Karvel climbed through the hatch and studied the instrument panel. The critical capsule was missing; Haskins was taking no chances on another accident.

"I'd like the photos of the original settings," he said. They were passed through to him, and he checked the instrument settings meticulously. "All right," he said finally, and handed them back.

"You're to read this, Major. Scientific descriptions of the U.O. passengers. You haven't seen them, have you? Mr. Haskins thought not. You should know what sort of animals they are, so you'll know what to look for."

Karvel read the two typewritten pages twice. "I don't know what some of these words mean," he said, "but at least this second passenger won't be difficult to recognize. Do I take this with me?"

"Better not. If the subjects were to get ahold of it, they might not find the descriptions flattering."

"All right. I'm not planning on dissecting them, so most of the information wouldn't be of any use to me. How much of this equipment will arrive in a usable condition?"

"I'll put it this way," the scientist said frankly. "If *you* arrive in a usable condition, most of your equipment and supplies should be all right. If you don't, their condition isn't likely to worry you."

"Fair enough. I'm ready. Are you?"

The scientist glanced at his watch, and nodded. Karvel climbed into the cylinder, and the radio clicked twice as the scientist closed the lid. Haskins said, "Are you there?"

"Tell them to throw in my cane."

"It's in. Everything is ready."

"What are you blubbering about?"

"I'm not blubbering. I'm swearing at myself. I know this was originally your idea, but both of us know I maneuvered you into it."

"I felt the gun in my back all the way over here."

"Don't be sarcastic. All six radios are coming in clearly. Do you hear me all right?"

"Fine. Thank the man for tucking me in. Any last-minute instructions?"

"Here's Colonel Stubbins."

"Major Karvel? We're packing in the messages now. They're in different languages, just like the last time, but with one statement added. We've had enough of this nonsense, and if another U.O. hits a population center, even if it's one farmhouse, we're sending it back with an atomic warhead. Got that?"

"What's to prevent them from answering with *two* warheads?" Karvel demanded. "Or two dozen, for that matter. You send the first one, and you'll put yourself permanently on the receiving end."

"They wouldn't dare count on that," Stubbins said grimly. "Anything else?"

"We're going to name an air base after you. Thought you'd like to know."

"One in Antarctica, I suppose. I'm glad I won't be there to hear the speeches."

"One more thing. I won't say we don't want you to return. We do—we want it very much, but only if you can be 100 per cent positive of hitting an unpopulated area."

"I understand that."

"Unless—" Stubbins chuckled dryly. "Unless you can manage a bull's-eye on the Kremlin."

"How about the Pentagon?" Karvel asked.

Stubbins sputtered something about a happy landing, and Haskins's voice came in crisply. "We're ready. How about you?"

"Ready."

"There's probably a lot I should say, Major, but I won't even try. We all wish you Godspeed and a safe landing, and Captain Morris has just asked me to tell you he is praying that the direction will be up. Up the mountains, I suppose."

"Tell him," Karvel said, "that I hope to leave the whole dratted range in his custody."

"Will do. Ready for countdown. Ten, nine, eight . . ."

Karvel counted with him. At zero he felt a slight jerk. He continued counting, "One, two, three—" Then he broke off. The only voice he heard was his own.

Part Two

1

Silence.

Then, almost imperceptibly, pressure.

Twisting in alarm, Karvel moved his hands across his chest and touched his face. There was nothing to brush away, nothing tangible to fight.

The pressure continued—light, insistent, all-embracing.

As he weighed his chances for survival, a remark echoed hauntingly in his mind. Gerald Haskins's remark: "Time? Well, you can have a shot at designing a protective device that would keep out time!"

Now he understood the fallacy that had undermined all of their planning. It was not a question of keeping out time, but of breaching time, of breaking a path through it.

He was moving through time, and time resisted his passage.

And there was pressure—feathery, intangible, but nonetheless relentless.

He lay quietly, and suppressed an urge to escape from the cylinder, to find out what was happening outside. The limping, time-compressed minutes slipped away, and slowly, tediously, the pressure increased. Karvel began to wonder about the meaning of time when one was passing through time. Was his wristwatch actually marking off seconds and minutes and hours? He lay in the tightening grip of time and pondered its measurement. When finally he decided to perform an experiment, he found the luminous hands of his watch immobilized under a pressure-warped crystal.

Pressure—and then pain. Karvel's calm resolution faded. He began to struggle, and each movement, each tightening muscle encountered stubbornly unyielding force. In a surge of panic he heaved himself against the cylinder's lid. The tremendous pressure without had sealed it rigidly. Karvel sank back, muttered, "When I called it a coffin I thought I was joking."

Still the pressure increased, until it was a swollen, vicious thing that held him in a vise of torment. The slightest movement required a prodigious effort, and he underwent a prolonged and exhausting struggle to bring his hands to his face in an attempt to alleviate the intense pressure on his eyelids.

Each breath became a grim toil to move the overwhelming weight that crushed down upon his chest. He gulped oxygen in shallow gasps, and became dizzily aware that he was suffering a protracted, tortuous suffocation. The convulsive pounding of his pulse wracked his entire body. He may have lost consciousness; afterward he had no recollection of what had happened, or what he experienced, in those final seconds when the pressure moved relentlessly across the excruciating threshold of unendurability.

He remembered only the delightful sensation of release, and his first triumphant, unburdened, life-giving inhalations.

He asked nothing more than to lie there endlessly on the wonderful softness of the foam padding. He had to force himself to move his hands, to raise the lid. The cylinder opened easily. He climbed out, and kicked open a supply cylinder. He glanced through the hatch, and then tossed out his emergency equipment and quickly followed it, leaving the multilingual ultimatums spilling about the U.O.'s interior.

As his feet touched the ground he heard distant crashes and a muffled upwelling of screams of pain and terror. He stood in a broad expanse of park. A small stream tinkled musically almost at his feet, its path as geometrically precise as that of the tree-lined avenue that bordered it. In the opposite direction a city loomed, an enormous complex of which he could see neither beginning nor end. It was shimmering white in color, with angular tiers piled up like precisely arranged boxes, and with a multitude of truncated, slightly conical towers rising above it. The towers looked like misshapen chimneys, and the whole had the appearance of an ultramodern factory.

And Force X was smashing through it.

Walls sagged, swayed, collapsed as their supports were ripped away. Towers teetered crazily and toppled, and flailing bodies momentarily fell or leaped clear of the wreckage. The relentless, widening lashes struck again and again, and each successive blow wrenched simultaneous cries of anguish and fear from additional terrified thousands. The ground level exits and the breaches in the outer walls were quickly jammed with frenzied humanity, which swelled toward Karvel like a mindless tide of ants rushing from a threatened anthill.

Karvel stood watching it, paralyzed with helpless horror.

The mob should have lost its momentum as it fought free of the collapsing city and spilled into the spacious park. It did not. Karvel realized abruptly that its leaders were no longer running away from the city—they were running toward him. Singly and in small groups they detached themselves with bursts of speed and altered course to converge on him.

So heartsick was he at the catastrophe he had precipitated that for a long moment he stood his ground, waiting resignedly to welcome whatever vengeance they chose to wreak on him.

Then he remembered that this same fury might next strike New York, or London, or Moscow, and that nothing would then prevent the military from returning the U.O. with an atomic warhead. He had a mission to perform, and he could settle with his conscience later.

He gathered up his equipment, splashed through the stream, and fled.

But he did not run. He moved with an easy, swinging

limp, glancing back frequently. The park was filling with a
widening ooze of incoherently screaming humanity. Karvel's immediate pursuers were now far out in front. They
had covered more than a mile, first in headlong flight and
then in furious pursuit, and they could not maintain that
pace indefinitely.

He lengthened his stride and struck off through the stubble of a harvested grainfield that stretched in flat monotony
to the horizon. Another backward glance showed him that
his pursuers were still running at top speed. The sunlight
gleamed on their bald heads, and their odd-looking, brightly
colored garments billowed and flapped in the breeze.

Several strange aircraft had lifted above the city, effectively sealing the hopelessness of Karvel's flight. In defiance
of all logic he began to run in earnest.

His cane was useless on the soft ground, and he tired
quickly. He stopped, turned slowly, faced his pursuers. He
made no motion to unsling his rifle or draw his pistol. He did
not know if the weapons had been damaged by pressure,
but in any case he could not bring himself to inflict further
harm on these people. The screams he had heard rang
hauntingly in his conscience, and in the background the
cruelly lacerated city loomed like a monstrous accusation.

He waited. His pursuers ran faster, ran with the churning
speed of sprinters taking off on a short dash until, only a few
yards from him, they came to a stumbling, indecisive halt.
One of the strange aircraft floated to the ground beside Karvel. There was no mistaking the pilot's gesture, but Karvel
stood motionless, staring at the plane. It was a mere circular
box on a thick, circular platform, and seeing it land did not
wholly convince him that it would fly.

The pilot gestured again, and took off while Karvel was
clambering over the side. They shot upward a dozen feet,
and then moved slowly. The men on the ground drifted
together into a tight group, and stood looking after them.
It was not until they began to gather speed that Karvel realized they were traveling *away* from the city.

He asked a question, looking closely at the pilot for the first time.

Excitedly the pilot spoke gibberish, waved an arm, spoke again. His left hand rested on a pattern of raised, rectangular surfaces, and he fingered this keyboard as casually as a skilled musician would play a piano. Their course altered slightly; their speed increased. Curving wings on their seat backs folded forward and encircled them snugly. A transparent canopy glided over them. The pilot grinned a leering, toothless grin.

"Look, friend—I don't want to run away," Karvel said.

The pilot grinned, and spoke more gibberish. Karvel gestured unavailingly in the direction of the rapidly receding city. They sped onward, still at a nerve-shattering twelve-foot altitude.

"Am I being rescued or kidnaped?" Karvel demanded. He glanced backward, and snapped, "Get some altitude, you fool!" The other aircraft had taken up their pursuit.

Several large planes converged above them. One at a time they began to dart down in swooping passes. Head twisting, eyes aglow with ecstatic delight, the pilot wove his way skillfully between the thrusts, changed direction, stood the plane on edge, even managed to gain a little altitude. The city was far behind them, now—no more than a reflected glow on the horizon. Ahead of them the level stubble of the grainfield ended abruptly at the feet of heavily forested hills.

Seconds later two of the pursuing planes managed a coordinated attack, boxed them in neatly, and forced them down into the forest. They plowed through heavy foliage, tilted, spun crazily, and slid to the ground, coming to rest wedged at a steep angle between two trees.

The canopy opened, the seats unfolded, and the pilot stood up to peer about him in apparent perplexity.

"This is what comes of not taking altitude when you can get it," Karvel told him disapprovingly.

It was no mere forest that they had crashed into, but a dense jungle. The trees were enormous, and their huge leaves blotted out the sky and produced an effect of eerie twilight. Their trunks bulged with strange fungus growths, and thick curtains of leaves hung motionless on long, rope-like vines. A noisy cloud of small insects churned in a shaft of sunlight.

The pilot leaped to the ground and studied the plane with cocked head.

"If it's a question of getting out of this predicament," Karvel said, with a mystified glance at the control keyboard, "you'll have to work it out for yourself. I move that we start walking."

He climbed down himself, lifted out his knapsack and rifle, and took a few suggestive steps. The pilot, still surveying the plane from the vantage point of his eight feet of height, ignored Karvel.

A curtain of vines parted, and a man stepped through. Enormously tall, bald, toothless, he could have been the pilot's brother except for his dark-hued skin and his clothing. He wore the same type of flapping garment, but his was a dark brown, irregularly splashed with darker blotches. He carried two long poles, each of them tipped with a long, vicious-looking barbed spike.

Other men appeared noiselessly. Soon there were seven of them, standing beside the plane and talking excitedly with the pilot. Karvel withdrew to the opposite side, where he could feel somewhat less like a midget.

The pilot climbed back into the plane and closed the canopy, and it lifted slowly. As it turned edgewise and drifted free, the forest men went to work with their poles, hooking vines away from it and clearing a path. The plane floated off through the jungle at a walking pace, with the men moving ahead in relays to clear the way for it.

Quickly they disappeared. Karvel stood contemplating the wall of greenery that closed after them, but only for a moment. He had lost his sense of direction in their spinning descent, and the forest impressed him as an excellent place in which to get lost. He hurried to overtake them.

The ground began to rise steeply. The procession zigzagged among the trees, and finally, after a long climb, broke through into a small clearing where vines and undergrowth had been removed but the dense overhead foliage left untouched. Three forest roads converged there, broad, arched tunnels that vanished in sweeping detours around the gigantic trees. The pilot set the plane down and climbed out, and the entire party moved single file up a ramp that spiraled around a tree at the edge of the clearing.

Karvel followed gingerly, and cursed his curiosity long before he reached the top. The ramp was woven of thick fiber and supported by huge pegs driven into the tree. It sagged alarmingly between its supports, and the fiber parted when Karvel attempted to use his cane. The tree's bark was too smooth and slippery to afford a handhold. Karvel fell far behind the others, but eventually he caught up with them at a platform fixed high up in the treetop.

The jungle stretched away at his feet like a green sea stirred whimsically by a gentle wind. Beyond lay the harvested grainfield, and drawn up near the edge of the forest was the vanguard of an army. Large aircraft were landing, disgorging their cargos of men, taking off again. The newcomers hurried to extend the long ranks of waiting troops.

On the crowded platform the forest men talked quietly. One was studying the assembling army with an optical device. The pilot grinned at Karvel, signaled with a jerk of his head, and turned away. Karvel stepped cautiously after him, and found the descent even more nerve-wracking than the climb.

As they gained the clearing again a group of men approached along one of the roads, their poles shouldered like enormous rifles. At a shouted command they vanished into the forest, leaving not so much as a swaying vine to mark their passage.

The pilot beckoned to Karvel from the plane, but he stood watching dumbly as another group of men approached the clearing. No one, he told himself, not even a Bowden Karvel with mountains in his soul, could possibly blunder an important diplomatic mission *this* badly.

His arrival had smashed a city, and killed or maimed untold thousands of its citizens.

And then, within two hours, his presence had precipitated a war.

Wearily he climbed into the plane. Tilted at a steep angle, they flew off along a forest road. The packed earth of the road unrolled monotonously beneath them, and the dim, unchanging greenery of the tunnel walls floated past in a hypnotic blur. Karvel found himself struggling to stay awake. He needed urgently to plan, to make decisions, to act, but fatigue had paralyzed his mental processes. He felt an overwhelming weight of exhaustion from the centuries he had—perhaps—passed through. His head nodded again, and he succumbed to the drowsiness that was enveloping him, and slept.

The eerie forest twilight was shading into forest night when the pilot shook him awake. Dimly he could make out another clearing, with several aircraft parked around its perimeter. He gathered up his equipment and followed the pilot, attempting to stomp himself awake. The footing changed abruptly from soft forest turf to hard ground, and ahead of them a door creaked as the pilot opened it. A few steps in total darkness, and another door opened onto a blaze of light.

Karvel's eyes quickly recovered, but the shock he received from his surroundings lasted longer. Future man had returned to the cave.

He blinked incredulously at the high, jagged arch of the ceiling. Bands of brilliant yet soft artificial light crisscrossed it. An alcove contained what appeared to be startlingly advanced communications equipment. At one side of the room food sizzled on an enormous, gleaming grill, and the men of the forest were helping themselves with casual dips of long-handled tongs—and dropping the portions of food into crude wooden bowls, from which they ate with their fingers.

Long, wicker-like benches were scattered about the huge room, and the grinning pilot led Karvel to one of them, and got him seated. The forest men gathered around him. With the open curiosity of children they touched his hair, touched his clothing, ran their fingers along the barrel of his rifle, seemed fascinated with his cane. As one stepped back, apparently satisfied, another took his place.

The pilot returned to offer Karvel a bowl of deeply browned balls of food. He accepted with a nod of thanks, and cautiously placed one in his mouth. It disintegrated into a thick paste before he could begin to chew it. A highly appropriate food, he thought, for a people who had no teeth and—what was it the report had said?—no stomachs. "Prechewed and predigested meat balls," he told himself wryly.

But he doubted that they were made of meat. The taste was strong and not unpleasant, with a vaguely familiar flavor that he could not identify. He washed the mouthful down with a drink of a mildly fermented fruit juice, and began to eat hungrily.

The pilot had disappeared; the forest men drifted away and went about their own affairs, which involved much coming and going. In the full light Karvel realized for the first time that their dark faces were green-tinted, as were the blotches on their clothing. There were fewer of them in the room than he had thought. Their tremendous size, and his dazzled senses, had combined to magnify an understrength platoon into a company.

He searched vainly for a sign that one of those present was a person with authority, and regretted that he could not ask, tritely, to be taken to their leader. His first brushes with the language barrier had left him shaken and discouraged, and convinced that Haskins should have sent a linguist.

For a time he occupied himself with checking over his equipment. Nothing seemed damaged, not even his flashlight. He packed it away again, wondering if the pressure he experienced could possibly have been a sensorial illusion.

Certainly there had been nothing illusionary about the condition of the other U.O. passengers.

The night wore on slowly, and Karvel stretched out on the bench's uncomfortably ridged surface and attempted to inventory the errors he had made since his arrival. Finally he reduced them to one: he should not have left the U.O.; but he could not retrace his steps without passing through, or over, two hostile armies.

Dawn was no more than an hour or two away when the pilot came for him. He allowed himself to be led without protest through the Stygian forest night to the plane. The seat closed about him, the canopy closed, and they waited silently in the darkness.

A star flashed overhead and disappeared. Karvel stared in that direction, and saw it again. And again. Planes were taking off, parting the forest foliage as they ascended. Six times he saw the star, and then they rose slowly and brushed through the trees into the night sky.

There were patches of stars visible through the clouds, but no moon. "Moon?" Karvel exclaimed. "How do I know that there *is* a moon?"

He squinted into the darkness, trying to pick out their escort, but there were no shadows hovering near them. Probably the six planes had been decoys, sent out to draw off any pursuit.

"Get some altitude!" he growled.

They were skimming low over the forest, and soon the first light of dawn showed in what Karvel hoped was the east. Then the forest ended abruptly. There were cultivated fields below, and on the horizon loomed another city.

2

First an ultramodern factory; then a surrealistic cathedral.

The city glowed with a softly rich, stained-glass blending of colors. Its spirally fluted towers culminated mushroom-like in great, circular platforms that marched in ascending order toward the looming authority of a central tower. It was a single enormous building that covered square miles, and yet Karvel's remembrance of the unending expanse of the first city made it seem tiny.

They settled slowly onto one of the towers, hovering for a moment until the waiting throng parted to give them landing room. As soon as his seat released him Karvel climbed out with as much dignity as circumstances permitted, snapped to attention, bowed.

Here, finally, were the men he was seeking.

They were old, old men, with gaunt, deeply wrinkled faces, and each face was ludicrously ornamented with a brightly colored, flowing beard. One of them—his beard was a lovely robin's-egg blue—stiffly returned Karvel's bow, and spoke gibberish. His hands waved excitedly and his long, meticulously shaped, polished fingernails flashed knifelike with every gesture.

The oration attained a bleating climax, and subsided. Karvel bowed into the expectant silence that followed. "I don't understand," he announced.

Bluebeard returned the bow, and the entire company followed a spiral ramp far down into the tower. Karvel prudently carried all of his equipment with him, and no one objected, or even showed signs of curiosity.

They gathered in a windowless, octagonal conference room, where multicolored walls and ceiling diffused flowing patterns of colored light. Unbearded attendants passed among them, distributing bowls of food that looked and tasted like diluted, predigested mush. To refuse could have been a breach of etiquette, so Karvel accepted one, and drank its contents, forcing himself not to gag.

The long-bearded elders of the reception committee retired to the background, and a procession of men with shorter beards took their places. They spoke and chanted and sang gibberish at Karvel, and eventually he realized that they were trying different languages on him. He failed to isolate a single intelligible sound. After each performance he shook his head, and said, "I don't understand."

When he could no longer contain his impatience, he strode over to the longbeards, tapped himself on the chest, and announced, "Major Bowden Karvel."

The longbeards went into conference; the shortbeards were summoned one at a time for consultation. Then attendants appeared with more food, and the conference was forgotten in the orgy of lip-smacking and slurping that followed.

As soon as they finished, Karvel tried again. "Major Bowden Karvel," he said, pointing to himself. Then he pointed at Bluebeard. "And you?"

Bluebeard convened another conference. Dejectedly Karvel retreated to the far side of the room and perched on the edge of a mushroom-shaped stool. "Haskins should have sent a linguist," he muttered.

They were probably trying to find out where he came from, but even without the language barrier he could not have told them. Had he traveled in time, or space, or in some previously unknown dimension? He would not know until he found out where he was.

The flow of gibberish continued, interrupted at regular intervals by the mush break. Karvel developed a wholesome

respect for his own stomach while watching the eating habits imposed by the lack of one: small quantities of fluid
nourishment imbibed every half hour or so. It was no doubt
fortunate that they had neither the appetite nor the capacity
for solid food, because the only teeth in the room belonged
to Karvel.

"Major Bowden Karvel," he told them wearily. "I came in
your spherical traveling device to ask you, please, don't
send us any more of them."

They considered that unworthy of a conference, and as-
saulted him with more gibberish.

By the end of the day he was groggy with fatigue and rav-
enously hungry. He forced himself to drink four bowls of
mush, an act that obviously astonished them. For an hour or
so he felt satiated, and then he was hungry again.

They escorted him to a nearby room, also windowless and
eight-sided, but much smaller and without furnishings of
any kind. A door slid out of the wall to close noiselessly, and
he was alone. He dropped his equipment, and sat down on
the floor. After a day replete with incomprehensible sounds,
the silence seemed blissful.

Suddenly it occurred to him that he was being left for the
night. He went to the door, intending to knock on it, and it
opened automatically. Two men with long orange beards
were seated on stools in an alcove nearby.

"Look," Karvel said to them companionably. "I don't know
if I'm an honored guest or a prisoner, but where I come from
even a prisoner gets some kind of bed."

They came readily when he motioned them into the room,
and when he stretched out on the floor they understood at
once. A sleight-of-hand gesture, and a bed folded out of the
wall. It lay flat on the floor, a thick pad three feet longer
than Karvel needed and narrower than he would have preferred, but it was a bed.

"Thank you," Karvel said. "Now I ask you to kindly direct
me to the nearest bathroom, and I'm darned if I'll act that
out for you."

They bowed politely, and left. The bow was the only

encouraging sign he could glean from the day's frustrations. The gesture was obviously alien to them; they bowed because Karvel had bowed.

He studied the room. Narrow gratings at wall and ceiling levels provided ventilation. A recessed panel in each wall looked like a sliding door, and one of them opened for him to reveal a tiny bathroom. Its furnishings were exotic in design, but still vaguely recognizable. He told himself philosophically, "At least there's one area where artistic fads will never triumph completely over function." The bathtub was small in circumference and extremely deep. He would have enjoyed a vertical bath, but he couldn't figure out how to turn on the water.

He returned to the other room, stripped off his outer garments, and stretched out on the bed. For a long time he watched the kaleidoscopic flow of color on the walls and ceiling. It waxed and waned continuously to form changing patterns and produce an effect of incessant movement. In a strange way it was restful, and soon he fell asleep.

He awoke abruptly, and scrambled to his feet in alarm. The walls were whispering gibberish at him. He went to the door, and looked out.

The orange beards regarded him inquiringly. "Do either of you talk in your sleep?" Karvel asked, and went back to bed.

He lay awake for a long time, listening to the whispered gibberish and worrying about many things. At that moment they might be preparing to launch his U.O. or another. He *had* to learn their language, or teach his language to them, and he did not know how to go about doing either.

Finally he slept again, and was awakened by the timorous touch of a hand on his arm. He looked up in bewilderment at the hairless, bearded head that bent over him.

"Good morning," the head said.

"Good morning," Karvel replied, and did not realize until he fumbled the pronunciation that he was speaking a strange language.

But the next words meant nothing at all as the other continued to speak, first with apparent enthusiasm, then with doubt, and finally with exasperation. Karvel deduced that he had been exposed to the language while he slept, that he had been expected to master it—and that the project fell just short of being a total failure.

He was aware of one small measure of improvement. The words no longer sounded like gibberish. They were merely unintelligible.

There followed a day when frustration piled on frustration with an inevitability that made Karvel think he had been entrapped in a badly written comic opera. His hosts stubbornly refused to believe that he could not understand them. They continued to toss words at him.

At intervals Karvel attempted to direct their efforts toward some kind of methodical instruction. He fingered the draping sleeve of one of their garments. "What's this?" he asked.

They brought clothing for him.

He indicated the curved bowl that had contained his breakfast mush. "What's this?"

They brought more food.

He walked; they took him to the platform at the top of the tower for exercise. He breathed; they brought in a wrinkled oldster with a flowing purple beard, who made like a doctor, performed some remote electronic listening to Karvel's chest, and left medicine.

They did not repeat words. They made no attempt to identify objects. His quest for simple verbs missed the mark so consistently that he began to wonder if their language had any. They seemingly possessed no concept of teaching a language according to Karvel's notion of how a language should be taught.

His neck became cramped from looking up at them. Whether he was standing or seated, they bent over him, orange beards dangling, with the smugly affected patience of adults lecturing a recalcitrant child. Their infernally incomprehensible words grated on his nerves. Their periodic slurping of mush disgusted him.

Long before midday he lost his temper. "What are you doing with the U.O.?" he roared at them.

They recoiled in consternation and returned him to his cubicle for a rest, which did nothing to improve his mental state. Solitary confinement served his purpose even less than did their babble of talk.

That night he received more lessons, or perhaps the same lessons. The sterile muttering of the walls blended grotesquely in his shapeless dreams with the haunting screams from the devastated city and Lieutenant Ostrander's youthful laughter. The next day he fancied that he had a precarious grip on a word or two, but he could think of no adequate way to test his knowledge. Were they saying, *Here is your breakfast,* when they brought food? Or *Eat this quickly so we can get back to work?* Or *May your digestive efforts be bountiful?* Was it a blessing that they intoned with his first sip of mush, or pointed commentary on his table manners?

Whenever he lost his temper they banished him into isolation. They themselves seemed wholly devoid of strong feelings. Their emotional life, he thought, must be as bland as the mush that they fed to him.

On the third day the longbeards gave him a short-bearded tutor, probably because they considered the education of such an impossible student beneath them. The tutor looked to be little more than a child. He was only two or three inches taller than Karvel, with slender face and build and a high-pitched, almost feminine voice. His orange beard was no more than a rakish goatee, but his fingernails were fully as formidable as those of the longbeards.

He casually unfolded a stool from the wall of Karvel's cubicle and sat down, and Karvel, irked with himself for his long hours of sitting on the floor, pointed and demanded to know what it was. The tutor spoke a word; Karvel repeated it, got the feeling of it firmly entwined in his tongue, and began to circle the room, mouthing the word and touching the walls at random. The tutor watched him in solemn incomprehension. Karvel began to shout the word angrily. Had these people no imagination whatsoever?

Abruptly the tutor arose and unfolded another stool. Karvel dropped onto it with a shout of triumph. He knew the approximate meaning of one word, and he kept repeating it until he had established that the room contained four stools, and he could produce them himself.

Next he mastered the bed, and then he wasted half an hour trying to distinguish between *head* and *face*.

An attendant appeared with food. The tutor sipped his mush leisurely; Karvel downed his with an impatient gulp. When the tutor had finished they made a long, spiraling descent to ground level and walked out into a small, completely enclosed park. The glowing walls of the city towered above it, and it looked as incongruous as a garden at the bottom of an elevator shaft.

They strolled back and forth, Karvel still hobbling with the aid of his cane, and he learned words for *tree, grass,* and *flower*. The tutor seemed pleased; Karvel remained impatient. His only thought was to find out what had happened to the U.O., and he did not even have a word with which to begin a question.

That night Karvel's sleep was flooded with words and meanings always just beyond his grasp. At long intervals came flashes of comprehension. ". . . grass . . . green." *Color* of grass . . . green? Or, *the* color of grass *is* green? And how could he say, "What have they done with the thing I arrived in?" At his present rate of progress it would be a dozen years before he could translate *unidentified object*. ". . . grass . . . green." Odd that they hadn't given him a textbook. How could he go about asking for a book? ". . . *long* grass . . . green." Or *tall* grass? But the thought— the *pictured* thought—came through clearly.

"Good morning," Karvel said. "Share breakfast?"

"Share breakfast," the tutor agreed.

An efficiency engineer had sneaked in and streamlined their language for them. Karvel had to think what he wanted to say in English, and mentally cross out superfluous words until the threadbare meaning spoke itself in translation. Surprise and suspense lurked in every phrase, because the concluding inflection could turn the meaning inside out.

But once he had mastered the basic essentials of grammar and acquired a smattering of vocabulary, the nightly lessons began to take hold with phenomenal effect.

They shared breakfast. They spoke of simple matters—the greenness of the short grass in the park, the tallness of the green trees in the park. Karvel found himself experiencing a hazy recollection of words he did not recall having heard before. He indicated that his health was good—it would have been better if he could have had some solid food, but he did not know how to say that—and that he would like more walking.

They returned to the park, and walked there. Karvel thought wistfully that a swim would give him the exercise he needed without placing undue strain on his knee. He mentioned a bath, a walking bath, an exercising bath, and made swimming motions.

The tutor understood at once. They left the park and followed a descending ramp, the tutor considerately shortening his stride to match Karvel's limping pace. On a lower level they entered a large, domed room, where perhaps a dozen nude bathers were swimming about leisurely in a circular pool. The tutor led him to the recessed ledge where the bathers had left their clothing, doffed his simple two-piece garment matter-of-factly, and gave Karvel the greatest shock he had sustained since his arrival.

The tutor was a bald and bearded woman.

Then she removed the beard, and dove gracefully into the pool.

Karvel stared after her dumbly, and when he began to remove his own clothing he found himself afflicted with a quaking modesty. Beside those sleek, hairless bodies his would be as conspicuous as that of an ape in a nudist camp.

He was politely ignored until he paused at the side of the pool to remove his artificial leg. *That* produced a sensation. One of the swimmers hurriedly dressed and went off to in-

form various longbeards of the phenomenon. They crowded
into the room, examined the leg almost awesomely, and discussed it with obvious puzzlement. Karvel enjoyed his swim
almost unnoticed.

Later there was another inquisition, the longbeards working laboriously to frame questions within Karvel's limited
vocabulary, and Karvel expending a like amount of effort in
attempting to find out where he was and what had happened to the U.O. Both concepts remained hopelessly beyond his verbal capacity. The meeting ended on a note of
mutual dissatisfaction, and Karvel was returned to the custody of the tutor.

She sensed his desperation, and began to make a sincere
effort to find out what was troubling her student. He stam-
mered through oblique explanations. "*Something* I *something* in." Damn the language! What could he do with the
word *walk* to make it mean *travel?*

He obtained a word for *circle* by tracing one on the floor
with his finger, but he failed utterly in his attempt to convert
it into a sphere. He needed a child's ball, but he had seen no
children since his arrival. Had children gone out of fashion
in this civilization?

The tutor watched his efforts thoughtfully, and returned
that night to lead him to the top of the tower and reveal to
him—the full moon.

The moon was . . . the moon. The familiar pattern of the
lunar *maria* was as obvious to the naked eye as it had been
in the twentieth century. At least Karvel could be positive
that he had not left the Earth, but precisely where he was on
Earth was not so easily determined. He searched the star-
studded sky and could not identify a single familiar constel-
lation.

For another three days Karvel labored vainly, until he
was able to seize upon a word meaning *thing,* or *object,* and
fashion a statement. "Thing brought me." The tutor combined this thought with his frantic tracing of circles, and
took him to see a circular aircraft like the one that had rescued him.

His frustration reached choleric proportions, the distressed tutor sent for the pilot, and after much fumbling of meaning they achieved understanding.

He was referring to the sphere he had arrived in.

They did not know what had happened to it.

3

"Time?" Bluebeard exclaimed. "You come to us from *time?*"

Karvel bowed an acknowledgement. "From the past, Sire. From an extremely remote past."

"This is a grievous disappointment to me," Bluebeard announced, fretfully combing his beard with his long fingernails. "I had hoped—but never mind. The historians will be pleased."

"*This* historian is not pleased," the longest pinkbeard said. "He comes from a time before history began. He can tell us nothing, nothing at all. He says—" Pinkbeard glared icily at Karvel. "He says that in his time man had not yet colonized the moon."

Bluebeard combed his beard again. "So remote a time as that?"

"He said *colonized.* And when I told him that man reached Earth *from* the moon, he would not believe it!"

"Indeed." Bluebeard eyed Karvel suspiciously. "You presume to deny the facts of our recorded history?"

"Before man could reach Earth from the moon, he had to reach the moon from Earth," Karvel said stubbornly. "Human history—"

"Prehistory," Bluebeard said. "You really know nothing but prehistory, and precious little of that. What a disappointment after our high expectations! I doubt that you were worth the trouble. Still . . . prehistory. Give him to Prehistory, and let them see what they can do with him."

"Prehistory does not want him, Sire," Pinkbeard said. "Prehistory 1 does not believe that he comes from prehistory."

"What are we to do with him, then?"

"Languages has requisitioned him, Sire. At least temporarily. His own language, or what he claims to be his own language, is unknown to them."

"Very well. Let Languages have him. Tell them to find out the truth about him, if they can."

Karvel took a step forward. "Sire, I must return to the city you call Galdu."

Bluebeard's head jerked. "Galdu? Barbarous place. Its people worship their physical selves, and neglect their minds disgustingly. Galdu would have no use for such an imperfect specimen as yourself."

"Galdu wants him, Sire," Pinkbeard said.

"Indeed! What do they offer?"

"Nothing, Sire. Galdu demands him. Galdu says that he and his machine arrived in Gald territory, causing much destruction, and he rightfully belongs to Galdu. Galdu says we stole him illegally."

"Tell Galdu he is not available for trade. We will consider their *offer*, but only when we have quite finished with him."

Bluebeard huffed himself from the room. The others followed, leaving Karvel alone with Languages 9-17, his tutor.

"I'm sorry," she said.

"I really don't care whether they believe me or not, if only I can make contact with the city that sent out the U.O.'s. How certain are you that it wasn't Galdu?"

"Galdu has no scientists, and no technicians above the fifth level. Its technicians would perhaps be able to build uncomplicated replacement parts, but I am certain that they would not have the knowledge and skill to make the thing that you describe."

"I *must* find out where the U.O.'s come from," he said despairingly. "Can't you understand that what happened to Galdu could happen here—and worse?"

She could not understand. Her people had no conception of catastrophe. They did not even have a word for it, though the Galds might recently have invented one.

They found the pilot waiting for them in the Languages Tower. "Nothing," he said unhappily. "The thing you call U.O. is no longer in the park. The Galds probably took it into the city, but no one knows for certain."

"Galdu demanded me," Karvel said. "Couldn't I demand the U.O.? It's mine."

They stared at him, as shocked at his bad manners as by his faulty grammar. He had not yet reconciled himself to the fact that in this strange university city of Dunzalo there was no concept of personal property. He could refer to his arm, but not to his clothing, and certainly not to his U.O.

In practice the citizens took whatever they needed from the city's stores, and no one would have thought of molesting the personal possessions of another—which undoubtedly accounted for the fact that Karvel's equipment was left in his possession. But the language did not permit him to call it his. It belonged to the city.

So did Karvel.

So did all of the citizens, up to and including Bluebeard, who was dean of all he surveyed by virtue of his number, zero-zero.

Karvel corrected himself. "Dunzalo could demand it. Dunzalo has me, and the U.O. brought me here. Isn't that sufficient basis for a claim?"

"It might be," Languages 9-17 said, "but I doubt that anyone would be interested."

"*You* would. In that machine is a communication in forty languages."

"Forty . . . *languages?*" she repeated breathlessly.

"Forty languages, all different and all of them guaranteed indescribably ancient. My own language is one of the forty."

"I'll see what can be done," she said, and hurried away.

The pilot, Communications 4-5, was regarding Karvel with amusement. He belonged to the city's service and maintenance contingent, rather than to the faculties of sanctified knowledge, and he seemed less than wholly sympathetic with their more obvious idiosyncrasies. "You're learning," he remarked.

"Languages 9-17," Karvel mused, looking after the tutor. "What a disgusting name for a young woman. Doesn't she have any other name?"

"You might call her Wilurzil."

"That's much better. Quite nice, in fact. What does it mean?"

"It means, 'Woman teacher of the one-sixteenth beard class.'"

"I shouldn't have asked. What about yourself? Surely your best friends don't call you Communications 4-5."

"Sometimes they call me Marnox, which means—"

"Something about a bird?"

"Bird-chaser."

"Very appropriate. Marnox you shall be. Couldn't the forest people find out anything about the U.O.?"

"No. The Unclaimed People do not get on well with the Galds. Long ago the Galds enlarged their fields at the expense of the forest, and the Unclaimed People have never forgotten."

"They were kind to me."

"You were fleeing from the Galds. The Unclaimed People do not often go near Galdu, and especially not now. There was a skirmish when the Galds attempted to enter the forest to find my plane—and you."

"Who won?"

Marnox grinned. "These days, no one defeats the Unclaimed People in their forest."

"You've traveled about a great deal, haven't you?"

"I have permission to practice flying," Marnox said. "We've convinced Old Zero-Zero that we need lots of practice. It's an excuse to get away from Dunzalo, where nothing ever happens."

"While you've been practicing, have you seen anything like the U.O.?"

"No."

"Or heard of anything like it?"

"No."

"Someone designed the thing, and built at least two of them, and presumably tested them, and finally sent them to the remote past—sent them out three times, with passengers, and got them back twice before I arrived, and they must have done some damage each time they returned. Isn't there any form of communication between cities?"

"What a city builds is its own business," Marnox said. "It wouldn't be talking about it to other cities unless it wanted to trade it."

"One of the passengers was a *nonperson*. An unhuman being, probably from a distant world. Do you know of such a creature?"

"The Overseer and his people are from distant worlds, but they are not *nonpeople*."

"What do they look like?"

The pilot's long forehead puckered in surprise. "Like people!"

"Then it couldn't have been one of them. Who is this Overseer?"

"Why he's . . . the Overseer!"

Karvel touched two stools from the walls. "Let's sit down," he said. "What I'm trying to do is desperately important, and Wilurzil doesn't want to talk about anything except word inflections. Tell me about the cities you have seen."

They were city-states, fiercely independent of each other in all except their disagreements, which were arbitrated by the mysterious entity whose title Karvel translated as *Overseer*.

Each city was the center of its own mechanized farm, and deep within its vitals each contained the automated factories that received the products of the farm and processed them into products and by-products and by-products of by-products.

Because they were so nearly self-supporting, they were able to specialize. Dunzalo was a university city; and somewhere there was a medical city, and a city of mechanics, and a city of agriculturists, and so on, through the entire professional spectrum. The largest city-states, such as Galdu, apparently specialized in producing the one thing all the others needed: people.

Most of the trade between cities was a trade in people. There were no children at Dunzalo. The university city traded its educated young people, and an occasional older specialist, to cities that needed teachers, or linguists, or mathematicians, or whatever Dunzalo could supply. In return Dunzalo received the doctors and mechanics and agriculturists and workers it needed to maintain itself and its farm—and more young people to educate.

"And yet, there is a sort of centralized authority," Karvel mused. "Where does this Overseer have his headquarters?"

"On the moon," Marnox said.

"Could I ask to see him?"

The thought shocked Marnox into speechlessness.

"How could I go about traveling to the moon?" Karvel asked.

"No one travels to the moon unless the Overseer's people take him there."

"Somewhere," Karvel said slowly, "there is a city of extraordinarily talented engineers, who built the U.O.'s. How do I go about finding it?"

"I don't know. We can keep looking, and asking people—"

"That would take too long."

Karvel was experiencing a disquieting sensation of uncertainty. If he had arrived in the wrong time, or the wrong place, how could he possibly go about finding the right one?

Dunzalo petitioned the Overseer, demanding the surrender by Galdu of one unidentified spherical object, Dunzalo's by token of its lawful ownership of the object's pilot. Galdu had already petitioned the Overseer, demanding the return of Karvel by token of its lawful ownership of the unidentified spherical object that had landed him in Gald territory.

"When will this Overseer act?" Karvel asked.

The tutor replied indifferently, "When he is ready."

"Will he come here?"

"Who knows? He travels where he is needed, but he is not likely to be needed to act on a simple petition. Probably he will send a message."

"Would I be able to see him if he came here?" He had shocked her again, so he changed the subject. "Do you mind if I call you Wilurzil?"

"Why do you wish to call me that?"

"I like it better than Languages 9-17."

"But Languages 9-17 is my name! There are many wilur-zils—"

"I know. I just happen to like Wilurzil better."

Karvel received a name of his own. He became Languages 20-249, the lowest number in the lowest classification. It carried no distinction and few privileges, and the wearing of a beard was not one of them. Because of this Karvel made his own modest contribution toward the rupture of the city's social structure—for he was wearing a beard. It was his own, and no amount of protest could halt its growth. He had left his razor in the U.O., and Dunzalo's otherwise ample resources were unequal to the task of supplying him with one. As the beard grew, the few Dunzals with whom Karvel came into close contact began to call him after a nickname of their own invention, which he painfully translated as "Little Fuzzy One."

During the next few days, while Marnox ranged far making futile inquiries, Karvel found himself forced into a decision. He did not know where he would go, but he had to leave.

And he would have to walk. He had reluctantly abandoned the idea of stealing a plane. Dunzalo might take little note of a missing Languages 20-249, but it would stir up all kinds of tiresome complications over a missing aircraft; and in any event Karvel could not get himself checked out on the weird keyboard controls without arousing suspicion.

He donned the native dress to make himself less conspicuous, and at every opportunity he went exploring. Bearded scholars paced the maze of corridors and ramps, engaged in endlessly ruminative discussions but never in arguments unless their beards were of equal length. They ignored the illegally bearded Karvel. He thought their status symbols ridiculous until he remembered the university ceremonials of his own time, and the colored robes by which professors flaunted their rank.

So large was the city, and so complicated its layout, that in three days of search Karvel made no progress at all in finding his way to an exit.

In three days of English lessons, Wilurzil proved herself a linguistic genius. There was no other way to account for the progress she made in the face of Karvel's inept teaching. No matter how carefully he expounded a point, her incisive questions soon had him muttering profanely that Haskins should have sent a linguist.

During the fourth lesson, while he was vainly attempting to explain the subtle distinction between *I walk, I am walking,* and *I do walk,* it occurred to him that a textbook would be an immense help. He decided to make one for her, but he had no words with which to ask for pencil and paper.

Neither had he learned a word for *write.*

He traced words in the air and on the floor, he described the nature of the U.O.'s messages, he explained and demonstrated to the extreme limit of his vocabulary and imagination, and finally it dawned on him that Dunzalo had no written language. Wilurzil only vaguely comprehended what it was.

"The silent speech," she said. "They say that the Overseer uses it."

And how did the university city preserve its accumulated wealth of human knowledge? In books, naturally. Talking books. Even the city's records were voice-recorded.

"I walk, I am walking, I do walk," he said resignedly.

Somewhere in the distance a gong sounded, and continued to sound. Wilurzil sprang to her feet and whispered an unfamiliar word.

Her obvious terror alarmed him. He opened the door and looked out, and above the deep reverberating *boom* of the gong he could hear distant shouts.

Marnox sprang into view at the end of the corridor. "The Galds!" he shouted. "Hurry!"

Wilurzil seized his arm. "The Galds have come for you. You must hide!"

Karvel jerked free and sprang to a storage bin for his equipment. He knew at once that he had a decision to make, and while he strapped on his pack and slung his rifle his mind worked anxiously.

He wanted to go to Galdu. He *had* to go there.

The Galds had come to capture him.

What could be simpler than to outwit the Dunzals, and give himself up?

And yet, though he had to go to Galdu, he did not want to go there *as a prisoner*. Probably a prisoner would command no more attention in Galdu than a Languages 20-249 did in Dunzalo. As long as he enjoyed even a limited freedom of movement, his mission had a glimmer of a chance. If he were to be thrown into a dungeon and forgotten, it would have none at all.

His mind made up, he let Wilurzil hurry him away.

The Galds were upon them before they reached the ramp. Marnox attempted to fend them off, and was flipped with the prettiest wrestling trick Karvel had ever seen. Karvel drove his rifle butt into the chin of one Gald, smashed another in the groin, and fired a shot past the ear of a third. The report rang out thunderously, and the Galds fled in terror toward the top of the tower. Wilurzil, equally terrified, darted off in the opposite direction. Marnox stared up at Karvel in stupefaction. The gong continued to boom gloomily.

Karvel stepped over an unconscious Gald and calmly strolled away.

The lower corridors were jammed. The nonbearded were attempting to reach the towers where they might be of some use; the bearded were in frenzied flight to the depths of the city. Arms flailed, beards were torn off, and the crowd surged back and forth in search of exits. The din was tremendous.

Karvel pushed through to the park and stood there for a moment, watching a large aircraft hover over the city. He could hear gongs booming on all sides. He circled the park until he found an exit that led into a deserted corridor, and followed it. A few nonbearded men passed him, hurrying toward the center of the city.

He strolled on. The noise of battle and flight receded into the distance, and soon he could hear nothing but the ubiquitous alarm gongs. The corridor divided, intersected others, turned, turned again. It led him into an enormous, vaulted room in which he counted twenty exits. He selected the one directly opposite, and kept going.

An hour later he stood at the mouth of a tunnel, looking out across a park at the city's undulating fields. An unmanned machine worked on in ignorance of the invasion, making unerringly straight furrows.

Karvel followed the city's outer wall for a short distance and seated himself in a fluted recess. A tree rendered the position invisible from above, and from the ground unless someone came within a few feet of him. He made himself comfortable and waited to see what would happen next.

When darkness fell he was still waiting incredulously. The Galds had achieved complete surprise, terrorized the city, and sucked its defenders up into the towers. They needed only a coordinated assault on the unmanned perimeter to take possession of the city. That assault never came.

He wondered if they were equally inept in their own defense. If the people of Dunzalo decided to retaliate—but he could not imagine Bluebeard planning an invasion. Given a few hundred adventurous men with a solid grudge against Galdu, Karvel thought he could capture the city.

Or at least the U.O.

He got to his feet and looked about. In the darkness the city gleamed with a ghostly phosphorescence. He hurried through the park to escape the effused halo of light, and then set off at an easy, plodding pace across the newly plowed ground.

The forest was less than ten miles away, and he had all night in which to reach it.

4

The Council of the Unclaimed People had been in session since early morning; it was now midafternoon, and Karvel, pacing restlessly at the far end of the cavern room, watched the proceedings with a deepening sense of panic.

Their speech was garnished with unfamiliar words and further confused by the fact that several councilmen spoke at once in an incessant, echoing hullabaloo. Eventually, though, Karvel was able to unravel enough of the discussion to know what it was that troubled them.

These green-skinned people could have pursued a gnat through their forest in the dark, but they were inherently unable to cope with a complicated mental problem.

Bowden Karvel represented a highly complicated mental problem.

As Unclaimed People they had a venerable tradition of extending refuge to all who desired it. Always in the past the refugees had been misfits, whose mere act of escaping automatically made them outcasts. Their cities would not want them back, and would not accept them if they attempted to return. They were Unclaimed People.

Bowden Karvel was not unclaimed. Not just one city, but two, were claiming him with a vehemence entirely beyond the experience of these simple forest men. Galdu had already petitioned the Overseer about him. Now Dunzalo had demanded Karvel's return, and threatened to make its own appeal to the Overseer.

The Unclaimed People were confronted with a problem

that had never occurred before in all of their history: Could a person who was claimed become an Unclaimed Person?

Tiring of his pacing, Karvel went to the grill and helped himself to a generous serving of cakes and a bowl of the fruit drink. He still hadn't been able to identify the strong, vaguely familiar flavor of the cakes, but after his ordeal with Dunzalo's mush they tasted delicious and made a highly satisfying impression on the stomach.

But his anxiety blunted his hunger. He had come to the forest seeking help rather than a refuge. He was unlikely to receive either.

Abruptly the Chieftain stood up. The debate stopped immediately, and the Unclaimed People crowded in from outside or from the depths of the cave and waited in hushed expectation. Someone touched Karvel's arm, and whispered to him, and he stepped forward and stood facing the Chieftain.

"Our decision is that you must leave," the Chieftain announced.

"Am I permitted to inquire as to why?" Karvel asked.

"You are claimed. Therefore you cannot become an Unclaimed Person."

"You have not yet permitted me to plead my own case. May I do so now?"

The Chieftain hesitated. The Council stirred restlessly. All of them looked surprisingly young. Either they did not show their age because of their superb physical conditioning, or they did not live as long as the city people. Their indecision, too, seemed youthful. They were not governed by a senile reluctance to act, but by doubt as to what their action should be.

"May I speak now?" Karvel asked again.

The Chieftain seated himself resignedly. "Speak, then."

"I do so with a question," Karvel said. "On what basis do these cities of Galdu and Dunzalo presume to own me?" He pivoted slowly, meeting the eyes of each member of the Council. "I was not born in either city. I was not acquired in lawful trade by either city. By what right am I claimed?"

Again he regarded the councilmen searchingly across an uneasy silence. "The right of possession? Galdu never possessed me. I was for a time the guest of Dunzalo, but Dunzalo did not rightfully own me and does not now. Your laws and customs are strange to me, for I come from afar. I ask for instruction. Do you not, on occasion, send a messenger or emissary to nearby cities?"

"On occasion," the Chieftain admitted.

"When that messenger or emissary arrives at his destination, does he then become the property of the city to which he is sent?"

Again there was silence. Karvel smiled. "I am an emissary from my people to yours. I have come an enormous distance, I have suffered a perilous journey, and my mission is of utmost importance to both of our peoples. I cannot fulfill that mission if, wherever I go, I am claimed as property. I ask to be instructed as to your laws and customs. By what right do these cities claim to own me?"

"That is not for us to decide," the Chieftain said.

"My mission concerns the Unclaimed People as well as the cities. I ask now—"

"No!" The Chieftain sprang to his feet. "Who owns you is no concern of ours. As long as you are claimed you cannot become an Unclaimed Person. Therefore you must leave."

He turned abruptly, and walked away. The councilmen drifted off, the room began to empty. Karvel hesitated for a moment, getting his disappointment firmly in hand, and then he picked up his equipment and marched toward the exit.

He had won a partial victory. The Unclaimed People were evicting him from their forest, but they were not presuming to decide the claims. He must leave, but at least they had left him free to go.

Unfortunately the victory was meaningless. He had no place to go.

A few aircraft were parked around the edge of the shaded clearing. Paths converged from all directions, some wide roads, some narrow, a few so infrequently used that trailing vines blurred their shape.

As Karvel hesitated a plane broke through the leaves and settled slowly. He recognized Marnox at the controls and Wilurzil beside him. Hurriedly he turned into one of the lesser paths and placed a curtain of vines between himself and the clearing.

He followed the path's meandering course for several miles, until it widened into a pleasant, deeply shaded forest glade. There he sat down to rest, and demanded of himself what he intended to do next. He could easily wander for days without finding his way out of the forest; and as soon as he emerged the nearest city was likely to claim him as its property.

He had been contemplating this bleak future for nearly an hour when the Unclaimed People appeared. They filtered noiselessly into the glade, and if they saw Karvel they deliberately ignored him.

One of the men held a pole high above his head, and drove its spike horizontally into an enormous tree on the opposite side of the clearing. He grasped it like a trapeze bar and swung up to stand on it. Another pole was tossed up to him, and then another, and he mounted a ladder of widely separated poles to vanish into the tree's lower branches.

Others swarmed after him. Poles were tossed up to them, and soon they had spread through the tree, reaching out with their poles, hooking with the barb, and sending nuts crashing through the branches to the ground. The nuts were the size of small coconuts, and Karvel backed away in alarm as they began to fall nearby.

One rolled in his direction, and he stooped to examine it. When he touched the rough husk his hand came away stained a dusky green—an Unclaimed People green.

He wiped his fingers on the smooth bark of a tree; the stain did not come off.

"So that's it," he mused. "They can't handle the nuts without getting stain on themselves, and rather than go about with blotchy complexions they stain themselves all over. They don't seem to care if they wear blotchy clothing. Odd. One thing is certain—they're nut eaters, and their cakes are made of nut meal. They're also pretty good acrobats."

They swung down effortlessly, the last one jerking out the poles as he descended. Then they formed a circle about the tree and stood looking up at it quietly.

"A religious ceremony?" Karvel asked himself. "Are they tree worshipers?"

Watching them, he had an idea. He'd been a total failure as a diplomat. Perhaps it was time he tried some rabble-rousing.

As the circle broke up he stepped forward boldly. "It's a beautiful tree," he remarked. "A noble tree. How unfortunate that it must be destroyed."

They backed away slowly, regarding him with amazement.

"A noble tree," he said, looking upward and raising his arms in what he hoped was a posture of veneration. "A strong, deathless tree. But a terrible strength beyond understanding shall smash it to the ground, and fire as hot as the sun shall consume it, and the winds shall scatter its ashes afar. And the same shall happen to that tree, and that tree, and that tree—between one breath and the next your forest shall be no more. I grieve for you."

He lowered his arms and stole a glance at them as he bowed his head. He had their full, their intense, their breathless attention. "I grieve for you," he intoned softly. "Your forest shall die. All of these noble, strong, deathless trees shall die."

The performance was placing a strain upon his vocabulary. He took a deep breath, and raised his arms again. "They could be saved. They will die, but they do not have to die. How unfortunate that your Council and your Chieftain would not listen to me!"

He searched their faces. They were less simple-minded than he had hoped; there were skeptics among them. "Have you not heard what happened to Galdu?" he asked. "The unnamed horror has already struck Galdu. The city was torn apart. People perished by the thousands."

"Galdu had too many people anyway," one of them muttered.

"Of course. But do you have too many trees?"

They stirred uneasily.

"First Galdu," Karvel intoned, "and then your forest. The green life around you will be crushed to dusty, dead ashes. I grieve for you." He was propping up his vocabulary with words of English, and it seemed to add to the harangue's effectiveness. "This happened among my people," he went on. "I have stood on a distant hill and watched huge trees smashed to the ground—like this!" He snatched the nearest pole, stepped back, and flung it to the ground.

He paused, waiting for some kind of reaction. There was none. "Between two breaths it will happen," he said. "One moment a lovely, deep, life-giving forest; the next moment searing heat and invincible force that leaves the barren ground choked with the ashes of death. It could happen tomorrow. It could even happen NOW!"

The last word shattered their immobility. Their stunned expressions twisted to terror. They surged forward, laid hands on Karvel, pulled him toward the path. He broke free only long enough to pick up his equipment before they seized him again and rushed him away. He soon began to lag, but they lifted him bodily and broke into a run. Some of them were speaking gurgling inanities; some were weeping. When finally they burst out into the central clearing they were a panicky mob.

They poured into the cave, filling it with echoing shouts of the impending doom. In a twinkling the room was jammed, and Karvel learned too late that a rabble-rouser could have too much success. For a suspenseful moment many seemed to think that the catastrophe had already occurred. They attempted to fight their way out of the cave while those still outside were struggling to enter and find out what had happened. The milling crowd surged this way and that, taking Karvel with it. A few of the calmer men were waving arms and calling for silence, but they only added to the din.

Karvel stumbled against a bench and managed to climb onto it. Immediately he lost his footing, and only the tight press around him kept him from falling.

"Let the Council meet!" he shouted. "We must act quickly to save the forest!"

No one heard him.

All unknowingly he had dredged up some archaic horror, or given reality to their most terrifying superstition. The force he had unleashed seemed about to engulf him.

He could no longer hear his own voice when he shouted. Hands seized him; he attempted to shake them off, but they persisted, and propelled him forward. Miraculously a way opened for him. He looked back as he gained the clearing outside the cave, and found Marnox beside him. The pilot rushed him to a plane. Wilurzil leaped in after them, crouching down behind the seats. The canopy closed. They shot upward as the Unclaimed People began to emerge from the cave.

Above the forest Marnox banked the plane into a wide circle. "What were you trying to do?" he asked Karvel.

"I was trying to get some help for a raid on Galdu. What went wrong?"

"What did you say to them?"

Karvel told him.

"You should have been more specific. They got the idea that you'd destroy the trees yourself."

Karvel said dejectedly, "Anyway, I've made some progress. They took me seriously—which is more than Dunzalo did. What's been happening there?"

"When the Galds couldn't find you, they left. We've complained to the Overseer and asked damages. Why do you want to raid Galdu?"

"To see if I can disable the U.O. before it's used again. I have to assume that my blundering has made me too late to stop U.O.-2, but with luck the generals might think I passed it en route. If U.O.-1 goes back they'll know I failed."

Marnox and Wilurzil were exchanging blank looks. "What I told the Unclaimed People was no joke," Karvel said. "That *will* happen to someone's forest, or someone's city, if I don't get to Galdu. Will you help me organize a raid?"

"On Galdu? The Unclaimed People wouldn't go there."

"Not even to save their trees?"

"Perhaps to save their trees, if the need were properly explained to them, but they won't need to. Galdu no longer has your sphere. The Galds traded it to Bribun."

"*Bribun?* A city?"

"Yes. We only heard about it this morning. Bribun learned of your sphere when Dunzalo claimed it. Bribun placed a counterclaim, stating that the sphere belonged to it. It also placed a claim for you, because you arrived in the sphere, its property."

"Its *property?*"

"It had it before, but somehow lost it. I don't remember exactly how the claim was worded. Dunzalo has filed another protest because Galdu traded the sphere to Bribun."

"It'll take your Overseer a year just to get all the claims sorted out. Could Bribun have built the U.O.?"

Marnox hesitated. "It's possible, I suppose. They are a city of mechanics. They make repairs and build replacement parts and machines for many cities. They also train mechanics for trade."

"I don't suppose the Unclaimed People would join me in a raid on Bribun."

"I think you'd best stay away from these Unclaimed People," Marnox said. "The tribe near Bribun might help you, if it were to their advantage."

"I didn't know there was another tribe."

"There are Unclaimed People everywhere—everywhere the nut trees grow. What is it that you want to do?"

"I want to either disable that sphere or steal it. I don't care how many cities file claims. It's mine, and I'm going to make certain that no one will be using it. I can straighten out the technicalities later. Have you ever been to Bribun?"

"Many times."

"Is it a large city?"

"Not as large as Galdu. How are you going to bring the sphere away? It's very heavy, isn't it? This plane couldn't carry it, and the Unclaimed People don't have cargo planes. Even Dunzalo doesn't have one."

"Does Bribun have one? Well, I'll steal that too, long enough to get the sphere to a safe place."

Marnox grinned delightedly. "I've never heard of unlawful theft on that scale. I'd like to see it done. We can go to the Unclaimed People near Bribun and ask their help, but you'd best let me do the asking. They won't be of much use to you if you frighten them witless."

"Just a moment. What will Dunzalo think about this? I don't want to make trouble for you."

Marnox exchanged glances with Wilurzil. "Our orders are to remain with you until we can bring you back to Dunzalo. It isn't unusual for the Unclaimed People to take days to make up their minds, and what Old Zero-Zero doesn't know won't make him or anyone else miss a meal. But we must start now if we're to get there before dark."

At half-night, or midnight, they were circling another forest, and the city that glowed in the distance was Bribun. Marnox flashed a signal, and answering flashes came from the six planes that were following them.

"Now?" Marnox asked. He was enjoying himself immensely.

"You're just a pirate at heart," Karvel said.

"What's a pirate?"

"If I told you, you'd want to be one. Give them plenty of time."

He watched the city uneasily. The Unclaimed People—after Marnox presented Karvel as "Little Fuzzy One," a venerator of trees—had been gratifyingly cooperative. Everything had gone so smoothly that he had a premonition of **disaster.**

That feeling was not eased by the presence of Wilurzil. "A raid is no place for a woman," he had told her, and she calmly cited her Dunzalo orders and climbed aboard.

They continued to circle, watching the gently glowing mass of the city. Suddenly a bright light gleamed at its outer base.

"They've opened up to them," Marnox said.

"Or at least come to investigate. I think we can go in now."

Marnox signaled again, and they banked out of their circle and flew toward the city. Long before they reached it the outer wall blazed with lines of light, starkly illuminating the dark figures of the swarming Unclaimed People. Karvel could not hear their shouts, but he could see the furious gyrations of their movements. He had asked for nothing more than a demonstration, and he feared that they were overdoing it. In two instances they seemed to have forced the outer gates.

The towers loomed below, truncated cones that recalled those of Galdu, and they drifted to rest on one of them. Three more planes landed beside them, and the other three settled onto another tower. Not until Karvel leaped out did he realize how badly he had blundered.

He had planned his raid like an assault on a medieval castle, and this city was an enormous building that covered square miles. The puny bedlam set up at its walls could not even be heard at the top of the tower. Those in the depths of the city would never know about it unless, in a week or so, someone got around to telling them. His strategic diversion had gone for naught.

"Ready?" Marnox asked.

"Go ahead," Karvel said.

Marnox led the way, and the sturdy volunteers from the Unclaimed People formed up smartly to follow him. They placed Karvel in the middle, where his diminutive stature and outlandish, hairy features would be somewhat concealed. He moved Wilurzil to his side, telling her that her orange beard made her unnecessarily conspicuous.

They walked quickly down the ramp that spiraled around the tower's circumference, and moved for a short distance along a large, dimly lit corridor. The party from the next tower joined them. The first Bribs they met passed them by with scarcely a glance.

They turned onto a series of long, descending ramps, with Marnox still leading the way. He knew Bribun, knew precisely where he was going. They were meeting an increasing number of Bribs, and one of them stopped to ask a question.

"Traders," Marnox said. "Emergency."

They emerged in a vast tunnel, turned, and found themselves at the entrance of a room the size of a football stadium. It was a machine shop on a colossal order, and so were the machines. Mechanics swarmed over many of them, looking like ants dismantling gigantic insects.

"Do you see it?" Marnox asked Karvel.

"No," Karvel said.

They moved slowly toward the center of the room and began to drift apart, looking searchingly in all directions. "A sphere," Marnox kept saying. "Does anyone see a sphere?"

"Let's not get separated," Karvel called sharply.

"I thought it would be here," Marnox said, "but I don't see it."

"Where else could it be?"

"I don't know. Anywhere."

"Then let's look for it," Karvel said.

They managed an orderly retreat, and huddled in the vast corridor. It ran straight and level, and in one direction vanished into infinity. In the other, people were milling about and a distant clamor of voices reached them faintly.

"Are we on the ground level?" Karvel asked.

"Yes," Marnox said.

"Then that's one of the main entrances, and the Unclaimed People are still stirring things up there. This must be where they move machines in and out of the city. Fly the aircraft along this tunnel, I suppose. Does it go straight through the city?"

"Yes. I think so."

"There must be other workrooms."

"That's the only one I know about."

"If the U.O. was brought into the city, it should be somewhere along this tunnel. All we have to do is keep looking. Suppose we split up, and search in both directions."

"And you wait here."

"Good idea," Karvel said. "It's a long way to infinity, and I'd rather not be at the opposite end of the tunnel when you find it."

They started leapfrogging from room to room, but they had not gone a hundred feet when natives suddenly poured into the tunnel from a dozen passageways and overwhelmed them. One of the groups was cut off immediately; the other found the tunnel blocked, turned back, and was surrounded before it had taken a dozen running steps. For a short time Karvel stood unnoticed. He began to edge toward an opening where he had seen a descending ramp, but before he had covered half the distance Bribs charged out of it and blocked it off. He regarded their efforts with grudging admiration. Unlike Dunzalo, Bribun had a scheme of defense and used it effectively.

Karvel had his pistol and knife concealed under his loosely hanging native dress, but he did not want bloodshed, and the Bribs were far too numerous to bluff. As they advanced he backed away slowly. No one touched him until he attempted a belated dash for safety, and then he was seized and held firmly.

Suddenly a whirlwind of flailing arms struck his captors. He caught the flash of an orange beard as Bribs piled up in ineffective heaps. Wilurzil went down with them, but her arms continued to flail, her lethally long fingernails producing howls of pain and rage. For the moment Karvel was forgotten.

Three leaps brought him to the descending ramp. It spiraled gently downward, and he followed it at top speed.

A Brib blocked the exit at the bottom. Karvel seized him, twisting an arm behind his back.

"The sphere from Galdu!" he snapped. "Where is it?"

The man screamed with pain, and fainted. Karvel dropped him and raced away. He was in a narrow corridor that lay at right angles to the tunnel above. There might be another approach to its rooms, but he would need a guide.

Two Bribs snatched at him as he ran past. He whirled, felled one with a blow, and pounced upon the other. "The sphere from Galdu. Where is it?"

Face contorted with pain, the Brib choked an unintelligible reply. Karvel eased the pressure on his arm. "Can you take me to it?"

"Yes . . . yes . . ."

"Let's go. If you try any tricks—" He gave the arm a twist.

They moved off, Karvel keeping both of the man's arms bent behind his back. Whenever the pace lagged he increased his pressure, with gratifying results. They ascended to the level above, and started along another corridor. Karvel could see a crowd of people beyond a distant opening. "Is that the large tunnel?" he asked.

"Yes . . . yes . . ."

"Isn't there another way to get there?"

"Yes . . ."

"Let's go that way."

They turned back, but the pursuit was already on. Up a ramp, along another corridor, down again, and Karvel's captive was so thoroughly subdued that Karvel was able to hold onto one arm and run at his side. The pursuers gained, and when they emerged both ends of the corridor were already blocked off.

The Brib halted. "There."

"Open the door," Karvel ordered.

A touch of the hand, and the door slid open. Karvel shoved his captive through it. The U.O. stood in the center of the room.

"Close the door!" Karvel snapped.

The Brib did so, and sank white-faced to the floor when Karvel released him.

Karvel leaped to the U.O. and tried to dilate the hatch. It would not open. The U.O.'s entire outer surface had been covered with a tough, transparent, plasticlike substance. Karvel dug at it futilely, beat on the hatch with his fists.

"Major . . . Bowden . . . Karvel?" a voice said.

Karvel spun around, staring. The pronunciation was ridiculous, but the words were recognizable. A man walked forward slowly, a tall, fair-skinned man of hefty build, costumed in a queer kind of baggy overalls. He towered over Karvel, and smiled down at him.

"I'm the Overseer here," he said. "I think it is time that you and I became acquainted."

5

Karvel reclined on the exquisite, billowy softness of a sausage-shaped lounge, and looked up through a transparent bubble at the alleged planet Earth—alleged because the gleaming globe in the sky bore no more than a hazy resemblance to the Earth that he knew. The continents were twisted and distorted, bloated where they should have been narrow, constricted where they should have been broad. The seas had swallowed them in great gulps, and regurgitated them where no land belonged. The first glance moved Karvel almost to tears. It was like returning home after a brief absence, and finding everything that one loved altered beyond recognition.

Or like glancing into a mirror and confronting a total stranger. He wondered if he should call himself the first of his generation to reach the moon—or the last.

The Overseer laughed softly as he occupied the adjacent lounge. "Do you enjoy the view?"

"Yes," Karvel said, "and no. The Earth has changed so much that I hardly recognize it."

"There is no lovelier planet in the galaxy," the Overseer said. "To me it is always a majestic sight—an old, old world, its resources exhausted, its people ridiculously backward, yet scudding about in this obscure corner of space quite as nonchalantly as if the universe pivoted upon it. In an oblique sense the universe does, you know. Earth is undeniably the birthplace of man. Tradition holds that for a long time men everywhere dreamed of returning to it, but those who did found themselves distressed even as you are distressed, and perhaps cruelly disappointed as well, for the reality was to their dreams as an insignificant grain of truth is to an enormous husk of legend. The dream and the legend were eminently more satisfying than the reality and the truth, and so eventually men stopped coming. I don't really know if I love the old planet for what it is, or for what it once was, but I remain here, and decline loftier and less vexing appointments, and look at that lovely light in the sky whenever the cares of my office permit."

Karvel grunted noncommittally. The cares of the Overseer's office impressed him not at all. He had seen the luxurious moon headquarters, with its outrageously-sized female contingent that he instantly and indignantly labeled a harem. He thought he understood why the Overseer was so frequently unavailable, and why the claims of Earth's cities went long unheeded.

He had formulated his own succinct appraisal of the Overseer's character. The man possessed a genius for words that rendered the threadbare Earth language rich and vitally expressive. He prated poetry and oozed good fellowship, and whenever he intoned, "My friend . . . ," Karvel had to suppress the urge to reach behind him and discover where the knife had been buried.

The Overseer meant to make some nefarious use of Karvel, as soon as he could invent one that he deemed sufficiently profitable. Karvel felt certain of that, and he had no intention of waiting around long enough to find out what it would be. In the meantime, he could in good conscience advance a few schemes of his own.

At the moment he needed the Overseer far more than the Overseer needed him, so he accepted the good fellowship and pretended not to notice when he found the other studying him calculatingly.

"Have you learned anything new?" Karvel asked him.

"I have decided to leave your U.O. at Bribun," the Overseer said, "but it will remain sealed until I personally order it unsealed. It may be that my superiors will wish a technical study to be made of it, and if so I promise that it will be done with care. You may rest secure that no one will send it . . . anywhere."

"And . . . the other U.O.?"

"There, my friend, we have a problem. There was no other U.O."

"That is indeed strange," Karvel murmured, not believing a word of it. "We counted two of them."

"My friend, I have inquired of every independent city on the planet, and of every tribe of Unclaimed People. That is what has taken me so long. Mendacity is virtually non-existent on this planet, and even if it were not the people would not lie to their Overseer. There was no other U.O. Not in this time, in this place."

Karvel said politely, "Then my mission is a failure. I have come to the wrong time and the wrong place."

"Perhaps. But let us combine our knowledge and see what results. One hundred and ten Earth-days ago a pilot of Bribun sighted a strange sphere in a tract of unclaimed land far to the north of his city—some seventy air units. I have this day examined the place myself. The traces of destruction are obvious if one is looking for them, but the land is wasteland, and neither the pilot nor those who came for the sphere found them remarkable. They took the sphere to Bribun, and examined it, and inside they found messages—"

"Messages!" Karvel exclaimed. "The messages were included when the French sent their U.O. back to you, and that was the second one. U.O.-2."

"Permit me to finish my own chronology before we consider yours. Prior to this finding, the sphere was unknown to the citizens of Bribun or to anyone else in this time and this place. No—hear the rest. The Bribs could not read the messages. They did not even recognize them as messages, because written language is a lost art on this planet, but they were eager to make contact with a people who could build such a machine. It is now too late to discover all of the steps in their reasoning, but they have almost an instinctive knowledge of machines, and they easily arrived at an empirical understanding of the instrument panel. The result was that they determined to reverse certain instruments and send the sphere back to where it came from, along with an emissary. When the emissary operated the critical control the sphere vanished, which naturally astounded them. A machine of such a capability was quite beyond their comprehension."

"Just a moment. You're suggesting that neither of the U.O.'s originated here?"

"I am not suggesting it, I proclaim it. I am positive that they did not. The Bribs saw no reason to consult their Overseer either before or afterward about a private matter that could concern only Bribun, but I am satisfied that your U.O.'s were unknown in this time and this place until the one arrived with the messages."

Karvel said incredulously, "Then my arrival was the second?"

"Wait. The second arrival occurred forty Earth-days after the first. Again, by miraculous good fortune, the sphere did no serious damage. It appeared in the grazing lands of Merrun, where live one of the three groups of meat eaters remaining on Earth. It killed only a few of their animals. Because it was a strange machine, and because the Bribs' craft with machines is justly celebrated, the Merrs sent to Bribun for advice. Bribun offered compensation for the dead animals, and in return received the sphere. That second sphere contained a dead passenger, though for reasons you will understand the Bribs learned very little about him. The remains were cremated with all of the reverence that the Bribs extend to their own dead, and the ashes returned to the soil."

Karvel bowed his head and murmured, *"And strange-eyed constellations reign his stars eternally.* Adieu, Phineas Ostrander." He said slowly, "You may not realize it, but you're describing a paradox."

"In what way?"

"The U.O. that we sent out first arrived here second. The U.O. that we sent out second arrived here first. But continue, please. Obviously Bribun returned that second sphere with another emissary."

"Immediately. They were much concerned about the possible fate of the first."

"They sent out another without any thought as to why our emissary died?"

"They thought, of course, but they did not think to do anything about it. And that, my friend, is as much as I can tell you. The U.O. did not originate in this time and this place. There were two arrivals here, and two sendings or departures, and your own arrival was the third. Now I would very much like to share your knowledge. I trust that you are positive that the U.O. did not originate in your time and place?"

"The possibility was barely considered, for a number of reasons. Well, the U.O. arrived, U.O.-1, complete with Bribun's emissary and also with one butterfly that helped to convince me that the thing came from the future. Bribun's emissary was in no condition to tell us anything. The butterfly was unharmed. This is another paradox, and we should have given more thought to it. How did the butterfly survive when the pressure was sufficient to smash a man?"

"Was the butterfly inside the sphere?"

"No. No, it couldn't have been inside, because it was flying about before the hatch was opened."

"Perhaps the movement of the sphere creates a vortex of normal temporal pressure, which could suck in and hold an insect without damage."

"Something like that, I suppose. Anyway, the U.O. arrived, and I witnessed the arrival. There was substantial damage to persons and property. I joined the scientists who were studying the U.O., and one night when I was checking what seemed to be a brilliant idea my assistant moved a control he shouldn't have touched, and the U.O. vanished. With him in it, naturally. Exit U.O.-1."

The Overseer waited silently.

"The second arrival occurred on the other side of the ocean. A very small city was wholly destroyed. This time the U.O.'s passenger was a nonhuman. An unhuman being."

"Unhuman being," the Overseer mused. "That is a difficult concept to grasp. An animal with intelligence?"

"I wouldn't refer to it as an animal, except in the way that humans are animals. I didn't see it myself, and naturally it wasn't in the best condition to be studied properly, but the scientists did learn some striking things about it. It had no separate head. The scheme of its skeletal structure was entirely different from that of any vertebrate life known to my time. It had incipient or vestigial wings. The brain was enormous, filling the central part of its body. And so on. The thing was utterly unrelated to any life on Earth."

"Indeed. And what conclusions did you draw concerning the possible origin of this unhuman being?"

"The scientists didn't commit themselves. Even after they studied it some of them didn't want to believe it. I thought the thing could have originated in the distant future, like Bribun's emissary, because by then man would have reached other worlds and possibly made contact with such a life form. Have you?"

"Let us postpone that question for the moment. Continue, please."

"Messages in forty languages were put into U.O.-2, and it was returned to you."

"I object to the use of the word 'returned,' since that was its first arrival here, but let us not quibble over terms. I assume that the U.O.-2 was given the same instrument settings you had previously given to the U.O.-1?"

"It was. Next U.O.-1 arrived again, fortunately in a wasteland, with Bribun's second emissary. More messages were prepared, a protective device was designed for a passenger, and here I am."

"They were very impressive messages," the Overseer said. "How did you manage to read them?"

"I placed them in a linguistic analyzer, and it had no difficulty in deciphering them. I do not know if that was because the machine actually has records of such ancient languages, or simply because it was given so many versions of the same message to work from."

"I'm glad to know that written language hasn't entirely disappeared."

"Only on Earth," the Overseer said. "The people of Earth have forgotten many things. Sometimes I think they are the happier for it."

Karvel nodded absently. He was attempting to sort out the complicated interweaving of U.O. arrivals and departures, and he said finally, "The unhuman being would seem to be the significant clue."

"I agree," the Overseer said immediately. "The unhuman being's arrival is the only one for which we do not, between us, provide a departure. Is this also your conclusion?"

"Yes. And once that fact is established, it follows inevitably that the U.O. with the unhuman being—U.O.-2—was the first to reach us. And yet it arrived a month after U.O.-1! My difficulty is that I've been trying to reason the thing out chronologically, and obviously this is impossible. Time travel renders temporal chronology meaningless. So U.O.-2 reached us first, even though it was second by thirty days."

"What are thirty Earth-days when an enormous span of time is traversed? It amazes me that the sphere managed consistently to strike the same year."

"Agreed. Even if the U.O.'s controls measure time in days, a microscopic error might produce a difference of many days at a distant point in time. Anyway, U.O.-2 reached us first, and once that is understood it is immediately obvious that there was only one U.O."

"This I have believed from the beginning."

"You didn't have a paradox of chronology to confuse you, and the Bribs operated without any scientific experts to confuse them. There was only one U.O. The one we called U.O.-2, which reached us second, did not have the marks our scientists put on U.O.-1. It couldn't have had them until it had been sent to the future and returned again—thirty days earlier. If you can follow that."

"Not precisely, but I agree with the conclusion. Where does such a conclusion take us?"

"To another question. Where did the unhuman being

come from? I guessed the future, because I felt certain that man would eventually encounter intelligent life forms on other planets."

"That depends on what you mean by *intelligent*," the Overseer said. "Man has explored far into the galaxy, but to my knowledge he has yet to find humanlike intelligence, with a civilization and a technology. I would not be so rash as to claim that he never will, but thus far he has not. The galaxy is a vast expanse of frightening distances, and its distances are not the most frightening thing about it. Man has not even explored half, little is known of much that he has explored, and no one man has mastered all of that. The reference center of such a minor planet is limited in its resources, but I will make inquiry about your unhuman being. I will also ask my headquarters to institute a search, though that will not help us immediately. Tell me, please, all that you can remember of this creature."

"An estimated five feet tall when standing," Karvel said. "It had a thick, barrel-like body, with an enormous brain located in the upper central part of it. There was no separate head. There were incipient or vestigial wings, the scientists thought vestigial. There was something strange about the blood—a question as to whether it really was blood, in the sense that we have blood. There were six limbs, but the scientists refused to designate them either arms or legs. They terminated in something that didn't resemble hands or feet. There was disagreement as to its visual capabilities, probably due to the fact that its eyes were no longer recognizable as such. They couldn't find any mouth, either, or figure out how it breathed. It did have a lung of some kind. I'm sorry I can't remember more, but the report was handed to me as I was leaving, and I only glanced at it."

"Surely that should be sufficient," the Overseer said. "If you will excuse me, please, I shall make the inquiry."

Karvel leaned back and attempted to concentrate on the serenely glowing planet Earth. A six-limbed, scantily winged, headless vision marched across it, and he damned Haskins for neglecting to show him the report until the last minute. If he'd had the opportunity to study it properly, perhaps his recollection of it would have sounded less like a secondhand description of a hallucination.

The Overseer returned to his lounge, and said gravely, "Your unhuman being is unknown to our reference center. I have addressed an inquiry to headquarters, but I very much doubt that it will help us. If such a creature existed, surely it would be important enough to merit description in any reference center."

Karvel nodded, keeping his eyes fixed meditatively on the sky.

"I greatly fear that the problem is unsolvable," the Overseer went on. "With the galaxy as vast as it is, it would be difficult enough to locate this creature in space. If we must also search for it in time, the situation becomes impossible."

"The fact that man hasn't made contact with such a life form doesn't mean that he won't," Karvel protested. "And since it reaches us out of time—"

"The unhuman being may come from an uncertain future. Possibly, but that is not really helpful to us. How would we begin to search for it? And before we began to search, we would have to ask ourselves if we really wanted to find it!"

"Your time, and mine, have been sending the U.O. back and forth through the simple expedient of reversing the instrument settings," Karvel said. "That couldn't possibly have worked with U.O.-2, because U.O.-2 didn't come from you. It just occurred to me that I don't know where the instruments were set when the unhuman being arrived, and I doubt if the scientists knew. They said U.O.-2 had been handled carelessly; probably the instruments were tampered with before they saw them. The instrument settings may have been meaningless anyway, because U.O.-2 arrived with an empty fuel tank. What if it arrived where it did merely because it ran out of fuel?"

"That would indeed be a paradox," the Overseer admitted.

"That's only the beginning. U.O.-2's empty fuel tank was refilled with fuel we made after we analyzed the fuel it contained on its second arrival, which came first. I think I'm getting a headache. If the future—you—hadn't returned the U.O. to us so as to arrive before we sent it to you, we wouldn't have been able to send it to you in the first place. Rather, in the second place. We wouldn't have known what instrument setting to use, and we wouldn't have been able to refuel it. Do you follow me?"

"I do," the Overseer said with a smile, "but I'm not certain that I want to. Was there no residue of fuel in the tank that could have been analyzed?"

"I simply don't know. I'm reasonably certain that it wasn't analyzed, because that had already been done. Did the Bribs have any difficulty with the fuel?"

"There we have another paradox, or at least a puzzle. The fuel used by the U.O. is identical to the fuel we use to maintain our cities and operate our machines. It brought you to the moon, and it has taken man far into the galaxy. Our scientists call it the perfect fuel. That your people could have evolved an extensive technology without it is more bewildering to me than your time paradoxes."

"Not to me," Karvel said dryly.

"My instinct demands that both time and the events it controls should be immutable, so I say that the earlier return of the sphere did not change events, but merely facilitated them. I say that, but I am not wholly satisfied with it."

"Neither am I. Because I'm convinced that man acquired the perfect fuel only because an unhuman being traveled in time."

"The instrument setting on the U.O.-2 must have in some way confirmed the conclusions you had already reached. Is it possible that the instruments were set twice as far?"

"And the U.O. was 'returned' by halving the settings? No, I don't think that could be possible."

"I agree, and I think that it eliminates the possibility that the unhuman being reached you from an even more remote future. Supposing the setting was identical with the one you had already used?"

"Identical," Karvel mused. "And if the French were handling the U.O. carelessly, they didn't photograph the instruments on arrival. Later they saw our photographs, and heard about our using an opposite instrument setting, and by that time the instruments had been fussed with and changed and they'd forgotten the original settings. Or perhaps they thought someone had already changed them to the settings we used." He paused. "The spiral! When U.O.-2 arrived, Force X spiraled clockwise instead of counterclockwise, which could mean that it arrived *from the opposite direction.* But in that case—"

"You say it, my friend."

"In that case—" Karvel's voice broke. He could not meet the Overseer's eyes, and his own whispered words rang thunderously in his ears. "In that case, the U.O. did not originate anywhere in the future. It came from the past."

6

A man compelled to climb mountains did his most exhausting work at night; and when the dead of Galdu forced him into perspiring wakefulness with their screaming concert, and when Lieutenant Ostrander's head jerked back through the U.O.'s hatch to vanish once again into the crush of time (what *should* he have said to him?) Karvel lay gazing at the dimly glowing ceiling, and climbed.

And climbed.

When he had quite convinced himself that the summit was hopelessly beyond his reach, he left his quarters and walked.

The moon base was enormous. A gigantic dome pimpled with observation bubbles, it lay at the jagged edge of the Mare Imbrium, in the yawning mouth of the great Alpine Valley gorge. At the other end of a connecting tube was a smaller dome, the landing dome, and the complex viewed from above gave the impression of a lopsided dumbbell. Nearby were a number of lesser domes, surmounting a complex network of underground tunnels.

The base was enormous—and virtually empty. At some time in the dim past it had been a thriving city, perhaps a crucial steppingstone in man's first awkward lurch toward the stars. Now human aspiration had passed it by, and it was as barren and meaningless as a monument to a forgotten battle.

The Overseer and his staff occupied the dome's two highest levels, and did not need a fraction of that space. The ground level was a supply depot, and much of the remainder of the dome was sealed off. But there were miles of corridors for Karvel to walk, and miles of ramps for him to descend and climb; and when the ghosts of Galdu screamed, and Lieutenant Ostrander's young face smiled, and clouds obscured the unattainable mountain peaks, Karvel left his sleeping pad to pace the corridors with the long, gliding strides that the moon's low gravity made possible.

It was another morning after such a sleepless night—a moon base morning but not a moon morning, because outside the base the sun would not rise for more than a week—when Karvel tiredly entered the Overseer's administration room. Sirgan, the Overseer's assistant, looked up from a food tray, nodded, and grinned between swallows. As in Dunzalo and the caves of the Unclaimed People, food was always at one's elbow. The Overseer and his staff members consumed ridiculously small amounts of food several times an hour. They thought Karvel's custom of eating three meals a day incredible, and the dazzling quantities of food he was able to dispatch at those Gargantuan repasts shocked them.

At least the Overseer's food was genuine food. It dissolved in the mouth, but it had meat in it, and more than an illusion of substance.

"Will you take food?" Sirgan asked.

"Thank you. I've already eaten."

"The Overseer is occupied."

"I know," Karvel said curtly. He had heard his laughter booming down the corridor from the women's quarters.

Karvel circled the vast room and turned away. He hadn't come there to see anyone. He was merely walking. He had trod down the nerve-wracking visions of the night, and now he was at work on the harsh facts of day—the facts he had acquired since arriving on the moon.

The Overseer had arranged for the compensation of the cities claiming Karvel and the U.O. The U.O. was now the property of the Overseer.

So was Karvel.

The Overseer was as coolly brilliant and as suavely unscrupulous a person as Karvel had ever met, and thus far he had made only one mistake. He had assumed that a man from the Earth's past would be as blindly naïve as the Earth people he was accustomed to dealing with.

Unfortunately, with Karvel virtually a prisoner at the moon base, the mistake was unlikely to cost him anything. Karvel still had his knife and pistol, but he could think of no effective use for them. What he needed was a plan of searching ingenuity.

Sirgan, still gumming his last mouthful of food, overtook him in the corridor. "The Overseer said I was to show you around, if you like, and tell you anything you want to know."

"Anything?" Karvel asked with a grin. He didn't believe it, but there was always the possibility that he might be shown, or told, more than was intended. "Let's go."

Sirgan was a lesser edition of the Overseer—a younger man, of a medium seven and three-quarters feet in height and the same sturdy build. His eyes were deeply sunken and gleamed a depthless black, as though they had looked upon the aggregate evil of the universe and found it wanting. Like the Overseer, he seemed at his sinister worst when he was trying to appear friendly.

Karvel found little of interest on the administration levels. The reference center was an electronic marvel that occupied a suite of rooms, but it had already failed to answer the one question Karvel wanted to ask. A bank of machines performed the clerical work for a planet. Only in the message center was there human activity. Half of the Overseer's staff consisted of communications men, and they worked in shifts to handle the supply orders and the claims and complaints of Earth's cities.

On the lower levels, an overweight villain named Franur ran the supply depot with an assistant, a small crew of Earthmen, and a large number of machines. Franur's bulk intrigued Karvel, who hadn't thought that anyone could gain weight on the diet he was experiencing. After a cautious question or two he attributed it to gland trouble.

"The depot handles mostly fuel, fertilizer, and metals,"

Sirgan said, "but it has to have a little of almost everything on hand for emergencies. The supplies they don't get much call for are stored below. Would you like to see them?"

Karvel said no, and Sirgan led him through a long underground tunnel to one of the small domes. A scientific detachment was at work there, three bored individuals wandering about in a maze of instruments.

"They're studying the sun," Sirgan said. "It's part of a galaxy-wide research project—of the known galaxy, that is. Suns of various ages are being studied, and there'll be experiments to learn to control a sun's expenditure of energy, or regulate its aging, or some such thing."

"What will the experiments do to the Earth?"

Sirgan shrugged. "I suppose the people would be removed if any danger developed. An old, exhausted system like this one can't be maintained forever. Earth has to import too many things. The quantity of soil nutrients needed just to maintain its agriculture is shocking. At present the trade is profitable to us, but this may not always be the case."

"What does an exhausted planet have to trade?"

Sirgan looked surprised. "Why—people! Earth natives are much in demand. The men make quite the best spaceship crews available—in positions of nonresponsibility, of course. Their self-contained city life conditions them to a crowded existence, I suppose, and they are trained to give complete obedience to whomever owns them. In certain specialized environments they are immeasurably superior to any other people. There is a substantial market for them. Earthwomen are also much in demand. They have a loyalty to their owners that isn't easily found in women these days." He grinned. "They have other qualities that are also justly famous, but no doubt you know about those from experience."

Karvel considered himself anything but a stuffy moralist, and that shocked him. He could only ask weakly, "Don't the cities of Earth take any interest in what happens to their citizens after they trade them?"

"Of course not."

"Are there other worlds where people are used in trade?"

Sirgan was thoughtful for a moment. "I don't know of any. That's another reason the people of Earth are so much in demand, I suppose. It's a venerable practice on Earth. They've been trading people among themselves for so long that it probably seemed perfectly natural to start trading them away from Earth when Earth's resources gave out. But all that is ancient history."

"The one thing I don't understand is where they get the people. I haven't seen a child since I arrived."

"There are no children at Dunzalo. The Unclaimed People are unique in that their women still bear children, but they keep the women and children segregated. Where else have you been? Bribun? I believe there is a small nursery at Bribun, probably a throwback to the time before the cities began to specialize."

"I wasn't there long enough to see it."

"Galdu has one of the largest nurseries on the planet, and fortunately it wasn't damaged. But you didn't actually go to Galdu."

"You make the production of people sound as easy as growing grain. Instead of trading for them, why don't you grow your own?"

Sirgan regarded him indignantly. "If you'd seen the nurseries, you wouldn't ask that. It's a horribly complicated process, the children require many years of highly specialized care, and the environment has to be precisely right if the adult is to be worth anything in trade. Really, it's much easier to trade for them."

"And—only the women of the Unclaimed People bear children?"

"The Unclaimed People are strange in many ways. It was once thought that they would make excellent pioneers for the settlement of new planets, but that didn't work out at all. We even supplied them with those silly nuts they insist on eating, but the entire colony died off. We still don't know why. Evidently something in their forest environment is lacking elsewhere."

Karvel nodded. "Trees. What do the Unclaimed People trade?"

"The products of their forests. They need very little themselves—fuel, very rarely a replacement machine or plane. They wouldn't trade their people even if we had a use for them. Would you like to learn about the sun experiments?"

"No," Karvel said. "I doubt if I'd understand them anyway. What else is there to see?"

"Very little, unless you'd like to explore the old mine. This was once the most important mine on the moon, which accounts for the size of the base."

"I suppose it's exhausted."

"Long ago. That's ancient history, too. The legend is that ore from the moon took man to the stars. 'Wrought of Mother Earth, fired with the strength of Luna,' an old saga goes. Or something like that. I don't believe a word of it, but there's no doubt that the moon once had many rich mineral deposits. The most important mining bases are still here. You can see the locations on the maps in the administration room. Things remain very much the same on the moon, unless man changes them."

"Is there anything to see in the mine?"

"Nothing but tunnels. I went down there once. It's a gloomy place."

"And a long walk, I suppose."

"Not when it was in use. It was fully automated and there were conveyors everywhere. Of course that was long before Earth had to start importing fuel. Earth's cities were once fully equipped with conveyors, I'm told, but when fuel became scarce they had to eliminate such luxuries and let their citizens walk. Speaking of walking, we're going to bring some doctors up to have a look at your leg."

"What for?"

"To see if they can give you a new one."

"I'm perfectly satisfied with the one I have."

"I don't mean an imitation leg. I mean a real leg. By surgery."

Karvel stared at him. "Is that possible?"

"Perhaps. It isn't often done here, because few citizens of Earth ever suffer such a loss. There's nothing very unusual about it. In your case we don't know if it's possible, you being . . . well . . . sort of a different species, and of an uncommon stature. We'll have to ask the doctors. Earth's doctors are old-fashioned and naïve, but what they're willing to undertake they do very well. Wouldn't you like a new leg?"

"Not knowing that such a thing was possible, I've never given it a thought. I wouldn't want an operation that required a long convalescence."

"You'll have plenty of time. Headquarters won't digest *that* report in a hurry."

They walked back to the administration room, and Karvel refused—again—an invitation to the women's quarters. "What I'd like to know," he said, "is something about the government. Does your headquarters supervise a number of worlds, or what is the system?"

Sirgan laughed. "Our headquarters isn't a government. It's a trading organization. It's located—but you wouldn't know the name of the star. I'll show you on a star chart if you're interested. We hold the franchise for the Earth trade."

He took his leave with a smile, and after he'd gone Karvel went slowly up the ramp to one of the observation bubbles. The Earth was still a beautiful light in the sky, though it was already waning.

"A slave world," Karvel muttered. "I wonder how long it's taken for humanity to sink so low."

An Earth Shuttle dropped slowly across his field of vision, headed for the landing dome. The Overseer's compact, errand-running spaceships looked like distorted models of the planes he'd seen on Earth, their elongated oval platforms having pressurized cabins attached. The strange craft should have fascinated him, but they did not. His mind was too fully occupied with the winged, headless hallucination from the past to give more than a passing thought to aircraft technology.

Had the Earth once nurtured a powerful civilization of such weird creatures? Some traces of it should have survived; but no doubt there were, even in the twentieth century, large areas of the Earth where such vestiges could have remained undiscovered. Under the Antarctic icecap, for example, or in inaccessible regions of jungle or mountains— or even under the sea.

Wherever it was, he had to go there. He had to reach the creatures before they started bombarding the twentieth century with U.O.'s.

Sirgan interrupted his meditation to announce with a grin, "Here are two old friends of yours."

"Friends? Of mine?"

"They think harshly of you for running off to the moon and leaving them behind. They say their city ordered them to remain with you. They raised such a fuss that the Shuttle pilot brought them up. As long as they're here, they might as well stay. Here they are."

Marnox and Wilurzil stepped into the bubble and looked about curiously. Sirgan stood in the background, still grinning. "Now I see why our women didn't interest you," he said. And departed with a wave of his hand.

Karvel rose to greet them, experiencing an embarrassment that verged on panic. Not only had he not seen them after the fracas in Bribun, but he had scarcely given a thought to them since. He said shyly, "I never had an opportunity to thank you. I appreciated your help—both of your help—deeply. My plan was not successful, but I did locate the sphere. Perhaps things will turn out all right. I hope so."

They did not answer, and the silence quickly became awkward. Karvel noticed a dark bruise on Wilurzil's face. "What happened?" he asked.

"You should see the Bribs who got in her way," Marnox said.

"I can imagine," Karvel said, with a glance at Wilurzil's fingernails. "She's fortunate she didn't get scratched herself."

"How would the Bribs scratch her? Men do not let their

nails grow, except the men of the Dunzalo faculties. If they did, how could they get any work done? To fly my plane I need fingers, not knives. Outside Dunzalo only women have long fingernails."

"That's understandable." It was probably a natural law. Deprive a woman of hair to fuss with, and she'd be bound to cultivate her fingernails.

"When will we return to Dunzalo?" Wilurzil asked.

"I suppose you can return whenever you like. As for me, the Overseer has claimed me for himself. Dunzalo and the other cities have already been compensated. It's too bad that you weren't informed. You've had a trip to the moon for nothing."

Marnox, untypical Earthman that he was, grinned happily. A trip to the moon was adventure of a sort, and an excuse to stay away from Dunzalo.

Wilurzil's facial expression was enigmatic. She said accusingly, "You promised to teach me your language."

"I know I did, but—" Karvel gestured helplessly. "There's no reason why I shouldn't continue your lessons at least until you return to Dunzalo. Certainly I have nothing else to do. Have you ever been to the moon before?"

Neither of them had. Wilurzil wanted to know where on the waning globe Dunzalo was located, and when Karvel could not tell her she lapsed into a brooding silence. Karvel began a lecture on the history of the Earth, attempting to point out the ways in which it had changed from the Earth that he knew. After a few minutes he glanced at them. Marnox had lost interest, and was studying the dark, jagged peaks of the Lunar Alps. Wilurzil was staring moodily at Karvel.

"My God!" Karvel exclaimed to himself. "I'd hoped that the baser emotions had been bred out of the human race by this time!"

Was it possible, was it even conceivable, that Dunzalo Languages 9-17 was in love with him? He wondered what her reaction would be if she knew how repulsive her appearance was to him. He would have much preferred her

with the synthetic orange beard on top of her bald head,
rather than on her chin. Her stark figure did not merely
deny her femininity, it defied it. And there was her toothless mouth to contend with, and—now that he thought about
it—her protruding and decidedly unfeminine ears.

She had lovely, deeply brown eyes, but the remainder of
her appearance very forcefully distracted from them.

The fault was not hers, but his. What was the old saying?
The beauty is in the eyes of the beholder. Sirgan had
thought her attractive.

"And what the devil do I look like to her?" he wondered.
"I'll probably never know. In fact, I'd rather not know!"

He must appear at least as strange to her as she did to
him, and for her to be in love with him—no. He rejected the
idea vehemently. She could not regard him as anything
more than an ungainly source for a new and fascinating
language.

"You mentioned forty languages," Wilurzil said.

"The Overseer has them. Unfortunately they are in the
silent speech, but I'll ask him for copies for you. What do
you two know about the government?"

The question startled them. Each city on Earth and each
tribe of Unclaimed People had its own system of government, no two of them quite alike, but the idea of a government of many worlds was hopelessly beyond their grasp.

Yet Karvel was positive that there must be one. The
Overseer's trading organization had obtained its franchise
from someone. Who, if not a government?

"I have something to tell you," he said. "You probably
won't understand, and even if you do I doubt that you'll be
able to help me. But I can trust you, I think, and it will help
a little just to be able to talk about it."

He told them. Watching their faces in the glowing earthlight he traced the confused history of the U.O. and the
basis for his bitter conclusion that he had traveled the wrong
direction in time. He added a brief but vivid discussion of
the evil use the Overseer was likely to make of the U.O.,

and his perfidy in selling the inhabitants of Earth into slavery.

"We have two problems," he said. "One of them is mine —to travel to the remote past and somehow prevent the unhuman beings from sending any more U.O.'s. Yours is much more difficult—to put a stop to this trade in humans. Somewhere behind the Overseer and his trading organization there must be a government, but I haven't any idea how you'd get in touch with it. Knowing what is in the Overseer's franchise might be a tremendous help, but it would be in the silent speech, perhaps in a language unknown on Earth, and even if you somehow obtained a copy you couldn't read it."

They were gazing at him blankly. Marnox protested, "The Overseer . . . the *Overseer* . . ."

"Look," Karvel said grimly. "I overheard a choice bit of conversation after I had a long talk with the Overseer about the U.O. He was incautiously speaking this Earth language, and he said to his assistant, 'That's as much as we're likely to get out of him. The only question now is how to turn a profit on it.' As long as he can have his profit he doesn't care how many people die. But never mind. I don't suppose these are the kind of problems you're accustomed to. It's time to sleep."

Marnox went off to the quarters Sirgan had assigned to him, but Wilurzil remained, demanding a language lesson, and Karvel gave her a language lesson. He made no further attempt to analyze her motives. He'd had difficulty enough in attempting to understand the women of his own time.

Finally she left him to the nocturnal ordeal with his mountains.

The Overseer had finally emerged from his harem when Karvel awoke, and was testily dealing with an accumulation of messages. Karvel moved about the administration room studying the large, tremendously detailed metallic maps of the moon that were posted on the walls, obviously a heritage from a time when a knowledge of the moon's surface had been important to someone. The Overseer rudely ignored him.

Then Marnox and Wilurzil entered. Face puckered roguishly, the Overseer sprang forward with effusive greetings.

He drew Karvel aside, and said, grinning slyly, "Now I see why my women don't interest you. But perhaps we can work a trade."

"*Trade?* But she isn't mine to trade! She's just my language teacher."

"I wouldn't mind being taught a language," the Overseer said, with a boorish laugh. "I'll trade you—three for one?"

"She doesn't belong to me! Dunzalo gave her the job of teaching me the language, and when I left they sent her to bring me back."

"Then you belong to her," the Overseer said. "That's even better. Excuse me."

He talked briefly with Wilurzil, and returned frowning. "Stubborn little thing—but no matter. I'll trade Dunzalo for her."

"Dunzalo might not let her go. She has a fairly high number. She's Languages 9-17, and she seems to be an accomplished scholar."

"She's one of the bearded ones, too. I suppose there's a taboo involved—life pledged to learning, or some such thing. I'll look it up. But these Earth cities will trade anyone, if they're offered enough. Languages 9-17, is it? I'll trade for her the next time I go to Dunzalo. She's even worth a special trip. Lovely thing—what she must look like without that beard! On second thought, though, maybe I like her better with it on."

Karvel turned a wondering gaze on Wilurzil. Was her face tapered more beautifully than those of other Earthwomen, or was it her unusually small stature that made her attractive? He'd seen so few women since he arrived in the future, and paid so little attention to those he had seen, that he had no basis for comparison.

"Have you eaten?" he asked Marnox. "The food here may not be to your liking."

"It isn't," Marnox said with a grimace. "They will send for some of our food if we stay long."

"I've already sent for some," the Overseer called. "You'll be here a long time—both of you."

Later that day a returning Shuttle brought a trio of doctors, gaunt, tall, solemn individuals with the most beautifully shaped, long-fingered surgeon's hands that Karvel had ever seen. With Marnox and Wilurzil looking on, they examined Karvel carefully, took measurements, pondered the stump of his right leg.

"Have you attained your full growth?" one of them asked.

"I should hope so!" Karvel exclaimed.

The answer disturbed them. They rechecked their measurements, and communicated their concern in long, silent glances.

"How long will I be incapacitated by this operation?" Karvel asked.

"That is difficult to say. We may be unable to find an adult limb of the proper size, which would mean that two operations would be necessary."

"*Two* operations? Yes, I think I understand. The alternative would be to have one knee fifteen or twenty inches higher than the other, which I wouldn't like."

"The rule is to join only adult limbs to adults. If we were to violate the rule and join you to the limb of a child, that limb might continue to grow. I don't know if this is true, because to my knowledge it has never been necessary to violate the rule."

"Just a moment. Have you ever performed such an operation?"

"Certainly. Once when I was quite young, and again only seventeen Earth-years ago. It is a simple operation, and recovery is usually quite rapid, but few of our people ever lose their limbs."

"All right," Karvel said. "I'll have the operation. But no experiments. One operation, with a guaranteed short convalescence, or nothing doing. I hope to leave very soon on a long journey, and there may not be any surgeons where I'm going. I'd be worse off than I am now if one of my legs started to grow."

"Then it is a question of finding an adult limb as abnormally proportioned as yours. That will not be easy."

"You could take my leg," Wilurzil said.

They all stared at her, Karvel open-mouthed.

"I have my growth," she went on. "And my height is similar to his."

The surgeon carefully ran the beam of his measuring light over her leg. "That is true," he agreed. "There is not enough difference to matter. We shall join you to her leg."

"What would that accomplish?" Karvel demanded. "Then she'd have only one leg."

"She contemplates no such journey as yours. We could, at our leisure, join her to another leg, and it would not matter how much additional surgery were required."

"It would matter to me," Karvel said. "No. Positively no. Where do you usually get these spare limbs?"

"We keep an extensive stock of spare human parts," the surgeon said stiffly.

"Well, find me a leg in that extensive stock, or forget the whole business. And even if you find one, there'll be no operation unless you can guarantee a remarkably fast recovery. One thing more. Where were you planning to perform this operation?"

"Why, here. The Overseer said—"

"Have you ever performed an operation on the moon?"

"No, but—"

"Such an operation performed under low gravity would be exceedingly dangerous. I might not survive. I'm surprised you didn't know that."

The doctors exchanged startled glances. "No. No, we didn't know that."

"That's strange. It's common knowledge, where I come from. Tell the Overseer that the operation must take place on Earth, which is the only sensible place for it anyway— close to your stock of spare parts. We can't have you running back and forth carrying legs until you find one that fits."

"It would be much more convenient to do it on Earth," the surgeon admitted.

"And much safer—don't forget that. Tell the Overseer now. I'm ready to leave any time."

Karvel tossed out the suggestion on a quixotic impulse, with no illusions that the wily Overseer could be taken in by such an unsubtle ruse. He was dumfounded when the Overseer appeared a short time later to tell him he could leave immediately.

"It's only common sense to have the operation performed at Lewir," he said.

"Lewir?"

"That's the medical city. Anything they might need would be right at hand. I don't know where they got the stupid notion that an operation here on the moon would be dangerous, but they have it, and it's best to humor them. You can leave as soon as the Shuttle is ready."

"I'd rather have the operation here on the moon," Karvel said. If the Overseer wanted to snatch at the first feeble excuse to send him back to Earth, he was probably furthering some deep plot of his own. Karvel had naïvely allowed himself to be outmaneuvered.

"Nonsense," the Overseer said. "The Shuttle is almost ready. Don't keep it waiting."

Marnox appeared a moment later and asked, "What's the matter?"

"We're going back to Earth."

"Is that all? From the look on your face I thought you'd lost your U.O. again. I'll tell Wilurzil."

The Overseer came to the landing dome to see them off. Karvel and Marnox boarded the Shuttle; Wilurzil hung back.

"Aren't you coming?" Karvel called to her.

"The Overseer has invited me to stay," she answered.

The Overseer flashed a triumphant grin. "Good luck with the operation. I'll look in on you to see how you're getting along, but probably not very soon."

Karvel seated himself beside Marnox, shaking his head bewilderedly. An enormous lapse of time had altered woman's appearance almost beyond recognition, and changed her fickle nature not at all.

But that was no surprise to Bowden Karvel.

7

On the third day after his operation Karvel had three visitors: the leaders of the cities of Bribun, Galdu, and Lewir. These men were neither doddering oldsters nor naïve woodsmen. They were administrative heads of enormous cities, and they were intelligent, shrewd, and competent—and suspicious. Merely bringing them together in Karvel's presence represented a substantial diplomatic achievement.

Karvel watched their faces intently while he spoke, and learned nothing. He paused frequently for questions or comment, and received none. He had no way of knowing whether their solemn expressions conveyed shock, anger, or boredom.

They remained silent when he finished, sending fleeting glances about the hydrotherapy room, watching the foam bubbling around Karvel's immersed leg, studying Karvel, exchanging long, meaningful looks with each other.

It was the Galdu leader who spoke first. "*Individuals?* The Overseer trades our people to . . . to *individuals?*"

"He does."

"And . . . they are then the servants of the will of those individuals?"

"They are."

"What of their cities?"

"On Earth all people are the property of their cities. On other worlds this is not so. Men choose their own cities, change them at will, and follow pursuits of their own choosing. Their cities do not own them."

"They own each other?"

"No. Only the people of Earth are owned—owned by the individuals to whom the Overseer trades them. Had you no notion at all of what happens to those the Overseer takes in trade?"

"We knew that he traded some of our people away to other worlds," Galdu said slowly, "but we suspected nothing like this. There are cities on other worlds, and we naturally thought—" He broke off, and a moment later he said incredulously, "The Overseer trades the citizens of Earth to . . . to *individuals?*"

In a world where there was not even individual ownership of material things, the ownership of one human by another was inconceivable. Finally they began to understand, and with their understanding came anger.

"We did not suspect such a thing," the leader of Lewir said. "How could we? On Earth it would not even be possible."

"Your mistake was in having no interest in your people after you traded them."

"How could we have an interest in what was no longer ours? Anyway, many of the people the Overseer acquires in trade are traded to other Earth cities. And he does not trade only people—he trades everything. If we should have a temporary shortage of grain, for example, rather than attempt to find a city with a surplus we notify the Overseer. All of the cities tell him what they have to trade, and he obtains the grain, perhaps in exchange for fuel. We might trade him a young doctor for the grain. This is much more convenient than dealing directly with other cities, because the Overseer can supply whatever is wanted. An individual city cannot often do that."

"What would the Overseer do with the young doctor?" Karvel asked.

"He would trade him to a city that had a need for a doctor. He would receive in return whatever the city had in surplus, or—"

"People?"

"Yes. He might receive a hundred or more untrained young people for a doctor."

"Then your economy works on a barter system, and the common denominator is people. The Overseer sees that the needs of all of the cities are satisfied, and in the process he converts his own gains into as many untrained young people as possible—to be sold into slavery."

Karvel leaned back and watched the foam bubble around the leg. He still thought of it as *the* leg. Later, perhaps, he would accept its four-toed structure as part of himself, but after three days it still seemed more alien than the artificial leg it had replaced.

"There is the U.O. to consider," the Bribun leader said.

Karvel nodded. The leader from Galdu met his eyes, and said simply, "It must not happen again."

"It must not," Karvel repeated firmly.

"You wish to leave in the U.O.?" Bribun asked Karvel. "You will undertake to see that it does not come here again?"

"That is my intention," Karvel said. "I cannot promise success, because I do not know what I will find in the distant past. I do not know what manner of creatures these unhuman beings are. I do not even know if a man can survive such a tremendous journey in time. But I shall do my best."

"Is there anything that you require?"

"A few small things. The urgent need is to place the U.O. where the Overseer cannot take possession of it."

"That shall be done at once," Bribun said. "I will send a message."

"The Overseer might intercept it. His people frequently listen in on Earth messages."

"A messenger, then. May I have a messenger?"

Karvel waved Marnox into the room, and he listened to Bribun's message, grinned at Karvel, and hurried away.

"Thank you," Karvel said to Bribun. "I wish that the slave trade could be dealt with that easily. If you refuse to trade your people to the Overseer, the Overseer will not supply the fuel and fertilizer and other things you need. Earth is a worn-out planet. It cannot support itself. Its cities will starve."

Exactly how the problem looked to them Karvel could not guess, but to him it represented a horrendous injustice. Earth had spent its resources generously to send its people to the stars. Now, with its resources exhausted, its remaining people could support themselves only by selling each other. Earth was an aged parent that had impoverished itself for its ungrateful children, and it deserved better of them.

But Earth was not wholly blameless in the matter. The inception of the evil lay in the cities' ownership of their citizens. A man owned by a government was as much a slave as a man owned by an individual, and in some cases the government would be the more exacting master.

Clearly Earth's only hope lay in an appeal to the government of worlds—and the only way to communicate with it was through the Overseer.

Medical attendants interrupted them to remove the leg from the churning liquid, dry it, and cushion it into position under stinging jets of air. The doctors had finally conceded the practicality of two simultaneous operations, so that a normal male leg could be shortened at the same time that it was joined to Karvel. The leg was still immobilized in a brace, but there was feeling in it, and the toes moved easily at his distant command. He was aware of a persistent, searing itch in the small toe, which was missing, and lesser itches along the two invisible scar lines—but even this did not make the leg seem a part of him.

When Karvel turned again to his visitors he expected to find them sharing his pessimism. Instead they were watching him confidently. They actually believed that he was about to offer them a solution, much as an audience would expect a magician to produce a rabbit from a demonstrably empty hat.

He said weakly, "If there were one leader for all of your cities and all of the tribes of Unclaimed People, you would be better able to contend with the Overseer."

"I doubt that the cities would consent to such a thing,"

Galdu said. "Even if they did there would be difficulties. The distant cities have different languages, and we know little about the cities across the oceans."

"You must talk with other leaders, and see what can be done. Together you have at least a measure of strength. Divided you are helpless."

Finally they realized that he could give them nothing but advice. They arranged to meet with him again, but they were glum when they took their leave.

"It's their problem," Karvel told himself, though without much conviction. "I really can't take on any more mountains." He was fighting the numbing certitude that his own mission had been delayed too long, that a vengeful twentieth century might at that moment be arming a U.O. for atomic retaliation—in the wrong direction.

Marnox burst into the room, panting despairingly. "The Overseer beat us. His men got there this morning and took your dratted sphere to the moon."

"All right," Karvel said.

"If you'd let me go yesterday—"

"You couldn't have done anything. We needed the leaders' support, and we couldn't get them together until today. The Overseer isn't stupid. He couldn't be expected to let pleasure interfere with business indefinitely, and it was bound to occur to him that I couldn't be trusted on the same planet with the U.O."

"What do we do now?"

"Think of something else."

"We can't steal it unlawfully from the moon. The Overseer—"

"Controls the transportation. I know."

Marnox lifted his hands helplessly.

The leader of Lewir came in, and listened silently while Marnox repeated his story. "It would seem that the Overseer is suspicious," he said. "I have had a message from him. He asks when you will be sufficiently recovered to return to the moon."

"Will I really be able to walk tomorrow?"

"Of course."

"If you say so. In my time a cut finger took this long to heal."

"Do you have a plan?" Marnox demanded.

"A sort of a plan, but first I may have to learn to walk. Would you ask the Overseer to send the Shuttle for me day after tomorrow?"

"Certainly," Lewir said.

"How many men could we pack into it? Twelve? Could you find twelve young men who won't mind a fight?"

Lewir stroked his bald head thoughtfully. "Twelve men from Galdu, perhaps. The physical arts are stressed at Galdu."

"Get them. Get the roughest twelve young men they have. Marnox, I left my rifle and pack with the Unclaimed People near Bribun."

Marnox left without a word.

"We need an excuse for sending so many men to the moon," Karvel said. "Could you arrange an emergency trade of some kind?"

"It would be very irregular. Normally the Overseer keeps records, and people are exchanged only on a Day of Settlement."

"When is that?"

"The Overseer informs us."

"I see. When he has transportation for a new load of slaves, he asks you to settle your accounts. It saves him the trouble of feeding his slaves, and looking after them, between ships."

Lewir winced. "I could say that we have received more men than we need from Galdu in payment for the doctors we sent to replace those who were killed. I could ask him to take them now."

"Do that."

"It will be an unusual request. He might be suspicious. Do you really have a plan?"

Karvel smiled wistfully. "I have the feeling that I've dedicated my entire life to the theft of that damned U.O. One of these times I'm going to bring it off."

Karvel stepped forward cautiously as the Shuttle settled onto the city's tallest tower. The leg was no longer merely joined to him. It was his servant, it obeyed his wishes; but he continued to regard it as an honored guest, in delicate health, rather than as a member of the family. He babied it.

He also had a precarious sensation of lopsidedness. The people of the future had short, wide feet that were phenomenally flat. The shoe that he'd worn on his artificial leg would not fit his new foot, and probably would have been uncomfortable if it had. The wide, flat footwear they were able to furnish was extremely uncomfortable on his other foot. He retained his own shoe on his own foot, and wore an ovular, flat, hard-soled moccasin on the foot of his joined leg, and felt lopsided.

One of the doctors suggested, with more jocularity than Karvel had thought existed among these people, that they replace his good leg, just to even things up. "Nothing doing," Karvel told him. "It might start a trend, and before I knew it I'd be outnumbered."

The Shuttle's air lock slid open, and the pilot jumped down unceremoniously. "Where are the six men?" he asked.

"Twelve men," Karvel said. "Here they are."

"We have no use for twelve. The Overseer said to bring six."

"You heard wrong. Twelve men for trade, plus two passengers."

"Six," the pilot said firmly. "Come along. These two trips to Lewir have ruined my schedule."

Karvel looked helplessly at Lewir's leader. The Overseer had more than a dozen staff members at the base, plus an unknown number of Earthmen and the Shuttle and cargo carrier pilots who came and went. He had no idea what weapons they might have, and his rifle and pistol were the total armament of the planet Earth, where men fought with bare hands on the rare occasions when they came to blows, and had no word for *weapon*. He had fashioned blackjacks for his men, but even with the twelve he would have to rely heavily on surprise if his coup were to succeed. He did not dare to confront the Overseer in his lair with fewer men than that.

"I made an agreement with the Overseer," the leader said firmly. "The Overseer does not break his agreements, and neither do I. You will take the twelve men, or I shall not permit the departure of any of them, or the passengers either."

The pilot surrendered with a gesture of disgust. "If they don't mind being packed in, I don't see why I should care. Any that aren't wanted I'll dump wherever I touch down next, and you can worry about collecting them."

Karvel motioned the men into the Shuttle. He'd had to take the Galdu leader's word that these were the sturdiest physical specimens available. They were agile enough—they looked as though they could easily pole-vault twenty-five feet—but he distrusted their slender, willowy builds. On this operation he would have preferred a few fullbacks.

He also would have preferred more time for training. They'd learned the simple forms of mayhem easily enough, but they applied them as if they were maneuvering to embrace their sweethearts.

He slung his rifle, gave a last, affectionate pat to the blackjack hidden in his clothing, and followed them aboard. The pilot looked curiously at the rifle, but said nothing. Marnox bounded after him and took the seat next to the pilot. Karvel had told Marnox flatly that if he couldn't operate the Shuttle by the time they reached the moon they might have to remain there, and as they shot upward he was straining against the force of acceleration to scrutinize the pilot's every move.

Karvel was able to relax for the first time in two days. He slipped the moccasin off, and scratched futilely at his nonexistent, itching toe. "Two hundred and forty thousand miles," he mused, "and perhaps five hours for the trip." He dozed off thinking that these Shuttles would be worth an investigation, if only he had the time.

When Marnox nudged him awake they were above the moon and descending rapidly. He twisted in his seat to see if the Galds were in fighting condition. For a first trip into space they had borne up very well. There was not an upset stomach among them, which surprised Karvel until he remembered that there were no stomachs among them.

The vast, familiar panorama of craters and *maria* flashed toward them. The braking began—not the sharp, crushing deceleration of a rocket-driven ship, but a light, sustained pressure as of automobile brakes carefully applied. The base still lay in darkness, but sunlight flickered on the jagged fingertips of the surrounding mountains and the curved edge of day was approaching. To the north the vast circle of Plato was dark; to the south a strange-looking crater within a crater was ringed with light, and stared up at them like a ludicrously misfocused eye.

The landing dome had a large central berth for the great ships of deep space, and lesser compartments around the circumference for smaller craft. They hovered over the dome until one of the smaller openings yawned beneath them, and they drifted into it.

The safety lock clicked as air flowed back into the landing compartment. The pilot opened both air-lock doors and jumped out. With a nod to Marnox, Karvel followed him.

The landing engineer appeared, rubbing his eyes.

"Twelve men for Franur," the pilot said.

"Twelve? I thought it was six."

"They had twelve ready, so I brought them."

"Maybe Franur can use them. He wants to rearrange his stock on the lower levels. Take them over to him."

"*You* take them," the pilot said.

Marnox had joined them. Karvel fingered his blackjack and flashed signal to the Shuttle. One of the Galds slumped in the air lock, uttering a piercing scream. Pilot and engineer whirled in one motion, and Karvel flattened the pilot with an expert stroke. Marnox was only a second behind him in

felling the engineer. He stood over his victim, laughing delightedly.

"We're in business," Karvel said.

The Galds poured out of the Shuttle and leaped into action with a heartening efficiency. Two of them produced
lengths of rope, and trussed and gagged the pilot and engineer. The others moved to cover the doors. Karvel unslung
his rifle and walked cautiously into the next compartment. A
large cargo carrier rested there.

"Can you take us back in that?" Karvel asked.

"I don't know," Marnox said.

"Suppose you find out now. We couldn't get the U.O. into
the Shuttle."

Karvel circled the landing dome. He found two more
cargo carriers and another Shuttle, but no personnel. Marnox
caught up with him and cheerfully declared himself ready
and eager to pilot the cargo carrier. The Galds had the inert
pilot and engineer hidden in the Shuttle when they returned, and Karvel nodded approvingly, and said, "Let's
go."

They moved in single file toward the larger dome, with
Karvel leading. Franur, the obese supply administrator,
heard them coming and waddled to meet them.

"Are these my men?" he demanded.

"How many of them do you want?" Karvel asked.

Franur turned to count them and collided with Marnox's
blackjack. The Galds spread out through the supply depot
to find his workers. It took only a few minutes to round up
the bewildered Earthmen, but Franur's assistant resisted,
and was brought back tied up and unconscious.

"Behave yourselves," Karvel told the Earthmen, "and
nothing will happen to you."

They placed Franur and his assistant in one room and the
Earthmen in another, and blocked the doors with packing
cases.

"It's easy," Marnox said, sounding disappointed.

"It hasn't even started yet," Karvel told him.

He summoned the Galds with a wave of his hand, and began the long, cautious climb to the administration levels.

They met no one on the ramps, and at the Overseer's level they crept silently along the last corridor to look into an empty administration room. Puzzled, Karvel angled across to the message center, rifle held at the ready. He halted in the entrance, and a gasp whistled shrilly in his ear as Marnox came to a stop behind him.

Sirgan lay near the door, clothing ripped away, his body crisscrossed with deep slashes that terminated in gruesome ribbons of flesh. His face was torn almost unrecognizably. The body of an Earthwoman lay nearby, untouched except for a crushed skull. The horribly mutilated bodies of two communications technicians lay among their scattered instruments, their slashed faces still oozing blood. Equipment, smashed and spattered with gore, littered the room.

The Galds hung in the doorway, dazed and speechless. Karvel turned his back on the carnage, and thrust them away. "Did the Overseer keep some kind of animals here?" he asked.

They gazed at him dumbly.

"We'd better stay together," Karvel said. He led them out through the administration room, hesitated for a moment in the corridor, and then resolutely turned toward the ramps. On the ground level they released the supply personnel, and Karvel hurried everyone back to the landing dome and placed them in the cargo carrier.

"Don't open up to anyone or anything until I come back," he said. "If I don't come back—you work it out. You'd best return to Earth, I suppose."

"What was it?" Marnox asked.

"I don't know. I'll tell you when I find out—if I'm in any condition to tell you."

He turned away, checking his rifle again. A leopard or a tiger could have made wounds like that. If a ferocious beast were loose in the dome's maze of corridors, he didn't want his hunt impeded by thirteen unarmed men.

He found two more of the Overseer's staff in their quarters. Dead. Slashed horribly. He found another in a corridor beyond the administration room, and two in a small storage room. They had sought refuge there, but the light sliding door had been crushed in.

Reluctantly he turned toward the women's quarters. Where the corridor forked into two sections Karvel found the body of a man, so flayed with claw marks that only surmise told him it was the Overseer. He stepped gingerly over the body and the pool of blood that surrounded it.

In the farthest room he found the women, at least thirty of them—alive, huddled together, most of them with blood-soaked clothing, though their faces were miraculously untouched. All were in deep shock, some sobbing tearlessly, some moaning inanities, some staring sightlessly at nothing at all.

Then he noticed their hands, and their long, knifelike, blood-caked fingernails, and he understood.

He found Wilurzil in a room on the other corridor, crumpled in a corner as though flung there. The orange beard hung loosely from one side of her face. He straightened out her body and carefully rearranged her torn clothing before he realized that she was only unconscious.

He went for water and sprinkled it onto her face. Her eyes opened. She regarded him with horror, and raised her arms to defend herself before she recognized him.

"Is he . . . dead?" she asked.

"Yes," Karvel said. "What happened?"

She shuddered. "I don't know. Did you kill him?"

"No."

"The others . . . the women—"

"Yes."

"I talked to them about their cities, the way you talked to the Unclaimed People about their trees. They hated him, but they were afraid."

She lapsed into a fit of coughing. Karvel offered water to her, but she pushed it away. "He taught me the silent speech," she said. "It is very simple, once the symbols are understood."

"Yes," Karvel said. Simple for a highly talented linguist.

"I found the franchise, and was . . . was listening to it, listening to the silent speech—"

"Was it in an Earth language?"

"It was in all of the Earth languages. For the people of Earth to listen to, only the Overseer concealed it."

Karvel nodded. "He wouldn't want the people of Earth to know what it said."

"He found me listening to it. I ran, but he caught me and was choking me, and then the women came. They killed him?"

"Yes. Is the U.O. still here?"

"I . . . think so." She covered her face with her hands, and spoke haltingly. "The franchise. Don't you want to know about the franchise? You said it was important."

"It might be very important."

"He did not want to teach me the silent speech. He was suspicious, but I insisted . . . I refused—"

She broke off, and with a gesture the symbolism of which Karvel could only guess at, she stripped the beard from her face and flung it aside. "I should have done it before," she whispered, "but he liked me to wear it."

Gently Karvel pulled her hands away from her face, and held them. "What is in the franchise?"

"It is very long and difficult to understand. Many of the words are strange, and I cannot remember them exactly. It says the . . . something . . . is empowered—"

"Trading organization?" Karvel suggested.

"The something with a strange name . . . is empowered —no, is . . . something . . . to supply the needs of the planet Earth, and is empowered to accept in return—it is very complicated."

"Products?"

"Many things. The produce of mines, agriculture, manufacturing, forests—many, many things."

"Does it mention people?"

"I don't think so. No. Is that important?"

"Very important. Don't you understand? There *is* a government somewhere, and Earth is of special concern to it. The franchise is supposed to protect and help the people of Earth. The Overseer and his trading organization perverted it into an instrument of exploitation. If what you remember is correct, Earth can refuse to trade its people, and the trading organization will have to accept whatever is offered. How do you feel? Can you walk?"

"I think so."

"I'll go after Marnox and the others. Do you want to come with me, or would you rather wait here?"

She shuddered. "I'll come with you."

They found the U.O. in a storage room, still sealed, wedged to a circular platform. "How do we move it?" Karvel asked.

"It moves itself," Marnox said with a grin, and he stepped onto the platform and flew it slowly down the tunnel to the landing dome and aboard the cargo carrier.

The Galds searched the administrative levels for the dead, and brought them to the administration room. Finally there were fourteen—twelve men and two women. Six men were found alive in remote corridors where they had taken refuge. The three scientists in the distant research dome were unaware that anything had happened.

While they worked Wilurzil resumed her decipherment of the franchise. She spoke into a voice recorder what she could read of the strange symbols that were embossed on a long strip of flexible metal.

Karvel conferred with Marnox. "I'm placing you in charge of the base," he said. "I'll take the women and some of the Overseer's men back with me, and leave you enough Galds to look after the rest. If they give you any trouble—"

"They won't give me any trouble," Marnox said, caressing his blackjack. "But who'll fly you back?"

"The same pilot who brought us up."

"What if he won't?"

"Once he sees what's in the administration room, he'll be just as eager to leave as I am. There are a couple of Shuttles out, and at least one cargo carrier, so be on the lookout for

them. I'll send more men to you just as soon as I can. The
cargo carrier will transport at least fifty."

They left until last the delicate task of escorting the
women to the landing dome. Most of them went passively,
but a few became hysterical and had to be restrained. Wilurzil did not balk until her turn came to board the cargo carrier.

"You brought all these men here," she said accusingly,
pointing at the Galds. "You came to capture the Overseer."

Karvel made no reply.

"You would have captured him. There was no need to kill
him. You did not want him dead."

Again Karvel had no answer.

"But *I* wanted him dead!" she said defiantly.

Then she broke down completely.

At Lewir, Karvel turned the women over to the doctors.
He could only hope that their skill in psychiatry equaled
their surgical achievements.

He was immediately caught up in a frenzy of activity,
and he had no time for vain regrets, for soul-searching—even
for mountain climbing. So exhausted was he that for one
night he actually slept soundly.

A leader had to be appointed to fill the Overseer's role
in arbitrating disputes and managing supplies. The communications apparatus on the moon had to be repaired
and manned, careful plans made to deal with the trading
organization if it proved truculent, a mission appointed to
return on the next spaceship to establish a direct link with
the government of worlds. Karvel anticipated that the trading organization would not surrender without a fight, and he
felt certain that it would have potent political influence. He
did not find it easy to explain this to men who had no concept of politics, but he did his best.

And it was not his problem. As much as he would have
liked to help, to learn more about man's far-flung civilization, it was not his problem. He repeated that until he had
halfway convinced himself.

He collected an advisory board of engineers and technicians and went to work on the U.O.

He faced three inexorable terrors: pressure, time, and space.

If temporal pressure continued to increase as long as the U.O. was in continuous operation, it would kill him. It had come within a straw's weight of killing him on the journey to the future; the journey to the past would be twice as long.

If somehow he found a way to survive the pressure, time and space would kill him with disappointment and frustration—or old age.

He had no notion of the actual distance he would be traveling, but he knew that the most trivial of errors—say a mistake of a mere hundredth of a per cent—could be magnified to a staggering one hundred years on a journey that spanned a million. As far as he could tell, the U.O.'s instruments were not even designed to achieve that accuracy. If he made his instrument settings with an admittedly impossible precision, he could still miss his destination by a long lifetime!

He would take an extra supply of fuel and be prepared to make additional time jumps from his first stopping point, but in what direction, and how far?

If through some outlandish contortion of coincidence he did arrive at the correct point in time, he would probably never know it. The U.O.'s three landing places in the twentieth century had been a continent or a hemisphere apart. If Karvel opened the U.O.'s hatch and found himself alone on a lifeless Earth, should he assume that his error was one of time or space?

The empty fuel tank of the U.O.-2 and his uncertainty regarding the original instrument settings mocked all of his calculations. He must arrive at a precise time *and* a precise place—and the task seemed hopeless.

His advisory board had no suggestions. So remote to their experience were such problems that they did not seem to understand what he was talking about. He sent them home and called in a crew of Bribun's mechanics.

He had long meditated the fact that the pressure that almost killed him had not damaged the most delicate items of his equipment. The equipment had been packed tightly into small cylinders; the passenger cylinder had been designed for comfort, with ample room for movement and with wasteful inches of foam padding. Could the pressure within the cylinder be somehow related to its volume of empty space? He reasoned that it could.

The padding was ripped out and replaced with form-fitting armor built for him by the Bribs. Karvel would lie in Spartan discomfort in the tight embrace of a cylinder within a cylinder. If his theory were correct, the pressure would build up much more slowly in the cramped confines of the inner cylinder. If it were wrong, the discomfort would not bother him for long.

He would have to take his chances with time and space.

Three times he interrupted his preparations to call on Wilurzil.

She did not recognize him.

The ultimatums in forty languages he collected into a neat package, along with the Overseer's translation, and left it for her. On the back of one of them he carefully lettered, in English, a brief message of thanks and farewell.

Someday perhaps she would overcome her horror and attempt to decipher it.

Part Three

1

Karvel lay in supine discomfort in the armor fashioned by the Bribs, and his only sensation was a growing awareness of a protruding seam under his right shoulder. The sharpening pain in his shoulder helped to alleviate the monotony.

Time passed.

Then the pressure began to tighten. Its first feathery touch was like a door opening on a half-forgotten nightmare, and slowly, ever so slowly, it intensified.

Suddenly Karvel felt a vibration. In an instant it had become a violent pulsation that shook the cylinder and set his armor to rattling noisily. Alarmed, he cautiously pressed upward. The cylinder opened.

The vibration cut off as he was squirming out of his armor. He dilated the U.O.'s hatch and looked out.

The U.O. was revolving slowly, but for the moment he ignored that phenomenon. Twice before he had witnessed the ravages of Force X, and neither time had it struck with the pulverizing speed and fury that now spiraled away from him.

He was looking out from the top of a low, wooded hill—what had been a wooded hill. It was now almost bare, except for stumps. The shredded trees had been flung far down the slope. Toward the bottom a few scattered trees remained standing, spared by the gap between the spirals, and Force X rushed on to spend itself on a bleak, featureless prairie.

Something moved in the distance, something the fury had

missed. Karvel blinked at it. "Kangaroos?" he asked himself. The creatures did not hop, but walked with delicate, mincing steps, unaware of the crushing force that had just whipped past them.

Karvel ducked back inside and removed the U.O.'s critical activating instrument. He opened a supply cylinder and tucked the capsule into his knapsack. Then he squirmed through the hatch.

The U.O. was still revolving slowly, and the ground was three feet further down than he expected. The drop staggered him, and he backed off from the U.O., staring. It rested in a thick metal cup, like a golf ball on a tee, and the cup was revolving.

"A time beacon!" Karvel exclaimed.

A time beacon with a homing device, something to reach out through both time and space when the U.O. approached, and draw it back to its starting point. And the vibration . . .

"A signal," Karvel pronounced. "I hope whoever receives it has the good sense to wait until Force X has run down."

He circled the U.O. In one direction Force X was inflicting its final outrages on a sparse growth of trees. A small stream meandered toward him, curving around the base of the hill. In another direction the parched brown of the prairie merged with the horizon. Karvel moved on. A vast expanse of water gleamed in the distance, and the birds circling above it were slowly drifting specks in the sky. He moved again, and saw the water curve back to lose itself in the lush vegetation of an enormous swamp.

No direction looked promising, least of all the swamp; but from the swamp they came, bursting forth in a frenzied, stumbling rush. The vanguard suddenly went sprawling—perhaps Force X, now well above the ground, had whipped overhead—but it quickly regained its feet and floundered forward. They were too far away for Karvel to see them distinctly. They looked, in fact, like so many barrels scooting toward him, and that was indication enough that he'd found the unhuman beings.

Karvel thought wearily, "Another language to learn."

Haskins should have sent a linguist.

He restrained the urge to dash out and meet them. A freakish, four-limbed creature such as himself was probably the last thing they expected to see. Instead he moved out of sight behind the U.O. and continued to watch.

Some ran on all six limbs, some on four. A few were upright on two, but their straining eagerness kept tipping them forward. Many of them had been carrying long poles—"Not nut poles again," Karvel groaned—but they were losing them along the way.

A hundred yards from the hill they began to falter. By ones, by twos, by small groups they slowed to a halt, sifted forward, and finally arranged themselves in ranks, like ancient infantry massing for an assault.

Karvel retreated a short distance down the slope, seated himself on the shattered trunk of a tree, and waited. For a time he admired the distant, effortless soaring of a strange bird of slight body and enormous wingspread, and then he stared in disbelief at the buzzing gyrations of a cloud of enormous insects. Of all that he had seen, the tree whose trunk he was sitting on puzzled him the most. It was recognizably some ordinary species of elm.

When finally one of the creatures appeared, it did not approach the U.O. It moved directly toward Karvel and halted a long stride from him as others gathered just below the crest of the hill. Karvel, his carefully planned gesture of friendship forgotten, could do nothing but remain motionless and stare. Strange as the scientists' description had been, it had not prepared him for the incredible weirdness he saw before him.

Then the thing spoke.

Its voice was as unbelievable as its appearance. Karvel thought instantly of a bagpipe, for the thick wheeze of its speech was projected against hissing tones reminiscent of a bagpipe's drone. The sounds emerged from the creature's abdomen; rather, they originated and remained there. Its speech reverberated inside its body, and the longer it spoke the more blurred the words became.

And it spoke—English! It said, "How ... do ... you ... do. We ... are ... glad ... to ... see ... you."

Karvel managed to stammer a reply. "How do you do."

"You ... bring ... fuel."

It was not a question, but Karvel, struggling valiantly to maintain his composure, answered weakly, "I brought some extra fuel—"

Suddenly the others surged forward to surround Karvel and thrust their strange limbs at him. He did not immediately understand what they wanted.

They wanted to shake hands.

He pushed himself erect and clasped the first *hand* he made contact with, a large, pliant, fingerless membrane with an oddly gripping surface that completely enfolded his hand, pressed gently, and withdrew. He accepted another. After the fortieth he lost count, but he estimated that there were at least a hundred unhuman beings surrounding him, a hundred headless, six-limbed creatures of a scant five feet of height, with enormously thick cylindrical bodies and with two small, fan-shaped appendages that jerked or flapped when they made sudden movements.

The last of them stepped back, and a long silence followed. Then the spokesman—the one who had first approached Karvel—broke it with another wheezing statement. "U.O. ,.. did ... this."

It gestured at the devastated hillside. "We ... do ... not ... know ... it ..." It paused pantingly. "... damages. We ... regret ..."

The voice faltered. Karvel interposed, "You mean you wouldn't have sent it if you'd known? Where did you learn to speak English?"

"From ... you."

"From me!" Karvel exclaimed.

"We ... come ... from ... far ... place ..."

"You learned English from *me*? I know that time travel is complicated, but don't try to tell me I've been here before!"

"No. We ... learn ... now."

Karvel considered that briefly, and decided to ignore it.

"You come from a far place," he mused. "Another sun? Another . . . galaxy?"

"Far ... galaxy. Explore. Accident ... destroys ... fuel."

"Ah! Now I understand. You were marooned here. Shipwrecked a long way from home, with no chance of rescue. I don't suppose your people come this way often."

"Never ... come ... here."

"I understand. The only way you can get home again is to obtain more fuel, and spaceship service stations are hard to come by in this time and place. So you sent someone after it."

"Future ... evolution ..."

"Evolution? Of course. If your messenger went far enough into the future, evolution would have developed an intelligent form of life that might be able to supply the fuel you need. I understand. And I understand, now, why the U.O. arrived with an empty tank. You had only a little fuel left, and you sent your messenger as far as it would take him."

They remained grouped closely about him, some standing on two limbs and some on four. A few seated themselves, sitting as a dog would sit, their bodies braced by the middle pair of limbs.

There was something disturbingly reptilian about them. They wore no clothing, and their brown bodies had a soft, leathery texture. A ripple of movement ran incessantly about their abdomens, just below a band of mottled white, and Karvel guessed that this was somehow connected with their breathing. They took in air all around their bodies in a continuous, circular motion.

Another band encircled their bodies near the top, this one a darker brown, irregularly marked with large, blackish spots. There was no face, not even a suggestion of eyes, nose, or mouth. The terminal membranes were not the only weird feature of the six swiveling, multiple-jointed limbs. Karvel found it impossible to look at them without staring. He wondered if all of them were, in some eyeless manner, staring back at him.

The spokesman made another wheezing statement of

fact. "Messenger ... die." Its abdominal movement stopped when it spoke. It could not produce sounds while it was breathing, which accounted for the frequent pauses.

The spokesman gestured at the devastated hillside. "Many ... die."

"Many died," Karvel said quietly. "Many more than needed to die. There was a misunderstanding that would be difficult to explain to you. We feared—do you have another U.O.?"

"Only ... this."

"Your messenger was dead, so of course he couldn't tell us anything. We drew the wrong conclusions."

"We ... regret ..." It flapped four limbs futilely.

"You would not have sent it if you had known about the damage. I understand."

"You ... know ... we ... need ... fuel."

"But we didn't," Karvel said, puzzled. "Your messenger died before he arrived, so of course he couldn't tell us about your fuel problem. I brought extra fuel in case I didn't find you on the first try, and had to search further."

That produced another lengthy silence. "See ... fuel," the spokesman said finally.

Karvel nodded, and went to the U.O. They trailed after him, and waited anxiously around the hatch while he climbed inside. The Bribs had fashioned a duplicate of the U.O.'s spherical tank, and protected it with two concentric outer shells. Karvel knew nothing about handling the liquid uranium fuel, and hadn't wanted the trouble of learning. When the tank was empty, he simply intended to replace it. The spare tank held little more than a gallon, but it was unbelievably heavy. He removed the protective shells and managed to roll it up the U.O.'s curving side, although the weight staggered him.

A cluster of groping membranes was waiting to receive it and lower it to the ground. Karvel climbed out.

"No ... more?" Even in the spokesman's tinny, inhuman voice there was a note of very human incredulity.

"That's all," Karvel admitted. "We didn't think about having to supply a spaceship, you see. We were just thinking in terms of the U.O. I take it that you need more than that."

"Cannot ... leave ... planet."

A pathetic, four-limbed gesture. "Cannot ... leave ... horrible ... planet."

They drew back dumbly. Whatever their equivalent for weeping was, that was what they were doing, and Karvel felt like weeping himself. He had built up their hopes by announcing that he'd brought fuel, and then he'd handed them a driblet that would barely suffice to get their ship off the ground.

And he did not dare to go after more.

2

They called themselves the Hras, with an *r* that fluttered unbelievably and an *s* that dissolved in a long, gargling hiss. Karvel was unable to learn whether the name referred to their species, the world of their origin, their expedition, or an involved family relationship. All of them were Hras, and each of them was a Hras.

Their spaceship lay on a long, slender hump of land deep in the sprawling swamp. Bringing its hulk to rest there after the freak explosion ruptured it had been a masterful feat of skill and resourcefulness. An error of a few yards, and both ship and Hras would have been swallowed up in the slimy ooze that bubbled around the narrow island. For that matter, moving the heavy U.O. and its beacon to a suitable launching site had been no mean feat of engineering.

From the spaceship the Hras had constructed trails in two directions, each of them crossing a mile or more of the swamp and its network of slow-moving streams. They secured the stout cables of their suspension bridges to infrequent protuberances of solid ground, and where there was no ground for support they anchored the bridges to huge disklike pontoons that rode high on the ooze of the swamp. Across the larger, lushly overgrown islands they cut roads forty feet wide.

They risked no halfway measures with the U.O., their only chance for escape. They moved it and its beacon far from the menacing swamp. They laboriously collected the dregs of fuel remaining to them, and scraped whatever film

of fuel still adhered to their rent tanks, and launched the
U.O. Then they repaired their ship and waited for their
messenger to return with the fuel that would lift them away
from this raging nightmare of an environment.

And waited.

And waited.

Finally, through another vagary of the U.O.'s instrumentation, Karvel arrived nearly a year after the messenger set
out, bringing a mere crumb of nourishment for their ship's
enormous engines. He marveled that they reacted so stoically to what was nothing less than a final, irrevocable disaster.

Karvel had ample fuel to return the U.O. to the future.
In two trips, by eliminating his supply cylinders and carefully packing the U.O.'s interior with fuel containers, he
could bring them an ample supply to take them to a star
system where they had already found uranium. What were
the chances that Force X would strike another population
center? One in a thousand? One in a million?

The Hras vetoed the idea emphatically. However slight
the risk, they would endanger no more human lives to save
their own.

Karvel agreed with them. The screams of Galdu still
haunted his dreams, and not a few of his waking moments.

Dawn the next morning found Karvel huddled in silent
meditation at the top of the spaceship's ramp. The swamp's
deafening night chorus was fading, but strange slaps and
gurgles still arose from it. As the growing light chased the
huge nocturnal insects to cover they were replaced by other,
equally grotesque swarms, and amid the lush tangle of vegetation brilliantly hued blossoms opened their petals to the
sun.

Day had never seemed more welcome to Karvel, for he
had just passed the most unpleasant night of his life.

The Hras insisted on bringing him to their ship. He argued
futilely that he would be safe in the U.O. There were dangers, they said. Many dangers.

The spaceship had not been designed to accommodate the proportions of an adult human. Karvel had to stoop to enter, and remain stooped as long as he was upright. His private quarters were a cramped, cylindrical room. The bed, an ingenious form of hammock, was designed to hold a sleeper in comfort regardless of the ship's position. Its ends ran in a track around the cylinder's circumference, and it contained an elaborate suspension system to cushion its user against the forces of acceleration or deceleration. The contraption intrigued Karvel, and he obtained some entertainment from performing acrobatics on it, and attempting to outwit it and tumble out; but it was at least twelve inches too short for his minimum requirements, and he could not sleep on it.

The ship's atmosphere was unearthly. Alien smells assailed him with every breath. They penetrated even when he held his nose and breathed cautiously through his mouth, a nauseous blending of cloying sweetness and acidity and pungent stench.

A few hours of such olfactory horrors convinced Karvel that even the moist, fetid air of the swamp had been deliciously fresh and exhilarating. He was up and prowling about long before dawn, looking for a Hras to show him how to open the air lock. He found none in the dim, tunnel-like corridors, and the diaphragm-type doors of their sleeping quarters were closed. Finally he solved the mystery of the air lock by himself and escaped.

The sun stood well above the swamp when the air lock whirred open behind him. Hras boiled out of it, the first nearly falling over him. They had discovered his absence, and they were alarmed.

"You ... must ... not ... go ... out ... alone," one of them wheezed, in the posture of a parent lecturing an errant child.

"I only wanted a breath of air," Karvel said. "I haven't left the ramp."

"Dangers! Many ... dangers!"

Karvel grinned, and patted his rifle. "I'm pretty dangerous myself."

During the return to the ship their tedious progress through the swamp had both irked and amused him. If there really were dangers, his own inclination was to get past them as quickly as possible. The Hras moved at a crawl, alert to the stirring of the smallest leaf along the path. Their weapons were the poles he had noticed, some of them nearly twenty feet in length, all of them with a short crosspiece at the end. They held them ready for action as they edged forward. Only at the bridges did they hurry; but they observed the slow waters for a long time before they ventured onto them, and when finally they did cross it was in a frenzied rush of small groups of four or five. On the wide island roads they moved in single file, keeping strictly to the center.

And Karvel had seen no dangers, none at all. He reminded himself that the Earth had spawned unspeakable horrors in its past, but even a moderate danger might seem terrifying to an unarmed alien. He understood their apprehension without feeling the least apprehensive himself.

"Do ... you ... begin ... your ... day ... with ... food?" one of them asked.

They had mastered his language with incredible rapidity. He was certain that they plucked it out of his mind—he had only to think a word they were groping for, and they seized upon it instantly—but they did so with a touching discretion, almost with a reluctance, as though this invasion of another's mentality was justified only by pressing circumstances, and even then must be managed with caution and respect. They took what lay on the surface, but they would not probe; and when one of them had a word it did not forget it. None of them forgot it.

But all of their voices vibrated with the same metallic wheeze, and they spoke always with the panting pause after every word. As eager as Karvel was to talk with them, he dreaded the tedious ordeal of listening to widely spaced fragments of a lengthy explanation.

"Will ... you ... share ... our ... food?" the Hras persisted.

"Thank you, no," Karvel said. He was hungry, but his taste of their food the night before had not encouraged him to try it again. A fragment of a thin wafer had puckered his mouth and brought tears to his eyes, and his effort to swallow it had gone for naught.

He still had all of his emergency rations, but he was determined to save them for a genuine emergency. "I'd like to try to find food for myself," he said. "Are there fish in these streams?"

"Fish. And ... other ... *things!*"

"I don't know about the other things. I don't even know about the eating qualities of a fish's ancestors, but it seems like a logical place to start. I'd need some equipment."

A hook, a piece of line, and a pole. They gave him one of their shorter T poles, which he examined carefully. The crosspiece had been mortised to the shaft and glued. The joint was solid, the workmanship impressive. For a line they offered a length of amazingly flexible wire; the hook, when he had explained its function, they manufactured for him. It was three times the size he wanted, and when he objected they expressed doubt that it was large enough.

"I'll have to catch something for bait," Karvel said. "Earlier this morning I heard plenty of frogs, so it shouldn't be difficult."

"Dangerous!" they wheezed, in a foreboding chorus.

"Frogs? Dangerous?"

"Other ... things ..."

"I doubt that even those other things are immune to rifle bullets," Karvel said lightly.

"We ... will ... come ... with ... you."

"That isn't necessary."

They insisted on converting his simple fishing trip into a major expedition. Some two dozen of them accompanied him, and their progress was as tedious as it had been the previous day. When Karvel pounced upon a small lizard for use as bait—narrowly avoiding being slashed by its vicious teeth—the Hras immediately formed a circular defense around him until he had secured it.

At the first stream he took up a position at the end of the bridge, baited his hook, and dropped it into the water. For a short time nothing happened, and then something struck with a force that very nearly jerked him into the water. As he struggled he felt at least six arms holding him securely, and two of the Hras moved up beside him to help with the pole.

Karvel's two arms and their eight barely sufficed to hold it. The fish fought viciously, and the water around it soon churned with other fish. When finally they hauled the catch ashore its tail had been bitten away, and awesome chunks of flesh torn from the soft underpart of its body. What was left was more than ten feet long, with an enormous head and protruding, multiple-toothed jaws that continued to snap dangerously.

Karvel clubbed the head with his pole, but it continued to snap.

"Do ... you ... require ... more?" one of the Hras asked.

"No, thanks," Karvel said dryly. "It's enough breakfast for an army, if the thing is edible. It's already been breakfast for a navy. This is no place for a quiet morning swim, not even for a fish."

"Now ... may ... we ... return?" the Hras asked.

Karvel nodded. He clubbed the fish until it stopped snapping, forced the T of his pole into the huge gill, and attempted to hoist it to his shoulder.

A Hras uttered a piercing scream.

From the tangle of vegetation along the path lunged an express train with long jaws. Karvel dropped the fish and stepped to meet it, fumbling for his rifle. The screams crescendoed in a wildly bleating chorus as other Hras joined in. Before Karvel could level his rifle he was looking into the widest mouth he had ever seen, and one of the screaming Hras coolly stepped around him and plunged the upright T of his pole into it. They both leaped back, Karvel snatching an arm from the closing jaws—but the jaws could not close. The beast's mouth clamped firmly onto the pole. It uttered a furious bellow, and swung the pole wildly. A glancing blow on the head dazed Karvel. At the same time the enormous tail whipped out of the vegetation and knocked a dozen Hras sprawling. One toppled over the bank and clutched desperately at a trailing vine. As the vine parted another Hras pulled it to safety.

Karvel leaped over the tail as it lashed back, and put six rifle bullets into the beast's head. It seemed not to notice. Jaws still clamped onto the pole, it slid over the bank and into the water. A moment later the broken pole bobbed to the surface.

"And that," Karvel said awesomely, "is what I'd call a crocodile. Forty feet long, at least. I hope there aren't any older brothers around."

The Hras were shaken. "Now ... return?" one of them pleaded, a pathetic tremolo in its wheezy voice.

Karvel did not answer. The strangest creature he had ever seen came paddling leisurely around a bend in the stream. Its body was almost entirely submerged, and its long, serpentlike neck probed the waters deeply, to emerge with a fish in its jaws.

Karvel had taken the encounter with the crocodile in stride, but this creature unnerved him completely. It was unquestionably a seagoing dinosaur, and his first clue as to how far into the future and the past he had traveled.

"Back to the ship," he said, and again attempted to hoist the fish to his shoulder. Two of the Hras helped him carry it. He walked warily, and kept to the center of the path quite as conscientiously as did the Hras.

Karvel cleaned his fish, gave it a thick coating of mud, of which there was ample available, and baked it for the remainder of the morning in a long fire that consumed much of the brush pile the Hras had accumulated from their manufacture of T poles. The result was a delicious, tender, flaky meat. The Hras politely refused to share it with him, but until he had eaten his fill and wrapped the remainder of the huge carcass in leaves in the hope that it would keep longer, ten of them stood poised between Karvel and the swamp, their T poles held alertly. He doubted that it was necessary, but when they said "Many dangers!" he was no longer disposed to argue with them.

The spokesman of the previous day, Hras Drawa, joined Karvel on the ramp when he had finished eating. Karvel was beginning to recognize subtle differences between individual Hras, in coloring, in stature, even, in a few cases, in mannerisms. Hras Drawa had two distinctively shaped spots on the breathing band, and an amusing habit of criss-crossing the four upper limbs.

"Have you had many casualties?" Karvel asked.

"Many. It is a horrible world."

"You must have had some experience with horrible worlds. Why didn't you bring weapons with you?"

"Our weapons were lost in the explosion."

"I could show you how to make some, but what you really want to do is to go home, where I presume that you don't need weapons."

Hras Drawa wheezed softly, but said nothing.

"Could you make your own fuel if you had uranium?"

"Yes. We are fully equipped for this, because we could not carry enough fuel for the distance we intended to travel."

"Uranium," Karvel mused. "Pitchblende ore. Have you tried to find it?"

"We have tried. There is none within two days' traveling time. The dangers are many, the world is impossibly large for those who must walk, and nowhere have we ever found uranium to be plentiful. The chance of success seemed so slight that we did not look further."

"If you had some kind of flying machine—"

"We did." Hras Drawa wheezed an enormous sigh. "A special machine for locating uranium. It was destroyed in the explosion. We used what remained of it in the repairs to the spaceship."

"I see."

"All in that part of the ship was destroyed except the U.O., which is difficult to damage."

"Fuel reserve, armory, aircraft—everything you needed for survival went up in that one blast. When you get home you should put in a recommendation that the ship's layout be redesigned."

"Such a thing has never happened before."

Karvel nodded sympathetically. If creatures brilliant enough to build a U.O. couldn't solve their problem, there wasn't much point in Bowden Karvel working at it. He changed the subject. "There's something I wanted to ask you about the U.O. What instrument setting did your messenger use?"

"The ultimate—the maximum. We did not know how long it would be before intelligent life developed on this planet."

"The maximum," Karvel repeated. He took a deep breath, and said slowly, "That means that it went as far as its fuel would take it. Then it arrived in my time with the instruments set—"

"We also removed one instrument. It is a . . . a *limiter.* It prevents the U.O. from going farther than there is fuel to return it to the starting point."

"That accounts for the empty hole in the instrument panel, but it doesn't help with my time paradox. If the U.O. arrived with its instruments set at the maximum, the French couldn't possibly have known how far to send it into the future if it hadn't already returned from the future."

"The U.O. did not arrive with its instruments at the maximum. It has . . . what would you call it? A clock? A measuring device? If the progress is stopped for any reason—in this case, by running out of fuel—the instruments set themselves to show how far the U.O. has traveled."

"Ah!"

"Does that reconcile your paradox?"

"No, but it makes it a bit less drastic. I've also been wondering what I would have done if the thing had landed in the ocean."

"It will not. It will . . . land . . . only on land. I know very little about the U.O. myself. It is a new device, and unfortunately its inventor died in the swamp shortly after we landed. We had used it on other worlds for traveling much smaller distances, and even then the operators proceeded in many short steps. They were studying evolution and the ultimate of mysteries, the origin of life. We knew nothing of the pressure, and of the Force X, because these things are not noticeable when the U.O. travels small distances."

"Then your messenger would not have been killed, and there would have been no Force X, if the trip had been made in a series of short time leaps. Why wasn't it?"

"We had too little fuel. It is the starting up, the beginning, that requires the most fuel. The U.O. would need an enormous extra supply to reach your time with the short leaps."

"A larger extra supply than I brought?"

"A much, much larger supply," Hras Drawa wheezed firmly.

"I see. Which brings us back to the important question: Where is there some uranium?"

"We have thought about this since you arrived," Hras Drawa said. "It is your world. Do you not know where uranium is to be found?"

"I have a general idea where the principal deposits are. Rather, I know where they will be in a hundred million years or so. I don't know how to go about locating them in this time because I don't know where we are. The landmarks I would need probably aren't in existence yet. How can I look for a uranium deposit in mountains that haven't been formed? Even if I did stumble onto one of those locations—and it might require a trek of hundreds or even thousands of miles—the uranium could be miles deep and inaccessible until millions of years of erosion have uncovered it. Or it could be at the bottom of the ocean. I don't know enough about geology to know if the uranium deposits of my time existed this long ago."

"We had not thought of those problems."

"I think it would be foolish to try to find the deposits of my time."

"I agree." The pause was much longer than usual. "It was our final hope. Then we must remain here."

"Not necessarily," Karvel said. "Do you have instruments to detect the presence of pitchblende deposits? Something like a Geiger counter?"

"Uranium detectors. Yes."

"Then why not use them? Two days doesn't represent much of a search. Make it a week, or a month, or even a year. What more important things do you have to do, except sit around and hope you'll live long enough to die of old age?"

"You do not fully understand the difficulties."

"Perhaps not," Karvel admitted. "But I fully understand the problem. You haven't really tried to find uranium. You've been waiting for it to come to you—waiting for the U.O. to bring it to you. Now you know that it won't, but you're satisfied to go on waiting. It doesn't make sense."

"What do you suggest?"

"Haven't I said it plainly enough?"

"Would you accompany such an expedition?"

"I?" Karvel exclaimed. "I wouldn't know how to begin to look for uranium. Don't you have geologists? Or mineralogists?"

"No," Hras Drawa said. "We had such specialists, but they were all killed—looking for uranium."

It seemed like an excellent time to change the subject again, and to Karvel's intense relief Hras Drawa did so. "You are not comfortable with us?"

"No," Karvel said. "I prefer not to live in a swamp."

"It is safe here."

"It is safe in your ship. I should have to leave it frequently to find food, and the swamp provides too many places for ambush. Also, your ship is not comfortable for me."

"Surely the U.O. would be less comfortable than our ship."

"I was just thinking of sleeping there," Karvel said. "I can look after myself when I'm awake. I'll build a cabin with those fallen trees, and put some kind of stockade around it, and if I can't cope with a dinosaur before it gets past those obstacles I'll take refuge in the U.O. I might not be absolutely safe, but perfect safety doesn't exist anywhere."

"You have made your decision?" Hras Drawa asked politely.

"I have made my decision. I would appreciate the loan of tools, if you have any."

"We will offer our assistance in the building of this cabin. There may yet be time to do it today."

The Hras built the cabin. They were amazingly strong, their tools produced phenomenal results, and Karvel, once he had given them a general idea of what he wanted, had little to do other than keep out of their way.

They built the cabin around the U.O., and further reduced its living space with an elaborate network of braces. They fitted logs together with artful precision, and covered them with a transparent adhesive that in a few hours' time became as hard as rock. When they finished Karvel had a weather-tight dwelling that no force less than that of a bomb could have disturbed. He asked for firing slots, rather than windows, and the only real problem was posed by the door—for which they had cut a neat circle before Karvel found out what they were doing. He spent an hour in trying to think of a way to cope with the circular opening, and then they installed one of the dilating doors from the spaceship.

There were not enough logs for a full stockade. Karvel suggested an abatis instead, and the Hras brought great armfuls of the saplings from which they made their T poles, and surrounded the cabin with a circle of sharpened stakes pointed outward. Karvel was convinced that even a tyrannosaur, if there were any about, would think twice before attempting to get past that obstacle.

"We did not envision such an arrangement," Hras Drawa admitted. "We agree that you will be almost safe here as long as you do not go outside this abatis, and as long as you remain alert. I caution you that not all of the dangerous things are large."

"I'm sure I'll be safe enough as long as the water holds out," Karvel said. The country was obviously suffering a prolonged drought, and the stream at the foot of the hill was a narrow ribbon of water threaded between wide banks.

The Hras hurried off as sunset approached, promising to visit him the next day. Karvel did not blame them for wanting to return to the ship before dark. He stood watching until their long file reached the swamp, and then he seated himself on a log before his circular door, and gazed at the distant, smooth surface of the sea.

It was, he thought sardonically, the first permanent home he'd ever had. His mind lingered on the word *permanent*. He was marooned here just as irrevocably as were the Hras, but that fact did not depress him. He would have sung fervent hosannas, if he'd known any, for his mission was accomplished. There was only one U.O., and it had made its final journey.

He had no worries, and no responsibilities, and—as long as he stayed out of the swamp—a restful primeval world for a residence.

A world without mountains.

He slipped his four-toed, flat right foot from its moccasin and scratched idly at the missing toe.

"How the devil *would* they go about finding uranium?" he asked himself.

3

They set out three days later. The unhuman castaways out of space and the human vagrant from time joined forces to attempt that which all of them knew to be impossible.

The longer Karvel thought about the expedition, the sillier it seemed. The Hras were certain it had no chance of success, and said so.

Nevertheless, the expedition left. It was one of the only two alternatives left to the Hras. They could search, and keep searching; or not search, and resign themselves to remaining where they were. They chose to search.

The entire company came to the edge of the swamp to see the expedition off. Karvel, eager to avoid an orgy of leave-taking, gave a last wave to Hras Drawa and marched away with a firm, steady pace. Not until they had topped the first low hill did he step aside to inspect and count the Hras following him.

There were twenty of them.

Karvel swore fervently. He had asked for six; Hras Drawa wanted to bring all of the Hras. Karvel vetoed that notion emphatically, and also refused to take Hras Drawa. Anyone whose skill was essential in operating the spaceship, he said, or for the production of the fuel, should remain in a safe place and wait. For what would be the point of a hazardous expedition to locate pitchblende if the only Hras who knew what to do with it were lost? And why produce fuel, if no one survived who could navigate the ship?

Eventually Hras Drawa agreed; but six, he said, was an impossibly small number.

"As few as possible, then," Karvel said.

There were twenty. They plodded past in single file, T poles erect, strange tools and instruments tucked casually under spare arms. If they took pride in the fact that each of them had been carefully selected for this expedition, they were keeping it to themselves. Already the procession looked uncomfortably like a death march.

Karvel had left their selection to Hras Drawa. He asked only that they be properly equipped, and have better than average dexterity in the use of the T pole.

Properly equipped. Karvel's bellow of indignation halted them in their tracks. "Where are your supplies?" he demanded. "Your food and water—where are they?"

The Hras bringing up the rear wheezed politely. "We do not need any."

"Of course you do! We may be gone for many days. You can't do without food and water indefinitely!"

But perhaps they could. Perhaps, like the camel, they had extra stomachs filled with water, and their barrellike bodies concealed sustaining humps of food reserve.

And yet he hesitated to accept this miraculous solution to a worrisome problem. Even a camel would have to have food and water eventually.

He shrugged, and strode to the head of the column. Already the expedition was shaping up as a nightmare, and nightmares, he told himself grimly, should be for sleeping, and not for marching into in the company of twenty unhuman beings.

"Where's the direction finder?" he asked.

His second-in-command, Hras Klaa—or Klaaa, or Klaaaa, for the name ended in a gargle of indeterminate duration—stepped forward, saluted, and handed the instrument to him. The salute so startled Karvel that he nearly dropped it.

"Where'd you get that idea?" he demanded.

Hras Klaa stood politely at attention, and did not answer.

Karvel studied the direction finder. Its complicated symbols were vaguely reminiscent of those on the U.O. instruments, but the device was absurdly simple to use. A line of red light widened in the direction of the base, in this case the spaceship. The accuracy diminished with the distance, Hras Drawa had told Karvel, but he did not think that they would travel far enough to be bothered by that. Karvel found some consolation in the assurance that he would have no difficulty finding his way back. He had uncertainties enough without having to worry about getting lost.

He selected a course, picked out prominent terrain features for the map he intended to sketch in his notebook as they traveled, and said, "Let's go."

At midday they were pushing their way through a forest of giant ferns. The low-lying ground had once been under water, but now the mud of the forest floor had hardened beyond recollection of moisture. A dry stream bed wound through it, and the ferns, too, were drying up.

The Hras wielded their T poles in a frenzied slashing at the enormous, drooping fronds. Karvel shouted a protest as a pole narrowly missed his head and another thumped him in the back.

"This ruckus will attract all the Carnivora for miles around," he told them.

They continued their terrified flailing until finally they broke out into the open. Karvel stood counting them as they emerged from the forest, and two of the Hras slumped into their sitting-dog positions at his feet.

"What's the matter?" Karvel asked.

Hras Klaa gave him the inevitable salute. "It is the heat."

"Heat?" Karvel echoed blankly. The day was warm, but not insufferably so. His own clothing was soaked with perspiration, but that was from the weight of his knapsack and the exertion of dodging T poles. The Hras did not perspire, and if they were being felled by the heat on a day such as this one it could mean only one thing.

"You must be accustomed to a cooler climate," Karvel said.

"Much cooler," Hras Klaa agreed.

"So that's why you don't wear clothing. The Earth should have a cooler climate somewhere, but we aren't likely to find it by walking. All of the plant life I've seen looks subtropical."

The Hras gathered about their stricken comrades, and Karvel, with an anxious look at the ferns, asked, "Can't we get them away from here?"

Impulsively he dumped water on them from his canteen. Some of it got into their breathing bands, and they scrambled to their feet, sputtering indignantly. The other Hras wheezed in amazement.

"What's the matter?" Karvel asked. "Didn't you ever try that before?"

They had not.

"Water is nice stuff to have around. I told you to carry some."

For a time he walked beside the heat victims, but they were apparently unaffected by their experience. Even so, the incident seemed ominous to Karvel. He envisioned himself facing a crisis with half of his company prostrate.

The Hras became increasingly listless as the afternoon wore on. Their pace, which had pushed Karvel uncomfortably when they started out, taxed him more severely when it lagged to a crawl. He knew that they were capable of sudden bursts of startling speed and activity, but evidently sustained effort over a period of time wilted them.

"Perhaps all they need is a siesta," he told himself hopefully.

He turned the column toward a clump of strange-looking trees that stood on the bank of a small stream. They were short and stubby, with armored trunks and palmlike clusters of small leaves on long stems. The shade that they cast was negligible and the stream held a mere trickle of water, but it was the only oasis that the bleak landscape offered.

Karvel got the Hras settled under the trees, and while they rested he refilled his canteen. Then he took the uranium detector and walked a circle with it. It was a heavy globe of milky crystal not much larger than a golf ball, and it was alleged to glow in the presence of uranium—shine like the sun, Hras Drawa had said. One of the Hras watched it constantly as they traveled.

Karvel did not really expect to find uranium on that parched, rolling plain; but he was certain he would find it, if he found it at all, unexpectedly. For all he knew, this plain of the Age of Reptiles could be the uranium-bearing mountains of the twentieth century.

But the globe did not flicker—did not even reflect the hot afternoon sun—and Karvel completed his circle and silently handed it back to its custodian, Hras Hrul.

They started off strongly after an hour's rest, but soon the Hras were lagging again. A heavy pine forest angled toward them from the west, sending out thick tongues of growth along the valleys, and Karvel cautiously detoured around them. The Hras seemed irresistibly drawn toward the forest. They kept veering in that direction whenever Karvel was not leading the march, and several times he had to hurry to the head of the column to get them pointed in the direction he wanted to travel.

There was life everywhere. The startlingly strange merged and blended with the unexpectedly familiar. Long-beaked, toothed birds circled above the trees, swarms of insects probed small blossoms in the dry, thick-bladed vegetation that crunched underfoot, and an endless variety of scurrying, lizardlike creatures fled their line of march or watched them warily from a distance.

Twice Karvel glimpsed dinosaurs: a long neck arching briefly beyond a rise of ground; several of an ostrichlike species skipping over a distant hill. He had seen nothing that looked dangerous, nothing that did not timidly seek to avoid them, and yet every faltering footstep the Hras took betrayed their dread.

Reluctantly Karvel began to look for a campsite.

He tossed a question over his shoulder. "Where would you rather spend the night—around a fire in the open, or in the forest?"

Hras Hrul, who was plodding directly behind him, answered immediately with a salute. "The forest."

Karvel felt doubtful. His instinct told him that reptiles would fear the fire, but his reason was less certain. He'd have to experiment before he risked it.

He turned toward the forest. "Pick your own place, then," he said.

They followed with alacrity, and abruptly broke into a waddling, panicky run. They were already at work at the edge of the forest when he caught up with them. They were bending young trees to the ground and wedging their T poles into place, and they'd made a good start on a formidable-looking barricade.

Karvel examined it skeptically. It would not keep out anything heavy that chose to crash through it, nor anything agile enough to jump over. He dropped his knapsack and said with a grin, "Carry on."

He made another wearisome circuit with the uranium detector and had the good luck to secure his supper along the way. It was a large, gaudily colored, saber-toothed lizard, and Karvel regretted his action as soon as he'd killed it. He had never seen a creature with such a nauseous appearance.

"But I'll probably be eating worse things before this is finished," he told himself, and carried it back to the forest.

The Hras had completed their barricade, a circle of some fifteen feet in diameter that looked vaguely like a huge nest. The one good feature, Karvel thought, was that nothing could break into it without awaking the whole camp.

"We won't post sentries until dark," he said. "Any of you care to share my lizard?"

None of them did. He gathered an armload of dead branches and soon had a small fire going at the edge of the forest. He relaxed in the fading light and watched the sizzling lizard meat. When he forgot what it had come from it looked and smelled almost appetizing. It tasted better than he'd hoped, but not nearly as well as he would have preferred.

It was dark when he finished eating. He drank sparingly and put out the fire. "Time to post sentries!" he called.

There was no answer. He forced his way through the barricade, and inside he found the Hras in doglike crouches, huddled tightly in a circle with their ridiculous little wings outspread protectively. All of them were sound asleep.

He shouted, he prodded and shook them, he tried to jerk their heavy bodies erect. They remained inert under his anxious hands, their deep, circular breathing producing an unbroken, faintly whistling hiss. Finally he desisted and sat alone in the dark, his rifle across his knees, shuddering at the unearthly noises that were flung through the treetops.

The Hras's fickle stamina was a nuisance he could tolerate, but this was sheer catastrophe. So deep, so hypnotic was their slumber that a hungry carnivore could help itself to one or several Hras steaks and the Hras would know nothing about it until what was left of them woke up in the morning.

He did not wonder that they had limited their previous searches to two days, and that they felt a compelling affinity for the forest as night came on. Even small carnivores would be a terrible menace when they were so helplessly asleep. Several of them could decimate the party—saber-toothed lizards, for example, such as the one he'd eaten.

He leaped up in alarm and played his flashlight over the sleeping Hras. It quickly drew a swarm of gigantic night insects, so he turned it off and glumly sat down again.

Their camp had to be guarded at night, and obviously the Hras could not do it. If Karvel remained awake at night he would have to get what sleep he could during the day, and even a bare minimum of sleep for himself would cut severely into their traveling time. Their trek would take longer than he'd expected.

And they could not go as far.

On the sixth day they reached the river. The broad, slow-moving, silty water coursed slowly between vast, encrusted mud flats that were crisscrossed with the spoor of enormous, tailed animals. The river, too, was drying up.

"We're about to renew our acquaintance with your friend the crocodile," Karvel observed grimly.

He watched the surface of the stream for a long time, but there were no telltale ripples, no signs of life. Fortunately the barren shores offered no concealment for an ambush. Unfortunately, neither the shores nor the bleak plain they had just left could provide any means of crossing the river.

They followed the bank for several miles. The river widened; the surrounding plain remained bleak. Karvel was about to turn back when they found a large oak tree stranded on a sandbar. The Hras unlimbered their tools and went to work on it, all the time keeping a fearsome watch on the water. Under Karvel's direction they sliced the log into a manageable length, attached outriggers to keep it from rolling, and mortised safety railings along the sides. They poled across the river without incident, and when all were safely ashore Karvel called a conference.

"The country seems to be getting drier all the time," he said. "We may be heading into a desert. How long will it be before you need water?"

"We will need some soon," Hras Klaa admitted.

"You'd better drink now. It could be a long time before you'll have another chance."

There was an awkward silence. "We cannot drink without . . . without special arrangements," Hras Klaa admitted finally.

"Why didn't you tell me before we started?" Karvel demanded.

"We did not think we would be gone so long."

Karvel regarded them incredulously. If they traveled to the limit of their endurance without even attempting to obtain food and water, how could they expect to return? "What sort of special arrangements do you need?" he asked.

"We do not drink as you do."

"Obviously. What do you need?"

They had some difficulty in describing it, but eventually it dawned on Karvel that all they really wanted was—a bathtub.

"Nonsense," he said, waving at the river. "There's a large tub, with plenty of water. Go get wet!"

"It is not safe," Hras Klaa said, with a visible shudder.

"It is too dirty," Hras Durr protested.

"The dirt you'll have to put up with, but I agree that it wouldn't be safe. Do you need food, too? We'll spend the rest of the day here. What do you have to dig with?"

The membranes that terminated the Hras limbs made sturdy scoops, and after they had broken up the dried mud on the flats along the river Karvel started them digging. Under the mud was gravel, and as they dug below the water level water began to seep into the holes.

"There you are," Karvel said. "You can have as many tubs as you feel like digging. Are you able to eat fish?"

They would not eat it by preference, they said, but they might by necessity—though they preferred that he did not burn it first.

"Take your baths," Karvel said, "and I'll catch the fish."

They dug deep holes in which they could lie almost submerged, coming up infrequently for a sputtering breath. Karvel stood at the end of their makeshift boat and caught fish, small fish, no more than a foot or two in length. He cleaned and boned them, and the Hras masticated the meat with their strong membranes until it was reduced to a dry pulp. This they pressed into thin cakes, and before Karvel's disbelieving eyes they tucked the cakes into pouches whose existence he had not even suspected. Only after he had seen several such performances did it occur to him that the pouches were mouths. They extended completely around the lower part of the body, and they enabled the Hras to absorb a week's supply of food in one mouthful.

He was curious enough to risk offending them with questions, and they did not seem to mind. He learned that they had no sensation of taste, as he understood it; nor did they have any means, or any necessity, of chewing their food. In actual fact, they chewed it with their hands and placed it directly into their stomachs.

When Karvel whimsically protested that such a shortcut

eliminated most of the pleasure to be derived from eating, a Hras pointed out that it also saved a great deal of time. Karvel, for example, had the bother of finding fuel, building a fire, and cooking his food. Then he ate with ridiculous slowness, since he had to chew his food with the most inefficient mechanism that the Hras could imagine. The end result was the same—the food reached the stomach—so why not place it there directly, and have done with it?

"With the kind of food I've been eating," Karvel said, "you have a point."

When all of the Hras had been fed, they dragged the log boat far up onto the bank. "If it's not here when we come back," Karvel told them, "I'll know that dinosaurs have talents I never suspected."

They collected driftwood for the fires he meant to maintain that night, for they would have to sleep in the open for the first time. The Hras protested vehemently, but the river's barren flood plain offered not so much as a clump of bushes with which to succor them. They protested until darkness fell, and then they quietly collapsed into sleep.

They started off again at dawn, and instead of the expected desert they encountered a swamp. Karvel guessed that the sea had curved back toward them, or that the river had channeled out across the flat land. They put in a frustrating day zigzagging around tongues of the swamp, and finally Karvel altered their base course to attempt to find open country. It brought them, late in the afternoon, to the shore of a shallow, curving lake, and when they turned aside to go around it the water bent back toward them.

They made camp that night on a knoll near the end of the lake. Behind them Karvel could see the distant, sinuous line of the river. Their day's march had gained them only a few miles. There were no trees for shelter and no wood for fires, but as the light faded the Hras formed their protective circle without protest. Karvel's attempt to build a fire with the long, brittle grass produced only a monumental smudge.

It was a peaceful night, with a bit of a moon, and the rackety night sounds drifting up from the lake were distant and unmenacing. For a long time Karvel restlessly paced around the circle of sleeping Hras, slicing up the darkness with random flicks of his flashlight. He was dreadfully tired —soon they would have to lay up for most of a day while he caught up on his sleep. He rested, nervously scrambled to his feet to resume his pacing, rested again.

The night was already diluted with the first dim light of dawn when he noticed the gap in the circle. At first he would not believe it. He counted the Hras, counted them again. There were nineteen. Instinctively he ran toward the lake. The night noises had subsided; the water was motionless. He followed the shore a short distance and then retreated in panic to count the Hras again. Nineteen.

Not until it was lighter, almost light enough to bring the Hras lurching out of their somnolence, was he able to pick out the telltale blurred path of crushed grass. Something heavy had passed that way, or been dragged, and Karvel followed the trail until it ended in a deep furrow in the soft mud of the lake shore.

The Hras were awake when he returned. They seemed to know instinctively what had happened. They asked for no explanation, and he was much too horrified and torn with doubt to offer one.

For a week he had been getting no more than four widely separated hours of sleep in twenty-four. Had he dozed off in the peaceful darkness? He did not think so, but neither did he think that the lake's unspeakable inhabitant could have made off with a creature as large and as heavy as a Hras without producing a noticeable disturbance.

However it happened, Hras Hnil, whom Karvel remembered only for abnormally small wings and a large irregular spot like an ink blot on the breathing band, had vanished.

Hras Klaa said politely, "It is not your fault. It is no one's fault. It is this horrible world."

The Hras, so uneasy at the slightest threat of danger, so queerly cool and panicky at once when it struck, were strangely unmoved after a tragedy had occurred. *Resigned* was a better word. They had been nearly a year **on this** violent world, they had seen their numbers steadily diminished by its savage attrition, and they regarded tragedy as inevitable.

"Shall we turn back?" Karvel asked.

"It is for you to decide," Hras Klaa said.

Karvel gestured across the lake. "We should at least see what lies beyond the swamp. Another day. Or two . . ."

He cautiously filled his canteen with lake water and drank deeply while they formed a protective barricade with their T poles. Then he strode off, and the Hras silently followed him.

4

At noon on the second day Karvel stood on a low hill and saw a dark streak on the horizon. The undulating land in between shaded away into desert, and it teemed with dinosaurs. At a distance the slow-moving, drably colored beasts looked neither remarkable nor menacing, but the Hras drew back in alarm.

For the moment Karvel was more interested in the horizon. He called Hras Klaa back to the hilltop and asked, "Is it mountains?"

"Tall hills, at least," Hras Klaa said, "and I think they soon become mountains."

Hras vision was still a mystery to Karvel. Apparently the dark spots of their upper bands were their organs of vision —he could not make himself call them eyes—and they saw in all directions simultaneously, but also very badly. But when there was something specific that they wanted to see, they invariably saw farther and much more clearly than Karvel. It was as though their organs did not focus automatically, and rather than devote their waking existence to a tiresome focusing and refocusing, the Hras were content with a blurred existence. They looked carefully only at those things they thought important.

"How far away?" Karvel asked.

"I could not say."

"Three days?"

"I could not say. The heat becomes worse. We would need to rest often, and there is no shade."

Doubtfully Karvel studied the barren terrain. The dinosaurs were of slight concern to him. The beasts were plodding across their line of march, and would soon be gone; and if they had anything specific on their diminutive minds it would be water, for they were just emerging from a westward thrust of the desert.

But the land looked terrifying. The sand would be soft underfoot, difficult to walk in. The heat would be formidable, and as Hras Klaa had pointed out, there was no shade.

And the Hras could not travel at night.

By pushing themselves the Hras might cross safely, but they would be in desperate need of water when they reached the hills. Karvel was much less certain about himself. He still had a full canteen, but he had not drunk for more than twenty-four hours. He estimated that his water would take him no further than halfway.

Even if they were able to cross, there was no certainty that they would find water in the hills.

Karvel took the uranium detector and made his customary, futile circuit. The Hras waited silently. He could sense their uneasiness, but he made no effort to understand it. He had long since abandoned any hope he'd had of understanding the Hras. They had been together for nine days, and he had learned their names and noted enough minor differences in their appearances to be able to tell them apart, but he was not—could not be—one of them. He had more kindred feeling for the dinosaurs. The reptiles had necks, even though some seemed unnecessarily exaggerated. They had reasonably organized heads. And they were *of Earth*.

Karvel found it impossible to develop even a feeling of comradeship for a being who could not be looked in the eyes, or—which actually seemed worse—who could be looked in the eyes from any direction.

He completed his circuit and returned the uranium detector to Hras Hrul. "We'll rest here," he said, "and then we'll start back."

The Hras said nothing, and he had no way of knowing what they were thinking.

They moved back down the slope, where they might partially escape the searing desert wind, and sat down to rest. They had formed up again and were starting to move off when Karvel heard a distant, unending roll of thunder.

He turned a questioning gaze on Hras Klaa. "Do you hear that?"

Hras Klaa did not answer. The other Hras stood fussing nervously with their T poles.

"I'll see what it is," Karvel said, and hurried toward the hilltop.

Suddenly he realized that the thunder was crescendoing toward him. The ground began to shake underfoot, and a wave, a torrent of dinosaurs swept over the crest of the hill. A glance told him that there was no escape. They could outrun the terrified monsters for yards, but not for miles. He screamed, "Stand still!" and stood his ground, hoping that the stampede would pass around him.

Long necks swayed over him and were gone. Armored monsters charged past with unbelievable speed, their lowered horns protruding like lances. It was an outpouring of all of the museum cases he could remember, their speculative restorations brought suddenly into the sharper focus of stomping, bellowing, snorting reality.

On and on they came, quadrupeds and bipeds, weirdly shaped heads and grotesque bodies, the tailed and the tailless, giants and midgets, a churning, dust-choked deluge of horrors.

Karvel made no attempt to unsling his rifle. He stood motionless and the dinosaurs flowed by harmlessly. The beasts kept their distance, wider gaps opened and closed between them, and there even seemed to be a certain jockeying for position, a drifting away from the vicious horns of the quadrupeds.

Then the crest was empty, and as the last of the dinosaurs thundered past Karvel turned, and hurried down the slope after them. They vanished over the next rise, leaving four of the Hras standing in paroxysms of terror.

Only four.

Before Karvel could ask a question a shadow fell across

him. Hras Klaa uttered a pathetic bleat, and jabbed weakly with a T pole. Karvel wheeled, snatching for his rifle, but the tyrannosaur was already upon them. The claws of its small forefeet slashed downward. Karvel leaped away and emptied his rifle into the horribly gaping mouth.

Tyrannosaurus lunged forward, but one of the Hras moved in boldly with a T pole. Karvel reloaded and got off three carefully aimed shots at the head. Tyrannosaurus teetered for a moment, and crashed to the ground amidst a wild scattering of Hras. Its jaws continued a jerky, reflexive snapping, its forefeet continued to slash, its tail threshed twice and subsided to a spasmodic quivering.

They all drew away from it, as though from a common fear that the miasma of evil exuded by such a horror must remain potent long after death.

Karvel leaned weakly on his rifle. "That's why they stampeded," he said. "It's some kind of migration across the desert, and Tyrannosaurus follows the herds to pick off the weaklings."

"This horrible world!" Hras Klaa wheezed.

"Cheer up," Karvel said bitterly. "All of them will be extinct in a few million years. Has this happened to you before?"

"Yes."

Three more Hras had joined them while they were occupied with the tyrannosaur, and another staggered into view as Karvel turned to renew his count. "Nine?" he asked.

"Fourteen," Hras Klaa said.

Karvel looked about him bewilderedly.

"Including you," Hras Klaa added.

"Then we lost six. But where are the other four?"

"They ran. They are returning now. Hras Drawa says—"

"Hras Drawa!" Karvel exclaimed.

"Hras Drawa says we are to continue if you think there is hope."

"To the hills?"

"If you think there is hope."

Another dust-covered Hras stumbled into view, one of its limbs dangling helplessly. "Ten," Karvel breathed.

"Three more are coming," Hras Klaa said.

They were telepaths, which should have been obvious to Karvel from the beginning. They never spoke audibly to each other, only to him. And yet Hras Drawa was nine days' traveling time away from them, which meant . . .

The tail of the fallen tyrannosaur threshed again, and the Hras cautiously retreated. "I'd better see if we have any more surprises coming our way," Karvel said, and returned to the crest of the hill.

A solitary tyrannosaur loomed hugely on the next rise. Spattered with gore from its last meal, it was seemingly intent on not being outdistanced by its next. Karvel fired from a prone position at five hundred yards, and it wheeled and snapped viciously. Six more carefully aimed shots brought it down, its powerful jaws still searching for an invisible attacker.

The thirteen Hras were standing motionless in a circle, as though patiently awaiting another catastrophe. Karvel counted them twice. "We must search for the dead," he said. "Will you want to bury them?"

Hras Klaa answered, perhaps after a long-distance consultation with Hras Drawa. "Yes. Bury them."

No search was necessary. The Hras *knew*. So intimate and continuous was their thought-sharing that they could move directly to every dropped piece of equipment and each broken body, and tell Karvel precisely what had happened up to the moment when death broke the telepathic connection.

Hras Krur had emulated Karvel and valiantly stood still, only leaping aside at the last instant when death seemed inevitable. Unfortunately, the dinosaur had swerved at the same time. Hras Maarl had run, and outdistanced the dinosaurs for more than a hundred yards before stumbling. Hras Hrul had been impaled by one of the lancelike horns.

"Hras Hrul was carrying the uranium detector," Karvel said. "What happened to it?"

They did not know. It had been in Hras Hrul's possession at the moment of death.

"Let's look for it now. If we can't find it, we won't have the problem of deciding whether to turn back. We'd be silly to go on without it."

They soon located Hras Hrul, but not the detector. They formed a line and attempted to retrace Hras Hrul's steps, searching carefully. It was Karvel who finally found it lying in a crushed nest of the brittle grass, looking like a glowing egg.

Glowing.

His shout brought the Hras crowding about him. Breathlessly he lifted it and held it cupped in his hands. It continued to glow.

"How close are we?" Karvel asked.

"Walk with it," Hras Klaa suggested.

Karvel paced a small circle. The glow neither brightened nor faded. He strode off in a straight line for a hundred yards, for five hundred, for more than a mile, with the Hras trailing after him. "Shouldn't it get brighter as it comes closer, and dimmer as it moves away?" he asked finally.

"Yes."

"It doesn't change at all. I suppose that could mean that the uranium is straight down, but I certainly wouldn't expect a deposit to be so large."

The Hras said nothing.

"I'm sure I walked through this area with it the last time we stopped. It didn't show anything then. And Hras Hrul carried it over this ground, and would have let us know if it glowed. So it didn't glow before. Now it glows everywhere."

Still the Hras had nothing to say.

"I think it's broken," Karvel said bluntly. "How much brighter should it get when it's really close to uranium?"

"Very bright," Hras Klaa said. "Like the sun."

"What does Hras Drawa think about this?"

"That the detector is broken."

"Tell Hras Drawa, please, that we'll be starting back today. I doubt that we could reach the mountains safely, and with a faulty detector there wouldn't be any point in trying."

The Hras scooped out a deep grave and buried their six dead comrades, and while they worked Karvel wandered off by himself. If the Hras wished to inter their dead with reverence, or even with ceremony, he would not be present to inhibit them, and he wanted to be alone with his conscience.

Seven of the Hras were dead because he'd neglected to study their limitations and to find out what they'd already learned about this environment. That was inexcusable, but so was the expedition. He asked himself how many important uranium deposits were known to the twentieth century. Fewer than a dozen, he was sure. That averaged out at less than two to a continent; and even if this Mesozoic Earth had ten times or even a hundred times as many, which he doubted, a haphazard search on foot, from a random starting point, could not have one chance in a hundred thousand of succeeding.

The expedition had cost seven lives, and the only thing he had learned for certain was that if one traveled far enough one would eventually encounter terrain that was hilly or mountainous. A moron would have taken as much for granted, and stayed home.

The interment was completed when he returned, and the Hras were waiting for him. He handed the softly glowing detector to Hras Klaa and wearily gave the signal. The Hras formed up behind him for the long walk back.

They wasted almost a full day at the river, Karvel resting and catching fish, and the Hras soaking up water and eating again, though they insisted that neither was necessary. The idea, Karvel told them, was to learn to take food and water when they were available.

They moved well away from the river for what Karvel hoped would be their last night in the open. The rolling plains, so empty of large life forms when they crossed them before, were now the stage for a grim battle of survival.

The great herbivores were seeking edible vegetation; the carnivores were pursuing them. Tyrannosaurus did not stalk its prey; it attacked in a raging, bloodthirsty frenzy until the intended victim was felled or hopelessly beyond reach. The dinosaurs scattered widely, but sometimes pressure from the relentless carnivores forced them into compact groups—and into a panicky stampede.

They had been six days reaching the river on the trip out; the return trip took them ten. They held tenaciously to the fringe of the forests, they crossed open spaces with caution and only after careful reconnaissance, and they moved much more slowly. The Hras were very frightened, and they were also ill. Their brown skin faded slowly to a sickly gray. Perhaps because of their weakened condition they were much more susceptible to the heat. They collapsed with such regularity that Karvel became obsessed with the fear that all thirteen might faint at once—in the open, in the face of a stampede.

In contrast, his own physical condition was improving. The slower pace and the frequent stops enabled him to have the rest he needed for his nightly vigils. He was eating much better, feasting each evening on dinosaur steak. Its toughness was unsurpassed by that of any steak he had ever eaten, but he had never enjoyed steak more.

The entire Hras company met them at the edge of the swamp, took firm charge of the weary Hras travelers, and, when Karvel declined the hospitality of the spaceship, furnished a small escort led by Hras Drawa to accompany him across the swamp to his cabin. The dinosaur migration had preceded them, and the swamp wore a strange auditory veneer of deep grunts, bellows, eerie cries. As they hurried over the bridges, fantastically-shaped heads arched up out of the slow-moving waters to regard them curiously.

The abatis was intact, though dinosaurs grazed the plain about it. Karvel inspected the cabin and the U.O., and then he wearily dropped his knapsack and sat with Hras Drawa on the log by the cabin door. The other Hras collected in the shade of the cabin and watched the dinosaurs.

Hras Drawa wheezed meditatively. "We should talk about this expedition. Why not talk now?"

Karvel glanced at the setting sun. "You might not be able to get back to the ship before dark. We can talk tomorrow or the next day—I'm not going anywhere."

"We could remain here for The Sleep," Hras Drawa said, "though the swamp may now be crossed with much less risk. The crocodiles have other than Hras to occupy them."

"Let's talk, then," Karvel said resignedly. If the Hras remained it meant another sleepless night for himself; but their unexpected willingness to spend a night away from the ship indicated a degree of impatience he would not have thought possible. "The expedition was a complete bust, of course. I learned a few things, but I could have learned most of them here, with less effort and at far less cost."

"We learned many things," Hras Drawa said. "I fear that I caused the failure by not thinking to provide more than one uranium detector."

"No. We couldn't have gone farther. We weren't equipped to cross a desert—which seems silly, because I half expected that we'd come to one. We should have talked our problems over ahead of time. Your worst mistake was in not giving me a better idea of what your needs would be. Mine was in not making an effort to find out."

"We are unaccustomed to this need for telling things," Hras Drawa said frankly. "Among ourselves we do not bother to tell things, because we *know*."

Karvel nodded glumly. "Whatever was learned, the cost wasn't worth it. All the way back I was kicking myself for not thinking of a perfectly obvious solution to your problem. You haven't enough fuel to get you *away* from Earth. Do you have enough to take you somewhere else *on* Earth?"

"Yes. There is enough for that."

"That's what I thought. I spent three weeks, and cost you seven lives, and accomplished nothing. And you could have reached those mountains easily with the ship."

"Why should we take the ship to the mountains?" Hras Drawa asked.

"To look for uranium!"

"Is there uranium in the mountains?"

"We know that there isn't any around here. You'd certainly be no worse off than you are now."

"We might be worse off. You do not know if there is water in the mountains."

"That could be determined before you land, couldn't it? If there weren't, you could land at the nearest river or lake."

"What we have thought," Hras Drawa said, speaking with a deeper rumble and great deliberation, "what we have thought is that we can make only one such journey. There is not enough fuel for two. There is not enough fuel to permit the search for alternate landing places. It would be best to wait until we know for certain where we wish to go. It would be best to find the uranium, and then take the ship there. Do you agree?"

"You have a point," Karvel admitted. "If you took the ship to the mountains and then found the uranium five hundred miles further on, it would be a long haul to get the ore back to the ship."

"Exactly."

"On the other hand, if you don't take the ship to the mountains, you may never get five hundred miles beyond."

"That is true, also."

"Then there isn't any easy solution. If you're to find the uranium before you move the ship, you must find it on foot. You must search as far as you can, in all directions. You must develop new travel techniques and new equipment. It may take you years just to reach your ultimate limits, because as you gain skill and experience you'll keep pushing those limits back. If you ever do reach them, *then* you can move the ship elsewhere and start over. You'll be resigning yourselves to an ordeal that will quite likely last all of your lifetimes, and cost you many casualties along the way."

"We agree. As you pointed out, the worst that can happen is that we'll die far from home. We can die waiting, or we can die searching, and we prefer to search. You will help us?"

"As much as I can," Karvel said.

"You have thoughts as to this equipment we would need?"

"A few thoughts. There must be a portable shelter for The Sleep. Perhaps the shelter could also serve as tubs for drinking. You must be able to carry a reserve of food and water, and you won't feel really safe until we've found a sure way to turn a stampede—which won't be easy. We'll work on it. We'll start tomorrow."

As the sun went down the Hras filed into the cabin, and Hras Drawa followed them. They formed a circle and quickly slipped into their deathlike slumber. Karvel made a slow circuit of the abatis, checking every post carefully, and then he went back to sit by the cabin door.

A small, ugly-looking lizard popped out of the ground nearby, glowered suspiciously at Karvel, and retreated. As the light faded it became bolder. Karvel stretched out his right foot and scratched its back, at the same time relieving the itch in his nonexistent toe. The lizard scurried into its hole, returned again, finally submitted to the scratching.

The Hras plan seemed wholly futile to Karvel. It amounted to nothing less than a lifetime of searching and not finding. Hras Drawa's grim optimism surprised him. Karvel's thoughts were an open book to the telepathic Hras. Surely they were aware of the tremendous odds against them.

But they were obviously an ethical race, and probably they were equally idealistic. They would fight the Good Fight, and damn the odds. He admired them, but he also pitied them.

The moon rose, full and splendid. Karvel had hardly noticed it in recent nights, confined as he had been to the forest barricades. He gazed at it nostalgically. A short time ago he had been there—a short time ago that was a couple of hundred million years into the future. The future was behind him, the past was the present, and Bowden Karvel was a derelict without purpose or destination.

He leaped up suddenly, wrenched open the dilating door, and dove through.

"Hras Drawa!" he shouted.

The sleeping Hras did not stir.

Karvel shook Hras Drawa impatiently, shouted again, and finally delivered a parting kick before he turned away disgustedly. His dash into the cabin had frightened the lizard. He sat down on the log and scratched his right foot on the edge of his left shoe while he contemplated the moon.

5

Dawn came at last, and with it the first tentative stirrings of the Hras. The shallow shafts of light from the firing slots had not yet chased the darkness from corners and from behind the thick braces when Karvel returned to the cabin. Hras Drawa, grasping drunkenly for complete consciousness, received Karvel's question with astonishment.

"The moon? You wish to go to the moon?"

The other Hras halted their efforts to shake themselves awake, and sounded a wheezing chorus. "The moon?"

Karvel was already beginning to suspect that his brilliant idea would fade to absurdity in the light of day, but he said stubbornly, "You said there wasn't enough fuel to get away from the Earth. Is there enough to go to the moon?"

"No." The answer was immediate, emphatic, and unarguable.

"It's a good thing I wasn't able to wake you up. Still—what about the fuel in the U.O.? If the rate of consumption decreases with the distance, there should be more than half a tank left. Would you have enough fuel if you used that?"

"I do not know. It would have to be calculated with care. Why do you wish to go to the moon?"

"I know where the mines are located. Where they will be located, I mean."

"What kind of mines?"

"That I don't know. By the time I got there they were exhausted. But the moon had been a very important source of minerals."

"Uranium?" Hras Drawa asked, after a long pause.

"'Wrought of Mother Earth, fired with the strength of Luna.' I don't know if that referred to men, or spaceships, or whatever, but it was quoted to me as a legend. I didn't think to investigate at the time, but last night the thought struck me that 'fired' could refer to fuel, which would mean that man reached the stars with uranium found on the moon. There must have been an enormous deposit there if the source was important enough to be remembered long after the uranium was exhausted."

"It is a possible interpretation," Hras Drawa wheezed ruminatively. "And you know where these uranium deposits are located?"

"Just a moment—I don't even *know* that they are *uranium* deposits. I can pinpoint several important mines, and give you a general idea as to the locations of quite a few more, and because of the legend I think it certain that one or more of them are uranium mines—will be uranium mines. I'm not claiming that all of them are, and I don't *know* that any of them are."

The other Hras seemed to have lost interest. They left the cabin, and after a meditative silence Hras Drawa followed them, and sat down by the door.

"Even if there is enough fuel to take us to the moon, there will not be enough to take us away again. There will not even be enough to change our location once we land. Either we find uranium—or we remain there."

"It would be a gamble," Karvel admitted. "I'm well aware of that."

"I have paid very little attention to your moon, but I feel that an expedition there would encounter difficulties much more severe than those you have just experienced. There are no dinosaurs, but neither is there an atmosphere. There would be no food, no water, no air to breathe. How far apart are these mines?"

"A considerable distance, I'm afraid. If we landed at the wrong one, we'd be stuck there. I agree. The terrain would be hopelessly rugged, the temperature extremes impossible, and we'd have to carry all of our air and food and water with us. We couldn't go trekking about from mine to mine hoping to find the right one."

"And yet—you favor this idea?"

"I sat here all night considering the odds. Against finding uranium here on Earth, several thousand to one at best. Against finding it on the moon, twenty or thirty to one at worst. I don't *favor* the idea—I have no right to gamble with your lives. I only think that you should consider it. The decision must be yours."

"Thank you. We will consider it."

"While you're considering it, consider this: The Earth is a living planet. It is constantly changing. I haven't the vaguest idea where I am, or how to go about finding minerals or anything else. The moon is dead. What we would find there now is almost exactly what I saw in the remote future—damn that paradox!—with the exception of the few trivial changes made by man. You can land your ship on top of a major mining site, and after that it's only a matter of odds. One chance in twenty or thirty. Think about it."

"You would accompany us to your moon?"

"Of course. How else could I show you where to land?"

"To us this gamble looks attractive. Your odds indicate that we would fail here on Earth. If we fail on your moon we should only die sooner, and we die on a strange world in either case. For yourself it is different. Why should you share this gamble with us?"

"No special reason. Just say I have a weakness for gambling."

"That does not say enough." Hras Drawa got to his feet and stood there for a moment, looking at Karvel or at the far horizon, depending on which of his vision spots were in focus. "We shall take the U.O. fuel and measure its weight carefully. If it is sufficient to take us to the moon, we shall talk again of this gamble."

Karvel walked with the Hras as far as the edge of the swamp, shrugging off their protests. He had reached the conclusion that an armed human was reasonably safe in this world of dinosaurs, as long as he bathed with care and avoided ambushes near water. He felt confident that he could maneuver a tyrannosaur dizzy, if necessary, and certain that if he remained in the open he wouldn't need to let one get close enough to put him to the test.

It seemed to him that the great dinosaurs were vastly overrated beasts. He recalled reading touching descriptions of the mammals' diminutive ancestors—of which he had seen no traces at all—hiding in terror while waiting for the dinosaurs to become extinct. Karvel doubted that the mammals were waiting for anything. Because they evolved from reptilian ancestors they were merely late in arriving on the scene. It was only an accident of Earth's evolution that the dinosaurs died out before man arrived, and thus spared him the task of finishing them off. Tyrannosaurus's bloodthirsty lunges were effective against the placid herbivores, but Tyrannosaurus could be lord of all it surveyed only as long as it surveyed nothing with the intelligence to fight back.

Before returning to the cabin Karvel stopped at the stream to fill his canteen. He had to scoop a hole to make the trickle of water deep enough to dip the canteen into, and he made a mental note to ask the Hras for some kind of container to store water in. If it did not rain soon he would have to bring his water from the swamp.

The Hras did not come again that day, nor the next. Karvel shot a small dinosaur under the mistaken assumption that its steaks would be more tender, and cut thin slices for an experiment in drying meat. He sat on the log by the cabin, scratching the lizard's back and feeding it tidbits while he waved insects away from a crudely fashioned meat rack and waited for a steak to cook. "Robinson Crusoe Karvel," he told himself. "And what a shock I'd have if I found a strange human footprint!"

It should have been a relaxing interlude, but it was not. "What does it matter to me," he asked himself, "whether these distinctively unhuman beings find uranium or not?"

Somehow it mattered. It mattered very much.

The Hras sent a delegation. One of its members was a pale Hras Klaa, and Karvel inquired as to the health of the exploration party, reminisced about their adventures, and offered small talk concerning neighboring dinosaurs. The Hras maintained an aloof formality, and, when Karvel gave them an opportunity, informed him that Hras Drawa invited him to the ship.

He had already formulated his own plans. He unpacked all of the emergency rations from the U.O. and passed them to the Hras to carry. If he returned from the moon he could bring them back; if he did not return he could at least enjoy a balanced diet while their air lasted.

He also removed all of the controls from the U.O. A lucky archaeologist might chance to excavate it in some future time when it could be supplied with fuel, and in Karvel's opinion human history already owned more time paradoxes than it could cope with.

He left the cabin without a backward glance. Its view had quickly grown monotonous, and he was not overly fond of his reptilian neighbors—though there were already signs that the dinosaurs were leaving. One species still wallowed thickly in the swamp, the weirdly-shaped heads plumbing the muck for food, but the others had exhausted the meager food supply of the plain and were moving on.

They crossed the swamp without difficulty and found Hras Drawa waiting on the ship's ramp with a reception committee.

"We have obtained a . . . a *photograph* of your moon," Hras Drawa said, and offered it to Karvel.

Karvel was too startled to accept it. It was a hollow hemisphere some three feet in diameter, and its surface was a perfect relief map, with every elevation precise and crisply formed, and every crater of pinpoint size or larger clearly shown. Karvel ran his hand over it and exclaimed, "I thought the moon couldn't be photographed when it's full!"

"Why is that?" Hras Drawa asked.

"No shadows."

"That is the best time to . . . to *photograph*. Shadows

would obscure many of the surface features. Are you able to locate the mines that you mentioned?"

"Of course. Easily."

So realistic was the reproduction that he could imagine himself descending over it in the Overseer's Shuttle. He touched the jagged ring of Plato, ran a finger over the queer-looking crater-with-the-eye, and then pointed confidently at the widening bay where the slash of the Alpine Valley debouched onto the Mare Imbrium.

"There. One of the mines was located there, perhaps the most important one, and it was—will be—the site of the most important base on this side of the moon."

"And . . . the others?"

"Let's see. One about here, a rather small one, in this mountain wilderness southeast of Tycho. One just out of sight around the western rim, straight west of Kepler. Here. And another between this alleged Sea of Tranquillity and this small sea whose name I can't recall. And another . . ."

They watched silently as his finger touched the hemisphere's serrated surface. Here, and here, and approximately here. He stepped back while the Hras silently studied the map.

"It is as we expected," Hras Drawa announced. "They are much too far apart."

"I remember a few on the other side, which of course you can't photograph from here. But don't forget this—the ones I've mentioned are only the mines important enough to justify the establishment of elaborate permanent bases. There may have been many lesser mining sites that were worked and abandoned."

"In choosing a landing place, we can consider only those mines known to you. Which do you recommend?"

Karvel did not answer immediately. Then he said slowly, "I feel certain that there's uranium on the moon, but I have no reason at all to say that you'd be more likely to find it in one place than another."

"You called this the most important mine," Hras Drawa persisted. "Do you think we should land there?"

"Your guess is probably as good as mine, and might even be better. But—yes. I think so. It was the largest base, and I'm sure I heard it referred to as the most important mine. And at the stage of human technology at which the base was built, uranium was by far the most important mineral."

"Thank you."

"What about the fuel situation?"

"If we achieve a high initial acceleration and precise-enough navigation to drive—coast—most of the way, we might have enough fuel left for the landing."

"A near thing, in other words. Risky."

"Risky, yes."

"A gamble trying to get there, and then another gamble on the landing place. That alters the odds."

"Then you think we should not attempt this?"

"I wouldn't presume to make the decision for you. If I were in your place, and there was only myself to consider, I think I'd go. If I were the head of an expedition, I'd take a vote—and perhaps leave behind anyone who preferred life here to a gamble with death on the moon."

"None of us has that preference," Hras Drawa said. "We have decided to go."

"When?"

"Today. Before darkness. The exact time is already calculated, and we have been storing air and water. The air requires much time because we cannot spare the fuel to operate our machines, but we will be ready at the chosen hour. We wish now only to give you our thanks and our farewell."

"Nonsense," Karvel said. "If you're going, then I'm going with you."

The onlookers stirred uneasily. Hras Drawa wheezed several times, and explosively demanded, "Why? You have shown us where to land. What further help could you give to us?"

Karvel did not answer.

"We cannot permit it," Hras Drawa said. "We have wrenched you out of your own time, and you have already risked your life for us. There is no good reason for you to share in this gamble."

"The best of reasons. It's my idea, so I'm going to see you through it—or as far through it as we're able to go. Do you think I'd be in your way?"

"No—"

"Then there's no good reason why I shouldn't come along."

"You have firmly decided. Very well. You will be welcome, but we do not understand why you wish to come."

Karvel smiled wistfully. "Call it another mountain that I'm compelled to climb."

It was possibly Karvel's last meal on Earth, and he wanted to consummate it with more ceremony than would be entailed in the opening of a military field ration. He asked the Hras to support him in the dangerous venture of catching a fish, and he baked it well and ate it slowly, savoring the sights and sounds and smells about him. Even the foul decay of the swamp had a vitality that he would recall nostalgically when entrapped in the alien atmosphere of the spaceship.

It was late afternoon when they came for him. Hesitantly they asked if he were ready to go, as though they fully expected him to change his mind. Karvel entered the ship without a backward glance and took his place on the hammock in the same cylindrical room he had occupied before. He would have given much to be able to watch this take-off from the control room, but he did not ask. They might have felt obliged to consent, and a control room on a touchy, fuel-conserving take-off was no place for spectators.

There was a rumble and a lurch. Karvel's hammock shifted smoothly as the ship rose to the vertical, and then gravity tore at him. For a few crushing seconds he fought the illusion that he was again in the throes of the U.O.'s pressure, and then the rumble ceased, the acceleration eased, and he was able to breathe freely. He lay panting on the hammock, and waited for his stomach to catch up with him.

Suddenly he realized that he was weightless. He caught himself drifting away from the hammock, and learned for the first time the purpose of the three indentations on either side. They were for hanging onto. Karvel hooked a finger into one of them and turned to watch the open diaphragm of the door.

The minutes passed tediously, and no Hras appeared. Puzzled, Karvel launched himself with a floating leap and looked out into the dim red light of the deserted corridor. He drifted through the door and propelled himself forward with a firm push. He reached the distant end, explored another corridor in increasing perplexity, and finally turned back.

Near his own quarters he noticed a dilating door that had not been completely closed. He glanced through it and was able to make out the figure of a Hras seated doglike on a hammock, clinging firmly with four of its six limbs but otherwise comatose.

A queasy sensation of panic smote him—the same sensation he'd had the first night out with the expedition, but of paralyzing intensity. The Hras had taken off just in time to get the ship safely on course before The Sleep, and Karvel was undoubtedly the only conscious individual aboard. If anything happened . . .

He banished his misgivings and returned to his quarters. The Hras were veteran space travelers. In spite of The Sleep they had reached Earth from a far galaxy, and they should be capable of planning a trip to the moon. Nothing could happen while the ship was coasting through space, and the Hras would be awake in time for the moon landing.

If they weren't there was nothing that Karvel could do about it. He wouldn't know how to cope with an emergency, and he knew that he couldn't arouse the Hras. He floated back to his hammock and tried to sleep.

He was still trying when the first Hras appeared. Karvel had passed the red-hued alien night in tense vigilance, and he greeted the red-hued alien dawn with the acute discomfort of exhaustion blended with the nausea of weightlessness.

"Landing soon," the Hras said, and disappeared.

Karvel tensed himself on his hammock, and a short time later the engines caught with a jar that slammed him into it. The Hras had waited for the last possible moment, when they had to brake their descent or crash, and the sudden, crushing change from no gravity to full deceleration was far worse than the pressure he had suffered on the take-off.

Just as abruptly the pressure stopped. The engines were silent, and *up* and *down* had meaning again. Karvel dropped to the floor and looked into the corridor.

Hras Klaa came bustling past, almost inarticulate with excitement. "We're sending out the first party. Would you like to watch?"

"Watch?" Karvel exclaimed. "I'd like to go along!"

"There is no clothing to fit you."

"Clothing? You mean a space suit. Yes, I suppose I'd better have one of those if I go outside."

"Ours would not fit you."

"True. I couldn't begin to get into one of them. Where do I go to watch?"

In a bulge at the top of the ship they found a group of Hras surrounded by a circular vision screen. Karvel looked dazedly this way and that, from the jagged, sun-flooded mountain peaks to bleak Mare Imbrium's shallow horizon, and back again. The Hras silently contemplated all of it with their circular vision.

The ship lay where Karvel had placed his finger on the map, its nose pointing into the valley. "Perfect!" Karvel exclaimed. "How did we do on fuel?"

"There is a little left," Hras Drawa said. "Not enough to leave this place, but enough to operate some of our machines when—if—we find the uranium."

A group of space-suited Hras came into view, their gleaming suits grotesquely magnifying their grotesqueness. The air tank was a bulging sausage that encircled them in the region of their breathing rings; the vision ring was a lesser bulge. The six slender limbs terminated in large disks, making them look like many-armed tennis players.

They marched straight for the base of the mountains, picked their way over chunks of rock that had eroded from the heights, and moved out of sight down the valley. Those in the observation room waited tensely, and Karvel watched the Hras rather than the viewing screen. They were mentally in contact with the search party, and the instant a uranium detector produced the smallest flicker they would know about it.

They remained silent.

The search party came into view again, returning from the opposite side of the valley. As it approached the ship the Hras abruptly left the room, leaving Karvel alone with Hras Drawa.

"Nothing?" Karvel asked.

Hras Drawa wheezed a lingering sigh. "No. Nothing at all."

6

They tried, of course.
They laid out search patterns with geometrical precision,
pacing off squares, and halving them, and halving the
halves, until it seemed to Karvel that no square inch of the
valley had not been tested with one of the damnably inert
detectors. They ranged far out into Mare Imbrium and far
up the valley. They scaled the mountains as high as they
could climb, and Karvel watched apprehensively as the
small figures edged their way upward, clinging to what
was, from his vantage point, the sheer face of a cliff.

All of the Hras searched. Karvel had never found out exactly how many there were of them, but he counted more
than a hundred at a time on the viewing screen, pathetic
figures that painstakingly plodded back and forth in small
groups, intent on the precious crystals that they carried
cupped in their flexible disks. They remained out for their
entire waking periods, and when they returned to the ship
for The Sleep Hras Drawa had always the same comment.
"No. Nothing at all."

"Is there any chance that something could be wrong with
the detectors?" Karvel asked. "The explosion, perhaps—"

"All have been tested," Hras Drawa said.

"How did you test them?"

"With uranium. The fuel."

"Oh," Karvel said, feeling absolutely like a fool.

The line of the sunset moved relentlessly up the valley
and left them in darkness. The glowing Earth reached its
first quarter and began to soften the jagged landscape with

earthlight. Aboard the ship there was no longer even a pretense that their gamble had not failed.

Hras Drawa summoned Karvel, and tersely outlined a plan to extend the search. They would be able to equip two small teams of explorers. One would proceed north along the edge of the *mare;* the other would go south. They could carry enough air for four Earth-days, two days out and two returning. Later there would be other parties, but unfortunately their extreme range could never be farther than two days of traveling. Did Karvel have any suggestions?

"You might work out a system of caching supplies," Karvel said. "You'd start with a larger team, but half of the members would leave their extra air at the one-day limit and turn back. When the others returned they would have that air waiting for them. It would increase their range slightly. If a stock were built up there, then some of it could be moved to the two-day limit, and so on. It would be possible, with careful planning, to build the range up to a week or more. A similar system was used by polar explorers on Earth."

"We will consider that," Hras Drawa said. "For a beginning, though, we shall limit ourselves to the two days. We do not know what problems we will encounter. You do not think such a short exploration worthwhile?"

"Of course. It's the only thing to do, since there isn't any uranium around here. I was just thinking that we're right back where we were on Earth, except that the conditions are infinitely more difficult."

"At least there are no dinosaurs," Hras Drawa wheezed. "And no crocodiles."

Karvel turned away.

"You must not feel badly about us," Hras Drawa said. "We knew when we determined to come that we were much more likely to fail than to succeed. We do not regret our gamble, but we are sorry that you insisted on coming with us."

They did not regret their gamble, but the atmosphere in

the ship, before the Hras collapsed in sleep, was downright funereal.

The two expeditions left as soon as the Hras awakened again. Karvel watched them out of sight—twenty Hras in each group, the same mystical number that had taken part in the Earth expedition. Through some trick of optics in the spaceship viewing screen the squat, bulging figures labored endlessly on the edge of the horizon before they finally vanished.

Later, pacing the dim corridors in edgy impatience, Karvel chanced upon Hras Klaa. "I want to go exploring," he announced. "I want to walk up the valley, and climb a mountain or two, and leave my footprints in moon dust. Couldn't you rig up some kind of a suit for me?"

Hras Klaa reacted with a rare enthusiasm, perhaps because the Hras had nothing better to do. A committee of space-suit tailors was assembled. Never had Karvel been measured so meticulously, and never had he received a worse fit. His head posed almost insurmountable problems for them, because they insisted on viewing him not as a human but as a misshapen Hras. The suit that they constructed looked like a cylinder with limbs haphazardly attached. He entered it by squirming in through the top, and he had to squat down slightly in order to see through the misplaced vision ring. The flexible limbs would not bend properly at the knees and elbows, leaving him both stiff-legged and stiff-armed.

"Splendid," Karvel said. "Let's try it out."

They insisted on running a lengthy pressure test; and anyway, it was time for The Sleep. As soon as they awoke, four of them, including Hras Klaa, suited up with him and accompanied him outside. They stood at the top of the ship's ramp, and Karvel enjoyed the majestic silence of the moon's surface for only a moment before he cursed, and motioned all of them back inside.

"I'd feel better about this if I could communicate with

someone," he said. "What would I do if my back needed scratching?"

They wheezed bewilderedly.

"Of course you haven't got any radios, because you don't need them, so there's no way you can talk to me. Can you receive my thoughts when I'm muffled up in this thing?"

"Certainly," Hras Klaa said.

"Fine. Then I'll think simple questions. You can tap out the answer on my arm—once for yes, twice for no. Got that?"

"Certainly."

Karvel slammed the lid on his suit and stooped down so that Hras Klaa could inspect it. The air lock diaphragm dilated, closed behind them. Karvel mouthed a question into the confines of his suit. "Shall we go up the valley?"

He felt one tap on his arm. They started out, moving with long, effortless strides.

The valley, a precipitous slash in the Lunar Alps, was heavily shadowed. Karvel stopped frequently to gaze in wonderment at the play of earthlight on the tremendous heights, and to marvel at the dazzling density and brightness of the stars. Once he looked back and found Hras Klaa scrutinizing a uranium detector.

He thought a question. "Hasn't this area been checked?"

Hras Klaa stuffed the detector into a pouch and did not respond. The wistfulness of the gesture broke Karvel's heart.

They moved slowly up the valley, the Hras waiting patiently when Karvel stopped to gape. In many places the mountains were split by fissures of tremendous depth, some only narrow cracks, others great crevasses that reached far down into the valley and pointed dim fingers of earthlight across the valley floor. There Karvel could see crisscrossing trails smudged in the moon dust—the mute record of the Hras's painstaking search.

After several miles they reached a point where an enormous rockfall had tumbled obstacles far out into the valley. Karvel turned back, made an experimental leap, and ran for several long, soaring steps. "What a place for a game of basketball!" he enthused. He stopped to wait for the Hras, and again saw Hras Klaa studying the uranium detector. Sobered, he walked on slowly.

At the head of the valley he veered off to the northern wall, picking his way carefully through fallen rock. He found a foothold and awkwardly began to climb. The wall was not nearly as sheer as it had looked from a distance, but the unyielding limbs of his suit soon thwarted him. He made a fast, half-sliding descent to where the Hras stood waiting.

A few yards further on he tried again, with less success. Then he found a natural projection that slanted upward. He followed it to its end, an unsettling hundred feet above. A narrow ledge dipped down toward him, and he edged along that for a short distance and then turned back. Doubtless the moon's low gravity and precipitous heights would some-day provide a paradise for mountain-climbing enthusiasts, but Bowden Karvel was not one of them.

They returned to the ship, and Karvel asked the space-suit tailors to fashion arm and leg joints that would work.

Life coursed along smoothly. Karvel ate his rations when he felt like it, slept usually, but not always, when the Hras did, and went outside frequently. He carried his own ura-nium detector, and he sometimes found himself, like Hras Klaa, gazing at it hypnotically and attempting to will it into luminescence.

Life coursed along smoothly, but there was an occasional disquieting omen.

The two expeditions returned, and no new ones were sent out. Karvel inquired about the plans for a system of caching supplies for a longer expedition, and Hras Drawa answered evasively. "Perhaps later," he said, and days slipped away.

One of the Hras, standing at the top of the landing ramp, suddenly went into a ludicrous dance and walked down the ramp on its central pair of limbs, waving the other four com-ically. The performance disturbed Karvel, but the Hras seemed not to notice.

On a walk along the mountainous shore of the Mare Im-brium, Karvel came upon a solitary Hras who was flinging rocks far into the sky and then apparently hurrying to stand

under them as they came down. Karvel watched for some
time, marveling at the ease with which the swiveling arms
were able, in the moon's low gravity, to propel missiles lit-
erally out of sight. The Hras was less to be admired in its
judgment of falling objects. It was fortunately unable to
place itself within yards of a rock's landing place.

The Hras were increasingly afflicted with a strange leth-
argy. They responded when he spoke to them, but only
after a long, inexplicable silence. They moved as quickly as
ever, but they contemplated an action endlessly before they
made it. When he left the ship, or returned to it, he began to
find a group of Hras clustered motionless about the landing
ramp, as though hypnotized by the magnificent light in the
dark, star-flecked sky. "Earth-struck," Karvel thought wryly.
The group became larger as time went by, and he began to
have difficulty in finding a path through it.

Except during The Sleep. When that time approached the
Hras shrugged off their trances with visible shudders and
lined up in orderly fashion to await their turns at the air
lock.

Karvel's contacts with them, his communication with
them, became less and less, but for all that he had a foreboding awareness of deepening despair and the steady,
corrosive growth of tension.

Earth's disk passed the full and slowly waned to a fragile
crescent. Karvel, emerging from the air lock, glanced up at
the sliver of light in the sky and decided that the moon's
long night must be nearly over. Soon there would be blind-
ing sunlight on the mountain peaks. He was beginning to
wonder how long the air supply would last, how many such
sunrises they would live to see. He had stopped asking questions of the Hras, for they no longer answered him.

He descended the ramp and hesitantly began to pick his
way among the dim, motionless figures. He had never seen
so many Hras standing there. It looked as if the entire company were gathered outside the ship, waiting for the mystic
impulse that would send it back inside to The Sleep.

He slowly threaded his way forward, and was almost

clear when a Hras unaccountably reached out and gave him a firm push. He spun into another Hras, who reacted with a shove that knocked Karvel off balance. He managed to recover and leap aside, but as he turned away he was pushed again and sent sprawling. He rolled, scrambled to his feet, and stepped into the viselike embrace of four Hras arms.

Karvel applied a knee to the bloated air tank, and after a brief struggle pushed free. All of the Hras were stirring. They milled about uncertainly, and several began a weird, jerky, arm-waving dance. Others drifted in Karvel's direction as he backed slowly away.

A Hras lurched forward and struck out at him. Karvel leaped aside, and immediately had to fend off another attack. He deftly side-stepped two more rushes, and in a sudden surge of panic it came to him that they were deranged. All of them had gone mad. He turned and fled, and the Hras swarmed after him.

With great, leaping strides Karvel raced into the deep, protective gloom of the valley, intending to lose himself in darkness. For a short time the Hras kept on his heels, but he soon left them far behind. He turned toward the southern wall, and when he glanced back he could just make out the dim glint of their silvery space suits where they had gathered uncertainly far out in the valley.

They hesitated only for a moment. They turned unerringly and rushed after him.

"They're following my mind!" he exclaimed.

He hurried on, clawing his way over rock slides, hearing nothing but his own labored breathing, until the mountain wall barred his way. He followed it, stumbling over fallen rock and expecting at any instant to feel Hras limbs closing upon him like a trap. He could only hope that the short-statured Hras would have more difficulty with the rock obstacles than he did.

His flight had been instinctive, and he'd had no time to contemplate the possible consequences of nonflight. Now he began to wonder, wryly, what difference it could make. All of the Hras were doomed, and Karvel along with them. If in a moment of madness they tore him limb from limb and bathed their silver suits in his blood, the act would neither shorten his life significantly nor leave undone anything of consequence that he might otherwise have accomplished. Some rations uneaten, some few hours or days or weeks of breathing alien odors, some lonely walks on the moon—that was the measure of his loss.

He relaxed, and slowed his pace.

He found a foothold on the mountain wall, climbed a few steps, and slipped down again. Yards further on he made another attempt, with the same result. The impulse to climb was also instinctive, and the idea of the Hras searching for the source of his mental emanations down in the valley while he perched safely on the mountainside appealed to him. He had only to hold out until The Sleep approached, when he was certain that they would file docilely back to the ship.

He moved on along the cliff, searching for footholds. Once he was able to climb perhaps twenty feet, but he could remain there only by clinging precariously, so he retreated. The climb wasted precious minutes, and he was certain, now, that they were close behind him.

He climbed again, found a slanting ledge, and edged his way along it. Once it crumbled beneath his foot, but he scrambled to safety and continued to climb. He reached the end and hauled himself onto a higher ledge.

As he cautiously felt his way forward the cliff exploded soundlessly in his face. Rock fragments showered him. An instant later his leg received a bruising blow, and a miniature avalanche of small rocks and fragments rained down on him from above.

He halted confusedly, and peered into the silent darkness. Then his arm was struck and more fragments pelted him, and he understood.

The Hras had located him. They were throwing rocks. They probably had the moon's airless air filled with them, but in the soundless night he could tabulate only their hits and near-misses.

He began to climb recklessly. The Hras could see him no better than he could see them, but all they needed was his general direction. His mind gave them that. If they threw enough rocks some were certain to hit him, and a solid hit with a large rock might knock him from the cliff. A worse danger was that the rocks would touch off a genuine avalanche.

He climbed through a hail of missiles until he found another ledge to follow. His lateral movement soon left the rocks behind, but in his haste he nearly stepped off the end of the ledge. He floundered briefly, gained a new foothold, and climbed higher. The ledge widened under a bit of overhang, and he crouched there to take stock of his situation.

The Hras were creatures of the sun. They had adapted themselves to Earth's day-night cycle—perhaps it approximated their own—but the moon's two-week night, with only an unvitalizing earthlight to sustain them, had driven them mad. Probably they had never been so long away from the warming light of a sun except in space, and there a properly fueled ship could supply some form of substitute.

In their derangement they lashed out at the chief architect of their disaster. Karvel felt no resentment for them—only pity.

They found him again. Rock fragments spattered down from above, but this time the overhang partially protected him. He waited resignedly. It seemed a damnably untidy way to die, but no more so than the death by suffocation that he would certainly suffer if he lived long enough.

"My thinking is too loud," he told himself.

They were ranging in on him with uncanny accuracy. A large rock struck his shoulder a painful, staggering blow, and others landed at his feet. Unconsciously he picked one up, and halted himself in the act of throwing it back.

He could terminate the fiasco instantly by opening the lid of his suit, or even with a short step forward, but both methods smacked repugnantly of suicide. Simple justice probably demanded that he climb down and let the Hras finish him off, but he wondered if that, too, might be called suicide. It was the kind of moral technicality that he would have pondered delightedly under circumstances that were less brutally realistic.

Rocks continued to crash around him, and a sizable slide from above buried his feet in a slow seepage of dust and fragments. Huddled back against the cliff, pummeled by rocks and rock fragments, Karvel began to laugh hysterically. The first human explorers of this area would have a sensational mystery on their hands. They would have to account for an alien spaceship, a crew of dead aliens, and one dead human. Eventually it might occur to them to connect the aliens with the unhuman U.O. passenger, and then Haskins, if he were still around, would produce whatever data was necessary to identify Karvel. Karvel regretted very much that he wouldn't be able to see the report Haskins's experts would write about his four-toed right leg (one copy only, to be handed to me personally).

The spaceship would yield valuable information, and probably speed man's conquest of space by centuries. It would—

Karvel jerked erect and nearly lost his balance. "Stop!" he shouted. "We haven't failed! We won't fail!"

A rock struck the overhang, and its ricochet caught Karvel squarely. He steadied himself and shouted again, "Stop, you idiots!" The words rang in his ears. "Stop! We're going to find it!"

A rock smacked into his chest, leaving him unhurt but shaken. He moved sideward and began to climb again, shouting as he fumbled for hand- and footholds, "Stop! Stop and listen, you idiots!"

The rocks chased after him. No one with an urge to throw them had ever worked with a better source of supply. Whatever finally stopped the Hras, it wouldn't be because they ran out of ammunition. Through all the eons since some mysterious force had gouged this valley, the mountains had alternately frozen and baked and slowly eroded an enormous accumulation of debris; and the Hras were throwing everything that they could move.

"Stop, you idiots!" Karvel shouted. "Don't you see? The future didn't find us. Their planes and ships are nothing like yours, and if they had found us—"

A ricochet staggered him, and in the instant while he was regaining his balance all of his ingenious reasoning crumbled. A hundred million years of development would have altered the Hras ship beyond recognition, and its discovery would have been buried deeply in man's forgotten history.

In angry frustration he continued to climb. He found another ledge, and quickly determined that it led nowhere. He could not climb higher, and sober reflection convinced him that he would never climb down again. He could not possibly remember the tenuous hand- and footholds that connected these ledges, and no amount of nerve-wracking search could locate them in the dark.

A rock slammed into his kneecap and left him writhing in agony. The knowledge that the Hras were sucking the pain from his mind, savoring it greedily, infuriated him.

"Is that the hardest you can throw?" he taunted.

They were ranging in on him in earnest, and he was struck repeatedly. He sent off another taunt. "Is that the hardest—"

Light flashed somewhere above him. He whirled to look upward, lost his balance, and fell.

For one blazing instant the valley was starkly illuminated. The Hras stood motionless, transfixed by light, some with arms frozen in the act of throwing. The rocks they had already launched still arched swiftly upward.

The light vanished as abruptly as it had appeared, and Karvel fell into darkness.

He lay on the hammock in the spaceship. Hras Drawa was there, and Hras Klaa, and the corridor beyond the circular door was crowded with Hras. Karvel spoke around the edges of a monstrous headache. "You caught me?"

"No," Hras Drawa said. "We tried to catch you—"

"You broke my fall, anyway. It looked like a long way down, but I suppose on the moon one doesn't fall as hard. Are there any broken bones?"

"We do not think so, but you will have many hurts."

"I already have many hurts," Karvel growled. He would be one unending bruise from head to foot. He shook his head, but the headache did not lessen. He said slowly, "That light . . ."

Hras Drawa waited silently.

"There must have been one of those crevasses above me."

"Far above you," Hras Drawa said.

"And one of you threw a uranium detector."

"Many of us threw them."

"Of course. They're just the right size and weight for effective throwing. But one of you missed me by the proverbial country mile, and the detector sailed far back into the crevasse. And before it landed and smashed itself it detected a fair amount of uranium."

"An enormous deposit," Hras Drawa said. "Deep in the mountain."

"You disappoint me," Karvel said bitterly. "I saw you climbing, and I assumed that you investigated the deep crevasses. You weren't really searching—you were just going through the motions."

"We searched as high as we could climb," Hras Drawa said. "We could not reach the crevasses."

"You'll reach that one now, won't you?"

Hras Drawa hesitated, and then said weakly, "Yes—"

"That's exactly what I mean. You went through the motions. You searched as high as you could climb conveniently, and not an inch farther. You expected to find the uranium piled up and waiting for you." He shifted his leg, and winced. Hras Drawa hovered over him anxiously.

Karvel said thoughtfully, "Your leaders—your *real* leaders —were killed, weren't they?"

"In the explosion," Hras Drawa said. "And when we first landed in the swamp."

"I suppose that explains your muddled searches, and your

U.O. blundering, and everything else. You needed someone to tell you what to do. If I'd had a suit when you were exploring the valley, I'd have told you." He shrugged resignedly. "Well, you've found your uranium. It's easy to see why the base was located down in the valley. Obviously they couldn't build it in the crevasse, and it was probably easier to tunnel after the ore than to put machinery up there and work in the open. Try to get the stuff out without leaving any traces, if that's possible. Man will encounter enough mysteries on the moon without having to wonder who's been mining the uranium."

"We will work with care. There will be no traces."

"That also applies to all the mucking about you've done since we've landed. Maybe a hundred million years will cover your tracks. If not, the first human explorers will think a herd of drunken moon cattle stampeded up and down the valley."

"The tracks will be removed," Hras Drawa promised.

"Fine. Carry on, then. Go get the uranium."

Hras Drawa did not move. None of them moved. The silence lengthened as Karvel looked from Hras Drawa to Hras Klaa and to the Hras crowded into the open circle of the doorway.

"It's all right," he said. "You couldn't help it. I understand."

Then they left him.

7

Most of the dinosaurs were gone. A few stragglers grazed futilely along the bare fringes of the swamp, but the vast herds had taken what they could of the scanty vegetation and moved on. The drought had intensified; the small stream at the foot of the hill was a twisting ribbon of sand and—where a few shallow pools had stood—dried mud.

On the plain the Hras ship loomed enormously.

"In any case," Hras Drawa said, "we cannot leave you here. There is no water. You will not reconsider?"

Karvel shook his head. "No. I'm honored, and very grateful, but—no." To live out his life sleeping in beds that were too small, and stooping through round doorways, and being served foods that he could not eat, and appearing to all and sundry as weird-looking as the Hras appeared to him—it had not required much reflection for him to decline their generous offer to take him home with them.

"What are you going to do?" Hras Drawa asked.

"I haven't thought about it. I really don't know."

"Do you wish to return to your own time?"

Did an escaped convict wish to return to prison? "There's Force X to consider," Karvel said lightly.

"You can now return without causing significant damage," Hras Drawa said, rolling out the word *significant* with a lilting wheeze. Of all the Hras, only Hras Drawa seemed to enjoy talking to Karvel. "We can arrange for you to take ample fuel. You could travel in many short time leaps, and arrive without the Force X."

"I'd forgotten about that."

"And we would give you instruction in the operation of the U.O., so that you could plot your distance accurately."

"You'd really leave the U.O. for my use? I don't think any human should be trusted with it."

"We could not leave you marooned in this terrible . . . terrible *environment.*" Hras Drawa wheezed out the word gleefully. "In any case, we cannot leave you in this place. There is no water. If you like we will move the time beacon and the U.O. to the mountains, where there is water and you will be safe from dinosaurs."

"Fine. If it isn't too much trouble."

"Not at all. We must replenish our own water. And we will build you another cabin. And fit the U.O. with reserve fuel tanks, so that you will have ample to return to your own time whenever you are ready."

"Fine," Karvel said. Return to his own time to do what? Take up astronauting again? After what he'd seen and done, a rocket landing on the moon would be, to put it mildly, anticlimactic.

And he foresaw problems.

The authorities, bless them, probably regretted their haste in dispatching the U.O. If they got their hands on it again, and learned that it could be operated safely, they would certainly proceed to operate it.

Like the Overseer, they would look for ways to turn a profit.

Hras Drawa was still wheezing. "—leave you any tools you want, and supplies—"

"Fine," Karvel murmured.

"—and a reserve of fuel to be stored at the time beacon, so that you can return there in case—"

"In case I go somewhere and then change my mind? Fine."

He felt superbly at peace with himself. His mountain peaks were still unattainable, and always would be; but he had climbed high, and the view was dazzling.

"What are you going to do?" Hras Drawa asked again.

"I won't know until I've given it some thought," Karvel said.

He needed new worlds, or new times, to conquer. He might find a tribe of primitive men and set himself up in the God business. Or probe the deeply remote past, and laugh hilariously as he watched man's distant ancestor drag itself out of the slime of the sea. He had stood on Earth long before the human race existed; it might be amusing to stand there again when man was not even an obscene memory.

First there was work to be done—to move the U.O. and the time beacon, to build a new cabin, to choose the equipment and supplies he would need. And then, when the Hras left, he must sleep. He had been unable to rest well on the spaceship, and he was desperately tired.

Tomorrow he would decide.

Lightning Source UK Ltd.
Milton Keynes UK
UKOW04f1041170214

226594UK00001B/89/P